# ODIN'S RAVENS

## THE BLACKWELL PAGES

# THE BLACKWELL PAGES

## BOOK 2

### K. L. ARMSTRONG
### M. A. MARR

Little, Brown and Company
New York  Boston

Little, Brown and Company

Hachette Book Group
237 Park Avenue, New York, NY 10017
Visit our website at lb-kids.com

Little, Brown and Company is a division of Hachette Book Group, Inc.
The Little, Brown name and logo are trademarks of Hachette Book Group, Inc.

The publisher is not responsible for websites (or their content) that are not owned by the publisher.

First Edition: May 2014

Library of Congress Cataloging-in-Publication Data
Armstrong, Kelley.
   Odin's ravens / K.L. Armstrong ; M.A. Marr.—First edition.
     pages cm.—(The Blackwell pages ; book 2)
   Summary: When Ragnarok—the apocalypse—threatens, the human descendants of the gods band together to fight monsters, and Matt Thorsen and his friends must journey to the underworld to save a descendant.
   ISBN 978-0-316-20498-9 (hardcover) — ISBN 978-0-316-25508-0 (electronic book)
   [1. Adventure and adventurers—Fiction. 2. Supernatural—Fiction. 3. Shapeshifting—Fiction. 4. Gods—Fiction. 5. Monsters—Fiction. 6. Valhalla—Fiction. 7. Mythology, Norse—Fiction.] I. Marr, M. A. (Melissa A.), 1972–  II. Title.
   PZ7.A76638Odi 2014
   [Fic]—dc23
                                                                      2013018519

10 9 8 7 6 5 4 3 2 1

RRD-C

Printed in the United States of America

M. A.: To Dylan—
I present to you a gift of goats
(and also a book written for and because of you).

K. L.: To Alex and Marcus—
Yep, another book for you.
It's almost as cool as having
your own Minecraft server, right?

# ONE

## MATT

## "WELCOME TO HEL"

If there was one thing worse than seeing a giant's head rise from the ground, it was seeing *two* giant heads. Belching fire. Still, if they killed Matt, his soul wouldn't have far to travel... considering he was already in the afterlife.

"At least it's only *one* giant," Matt said as they crouched behind a rock.

Fen gave him a look.

"What? It's true. A single two-headed giant is better than two one-headed giants."

And this, Matt realized, was what their world had come to. A week ago, his biggest worry was failing his science fair project. Now he was taking comfort in the thought that he faced only *one* fifty-foot-tall, fire-breathing giant.

It was a Jotunn from Norse mythology. The most famous were the frost giants, but *they* lived in a world of ice, and there was no ice in this smoke-shrouded wasteland, just rock and more rock, as far as the eye could see.

The Jotunn looked like a two-headed WWE wrestler on nuclear-powered steroids, insanely muscle-bound, with reddish-orange skin that gleamed as if it were on fire. The giant stood in a crevasse up to its thighs, but even so, Matt still had to crane his neck to look up at the heads.

Matt touched the amulet on his chest. It was vibrating, warning him that something dangerous was near, just in case he couldn't, you know, *see* a fifty-foot flaming giant. The amulet was Thor's Hammer, worn by all the Thorsens of Blackwell, South Dakota, because they really were "Thor's sons"—distant descendants of the Norse god...which is what got Matt into this predicament in the first place.

Matt dimly heard Laurie say that they would have to pass the Jotunn—answering something Fen had said. He looked over at Fen and Laurie—the Brekke cousins, also from Blackwell, descendants of the trickster god Loki. Matt was about to speak when a distant roar made him jump.

"It's okay," Laurie whispered. "The giant is still talking to itself. That was something else."

Of course it was. He laughed a little at how calmly she

had said it. She was right, though. The Jotunn hadn't noticed them yet.

"It's distracted," he murmured. "Good." Matt pointed at a line of jagged rocks to their left. "Get over there. Behind the rocks. Fast!"

"Shouldn't we—?" Fen began, but Matt waved him forward, and Laurie nudged him along.

As they raced for the rocks, Matt kept his gaze fixed on the giant. He herded the cousins behind the biggest boulders and motioned for them to hunker down. He did the same. Then he took another look.

"Shouldn't we have run that way?" Fen pointed in the other direction. "We could have ducked behind those rocks."

Matt shook his head. "That would lead us right to the giant."

"Um, yeah. Kinda the idea, Thorsen. How are we going to get the jump on it from over here? These rocks lead *away* from the freaking fire monster."

"Yes, because that's where we're going. Away from it."

"But Baldwin is that way," Laurie said, pointing past the giant.

They'd discovered that one of Laurie's powers was the ability to locate other descendants of the gods of the North. In this case, she was homing in on their friend Baldwin, who was stuck in the afterlife.

"Laurie's right," Fen said. "This is no short detour, and

we don't know what we'll find along it. Maybe more giants. We should just fight this one."

"Do you see how big that thing is?" Matt said. "It could swallow a troll."

"But we fought *three* trolls."

"And barely escaped with our lives," Laurie said. "Matt's right. We should try to avoid this guy."

"Great. Side with Thorsen *again*," Fen muttered.

Matt could tell Fen thought he was wimping out. A few days ago, that would have stung enough to make Matt reconsider. But he'd learned a few things since then. Sometimes being a leader *meant* wimping out of a fight. They weren't playing around here. They could die. Their friend Baldwin *had* died, and that's why they were trekking through the underworld, to bring him back to the land of the living. Even then, there was no guarantee they could.

Fen agreed to the long route. There wasn't much else he could do, being outnumbered, but he kept grumbling that they'd probably run into *two* fire giants now. Finally, Matt had to ask him, nicely, to pipe down before the giant overheard. Fen didn't like that, either.

Matt adjusted his shield over his shoulder and led the way along the row of jagged rocks. Sometimes they could walk upright. Sometimes they had to creep along bent over. Now and then they needed to dart between rocks. The closer they got to the Jotunn, the worse the smell got. Sulfur. Matt recognized it now, from chemistry. Soon, he couldn't just smell the fire—he could hear it crackling, deep in the canyon, and he could feel it, waves that made sweat roll down his face. The air shimmered with the heat, and he had to keep blinking to focus.

Laurie glanced over, but Matt waved for her to keep going. They were alongside the Jotunn now, the stink and the heat unbearable. Still, the giant was busy talking to...well, talking to itself apparently, its two heads deep in conversation. Matt could hear the voices, crackling and snapping and roaring, the words indecipherable, the sound like fire itself.

*It doesn't matter what they're saying. They're too busy to notice—*

One of the heads stopped talking. And turned their way...just as Matt was stepping from behind a rock. He stumbled back, arms shooting out to keep the others from doing the same.

"One's looking," he whispered.

Behind him, Laurie crept to the other side of the rock to peek out that way. Matt resisted the urge to pull her back. He could barely see from his direction—the angle was wrong. It seemed as if the heads were both turned toward them. One said something to the other, and the giant shrugged. As the heads talked, Laurie snuck back to him.

"I think they're trying to figure out what to do," she whispered. "If we want to make a run for it, now's the time."

Matt nodded. The heads did seem to be debating their next move. The left one obviously wanted to check out whatever it had seen. The right head wasn't interested. Then the massive left arm grabbed the edge of the canyon as if to pull the giant out. The right head shook and sputtered something, but the left half started pulling itself out of the canyon in a weird, lopsided climb. Finally, the right head gave in, hissing smoke, and the other huge, muscled arm reached up....

"*Now* can we run?" Laurie said.

Matt hunched over and ushered them to the next rock and then the next. When the ground shook, Matt thought it was just his amulet quivering. Then Fen swore under his breath, and Matt knew he felt it, too. He prairie-dogged up and saw—

A fire giant. Which was, of course, what he knew he'd see, but there was a difference between watching it from a couple hundred feet away and seeing it right there. Okay, maybe not "right there," but close enough. *More* than close enough. It was no more than twenty feet away, so near that Matt could smell fire.

When one head spoke to the other, wisps of smoke wafted out. Sparks flew as the other head replied. Matt could see flames inside their mouths. Did they *spit* fire? That wasn't anything he'd read in the myths, but they were learning not everything was the way it was in the old stories.

"A sword?" Fen whispered. "Seriously? It needs a sword, too?"

Matt's gaze dropped to the monster's belt. "No, it needs two swords, apparently. Flaming swords."

"Of course," Fen muttered.

"You still want to fight it?" Matt said. "'Cause now's your chance."

Fen scowled.

"Hey, you might distract it," Matt said, grinning. "Take one for the team."

"I thought that was *your* job, Thorsen."

"Stop it," Laurie whispered. When they did, she said, "Do you think we should run?"

Matt peeked over the rock again and then shook his head. "It doesn't know where we are. It's still just looking around. Follow me."

He set out, hunched over behind the rocks. When he dared peer out, the Jotunn was still moving, but slowly, looking from side to side. They reached a spot where the rocks were little more than boulders, and they had to almost crawl then, creeping along as they tried not to inhale dust and sand from the rocky ground. That wasn't easy, especially for Matt, with an ancient Viking shield on his back. He had to stay far enough from the rocks to keep from scraping the shield against them. His amulet wasn't helping, either. Now it was vibrating so hard that Matt swore he could hear it.

When they saw a row of taller rocks, Matt let out a sigh

of relief...until he drew close enough to notice the ten-foot gap between their row and that one.

"It's not too bad," Laurie whispered. "We just need to time it."

Matt nodded. "I'll watch the giant. You get in front of me. When I tap your back, run. Fen—"

"Follow. Yeah, I get it." Did he look annoyed? Matt couldn't tell, and this wasn't the time to worry about it.

Laurie inched forward and got into position, crouched as low as she could get, ready to run on his signal. Matt peeked over the rocks. The Jotunn had stopped. Each head looked a different way—neither their way. Matt tapped Laurie. She sprinted, with Fen right behind her.

Matt let them get halfway across the gap, then took one step out, his gaze fixed on the fire giant. A second step. A third...

Blue light flashed. That's all he saw, a flash so bright it was like a stun grenade. He staggered back. Laurie let out half a yelp before stifling it.

Both Laurie and Fen were staring at him. At his chest. He looked down to see his amulet sparking a brilliant blue. His hands flew to cover it. A roar boomed through the air—a crackling, unearthly roar. Matt swung around and saw the Jotunn coming straight for them. No, coming straight for *him*.

He glanced at the cousins. "Run!"

As Matt turned to the Jotunn and raced toward it, Fen

shouted, "Wrong direction! I really wish you'd stop running *toward* danger, Thorsen!"

As Matt ran, the amulet vibrated, but there was none of the usual heat. It was almost cold. The burn of ice. The amulet glowed so bright now that it cut through the swirling smoke and lit the dim wastelands like the midday sun.

The Jotunn had stopped running. It stood there, both heads tilted, looking at him in confusion. Matt pulled the shield from his shoulder and slung it over his arm. All four eyes of the Jotunn widened.

"*Vingthor,*" one of the heads rumbled.

*Vingthor. Battle Thor.*

Not exactly...but Matt still smiled. Adrenaline tore through him, sparking and sizzling like the amulet, and when his hand shot out, it wasn't even a conscious action. He just did it, as naturally as breathing. There was a deafening crack as ice shot from his fingertips. Yes, ice. A blast of white that froze into a shard of solid ice as it flew. It hit the Jotunn in the stomach and sent the giant crashing to the ground so hard the vibration nearly knocked Matt onto *his* butt.

Matt stood there, grinning.

*I can do this. I can really do...*

The Jotunn sprang up. It didn't struggle up, dazed, like the trolls had—it leaped to its feet like a gymnast and barreled toward Matt. His hand shot out to launch another ice bolt. And it worked—the ice flew from his fingers and whipped straight at the Jotunn. But the giant's massive fist swung, hit the ice bolt, and shattered it into a thousand harmless slivers.

"Matt! Come *on!*" Laurie shouted.

Matt turned and ran. Ran as fast as he could, the ground shaking under his feet. The Jotunn roared, and the heat of its roar scorched Matt's back.

"Run!" he yelled to Fen and Laurie. "Go!"

They took off behind the row of rocks. Matt veered to the left before he reached them. He was heading for another row of rocks, farther down, to keep the Jotunn away from the cousins. Then he saw the fissure—a crack in the rocks, maybe three feet across. If he could get down in there, the Jotunn couldn't reach him. He ran over and raced alongside the crack, getting a look down. It tapered off past the opening. The lowest point he could see was maybe ten feet down. Too far to jump. He should—

The Jotunn roared with a gust of heat that made Matt gasp. Sparks blasted him, burning his skin, singeing holes in his shirt. He spun, and the giant was right there, a flaming sword in each hand. One blade headed straight for him. Matt swung his shield up, but even as he did, he realized his mistake. Flaming sword. Wooden shield.

His amulet flared again, and cold ice shot down his arm and into his hand. There was a blast of white as snow whipped up and swirled around his shield arm. The flaming sword struck the wood with a thunderous *clang*. The blow knocked Matt clear off his feet. He fell backward, and as he did, he remembered where he'd been standing. On the edge of a chasm.

There was no time to grab anything. No time to even right himself. He fell backward into the fissure, his head hitting the rock side with an explosion of pain so intense he blacked out. He came to and found himself wedged as far down as he could get in the crevasse. He lay there, looking up, not daring to move, certain he'd broken something, probably broken *everything*. Then the Jotunn's two heads appeared over the edge of the chasm. One mouth opened. Fire blasted. Matt got his shield up just in time. A layer of ice snapped over the wood, and the fire bounced off.

The other mouth opened. Smoke billowed, and Matt thought, *That's it? Really?* Then the smoke hit him, so thick he choked and sputtered, eyes watering as he gasped for breath.

Matt yanked his shirt up over his nose and mouth. Then he flipped over and began to awkwardly crawl with his shield slung over his shoulder, protecting his back. Not easy to do when there wasn't a flat bottom. His feet kept sliding farther down into the fissure, and he almost got his shoe stuck more than once.

It felt like he had indeed broken everything, but he kept moving as fast as he could. The fissure dipped, getting deeper, and soon he couldn't feel the heat against his back. He glanced over his shoulder to see the Jotunn reaching into the chasm, but he was too far down.

"Hey!" a voice shouted. "Hey, you! Fire creep!"

Fen's voice echoed through the wasteland. When Matt looked up, he saw the Jotunn's two heads looking every which way, as if they couldn't find the source of the voice. Matt crawled faster. Fen kept shouting. Finally, with a grunt, the giant took off, ground shaking as it ran.

Matt grabbed the side of the fissure and began crawling up. When he popped his head out, the Jotunn was a few hundred feet away, looking around wildly.

"Matt!" It was Laurie, whispering loudly.

A hand appeared from behind a rock. Matt took one last look at the Jotunn, then heaved himself out of the fissure and ran for the cover of the rocks, where Laurie waited. When he reached her, he checked for Fen, to be sure he was safe. He seemed to be. He was keeping his distance from the giant and had gone silent now that Matt had escaped.

The Jotunn kept looking around, heads muttering to each other after each scan of the rocky plain. It checked the crevasse a few times, as if Matt might suddenly appear there. Finally, the giant lumbered back toward the chasm where it had first appeared. As it climbed down into it, Fen came along, jogging silently behind the rocks. Matt waited until he caught up, then the three of them set out again.

"You need to rest," Laurie whispered as they made their way across the rocky plain. The landscape had flattened out and the smoke had dispersed, but the ruined city was still a distant smudge against the endless twilight. The home of Helen, ruler of the afterlife. That's where they'd been headed, presuming that's where they'd find Baldwin.

"You can barely walk," she continued. "We've been up all night and hiking all day."

Matt shook his head. "We have a long way—"

"Fine." She raised her voice so Fen could hear. "I'm sorry, guys, but I really need a break."

Matt knew she didn't. He also knew that if he dared say so, Fen would snap and snarl at him for pushing his cousin too hard.

They settled on the rocky ground, because there was no place else to settle, not even a rise to perch on or a dip to hide in. They could only lower themselves to the flat ground in a circle, keeping a lookout for anything coming up behind the others. It felt good to stop, Matt's aching muscles sighing in relief. After falling into the chasm, he did need a rest, but considering their mission, he hadn't felt right saying so.

Their mission: to stop Ragnarök, the Norse end of days. In the old stories, the gods all died at Ragnarök. Except they were already dead. Odin, Balder, Loki...all gone. So Matt and the others needed to take their places, presumably without the dying part. If they failed? Then the world would be plunged into endless winter.

Matt rubbed his arms. Speaking of winter, there was a chill here he hadn't noticed when they had been moving. A damp chill. It seemed to settle over them, numbing Matt to his bones. He was going to say something, but Laurie was whispering to Fen, and Matt left them alone, falling back into his thoughts.

When his grandfather announced that Ragnarök was coming and Matt would be "Thor's champion"—to take Thor's place in battle—Matt had been...well, he'd like to say *honored*, but *terrified* was a better word. He knew everyone was counting on him, though, so he'd accepted his role and had been ready, to train, to fight, to win. Then he'd overheard his grandfather and the other elders saying they didn't expect Matt to defeat the Midgard Serpent. They actually *wanted* him to lose. Because if he lost, Fimbulwinter would come, and the world would be reborn, fresh and new...after nearly everyone on it died.

Matt still couldn't imagine how his grandfather could want such a thing. But he sure wasn't going to help it happen. So when he'd been sent to find the other descendants of the North, he'd taken Laurie and Fen and headed out.

"*Brrr*," Laurie said, shivering. "Does anyone else feel that?"

"Yeah," Fen said, looking at her worriedly. "We should get going soon."

He glanced toward the city, and Matt knew he was thinking about Baldwin. Their friend was the descendant of Balder, the most popular of the gods. According to the myths, after Balder's death, the gods went to Hel but failed to get him back, and that was the start of Ragnarök. That's why they were here. To change the myth. To get Baldwin back. To stop Ragnarök.

Matt looked at the distant ruined city. Yes, as Thor's champion, stopping Ragnarök was his priority. But as Matt Thorsen, he just kept thinking about Baldwin.

"We should go," he said.

"In a few minutes." Laurie rubbed her arms again and shivered. "You know what we need? A campfire."

"Those fire giants gave off plenty of heat," Matt teased. "We could go back and play with them for a while."

Laurie shuddered. "No thank you. I just wish my powers included fire-starting."

"I bet the twins could do it," Matt said quietly, staring into the middle of the circle.

Fen snorted. "I doubt it. They were useless. We'll find better replacements."

Laurie glanced at Matt, her expression saying she knew Fen was wrong. Even Fen knew he was wrong—Matt could tell by his blustery tone, as Fen tried to convince himself they were better off without Ray and Reyna, the descendants of Frey and Freya. Fen hadn't liked the twins much, but their magic had been useful, and they'd finally seemed to be making an effort to fit in with the group. Then Baldwin died, and the twins decided they weren't all that interested in saving the world after all. Not if it meant traveling to the afterlife. And certainly not if it could mean dying themselves.

"Okay," Matt said. "We really do need to get moving. Are you up to it, Laurie?"

She nodded, and they set out.

They walked for what seemed like hours until finally the city began to take form, and soon they could see the massive gates blocking their path.

"The gates to Hel," Matt murmured. "They say that once you pass through, you can never come out."

"So are we going to stand at the gates and yell for Helen instead?" Fen asked, sounding halfway serious.

Matt managed a wry smile. "I wish."

As they approached, they had to pick their way through ruined buildings. They ducked through doorways and climbed over rubble, and they were just about to crawl *under* rubble when Fen lifted his head and inhaled sharply.

"Smell something?" Matt said.

Fen's Loki-power was the ability to shape-shift into

a wolf, and he had a better sense of smell even in human form.

"Nah, just thought I—"

Laurie cut him off with a cry. "Matt! Watch—!"

Something grabbed Matt by the seat of his pants. He flew into the air, all four limbs working madly. Then, whatever had him let go, and he sailed onto a pile of rocks. Fresh pain exploded from every inch of his body.

Matt flipped over and looked up into a pair of eyes. Two pairs, actually, one right over the other—four red eyes glowering from matted black fur. Then the creature's jaws parted and white fangs flashed as it roared—the same roar Matt had heard when he was over by the Jotunn, now inches from his ears, making his head ring as his eyes squeezed shut. When he opened them again, he could see what was over him. A dog. A giant black dog with four red glowing eyes.

"Matt!" Laurie said. "Use your Hammer!"

Matt hesitated. He could easily work up enough fear and anger to invoke his power, but...well, his amulet wasn't vibrating, which gave him pause. It *always* vibrated for monsters. Unless this wasn't the same kind of monster as the trolls and the giants were...

Giant dog. Guarding the gates of Hel.

"Garm," he murmured as he looked into the beast's eyes. It snarled, drool dripping from its jaws, but it made no move to use those jaws on his throat. "It's Garm."

"I don't care what it's called," Fen said. "It's a big dog that wants to eat you for dinner, Thorsen. Now use your Hammer. Or do I have to rescue you again?"

"My amulet's not reacting," Matt said. "That means he isn't a threat."

"Right. He doesn't seem threatening at *all*," Fen said sarcastically as he raised his voice to be heard over Garm's roar.

Garm lowered his muzzle to Matt's face. Saliva dripped. Matt closed his mouth fast.

"Matt!" Laurie said. "Do something!"

Matt cleared his throat. "My name is Matt Thorsen. I'm a descendant of Thor, and I need to speak to—"

"Seriously, Thorsen?" Fen cut in. "You're trying to talk to him?"

"I need to speak to Helen," Matt continued. "I don't mean her any harm. If you could take me to her—"

Garm cut him off with a deafening roar.

# TWO

# FEN

## "PAVILION OF BONES"

Fen hadn't ever really considered Matt Thorsen a friend, not even when he'd agreed to join him on his whole save-the-world quest, but whether he liked the guy or not, he'd thought Matt was pretty smart. Watching him allow a giant monster dog to maul him while he chattered away at it made Fen seriously reconsider.

"Try using your Hammer, Thorsen!"

Matt just kept studying the beast, as if trying to decide whether the monster pinning him really did pose a threat.

Laurie scurried around looking for some sort of weapon. The terrain here was pretty desolate, so unless they developed troll-like strength to heft the giant stones or wanted to irritate the dog with tiny rocks, Fen knew that there wasn't anything useful. What he didn't know was how to fix this. He was—like Matt—more about jumping in to a fight than thinking it out. Thinking was Laurie's thing, but if *she* was looking for a weapon, they were in trouble. He glanced at his cousin and asked, "Ideas?"

The dog was now holding Matt in place with one big paw. Saliva dripped in a long, gooey strand, and Fen hoped that it wasn't some sort of toxic spit. Maybe the spit or some power in the dog's breath or something was making Matt think this wasn't a threat, but being pinned by a person-sized dog with spare eyes certainly seemed like an obvious threat to Fen.

"Get mad or whatever so you can use your inner Hulk!" Laurie demanded. Her voice had a desperate tone, but she wasn't foolish enough to charge the drooling four-eyed dog. *Yet.* She struggled to lift a piece of rubble that Fen knew she wouldn't be able to throw very far even if she did succeed in moving it, and then she paused and let out a yip as two giant black birds swooped down and landed on the rubble.

"Shoo! Go on. Go away!" She flapped her hands at them, and they tilted their heads as if they understood her. She turned back to Matt and said, "And you, defend yourself from the monster dog!"

Fen glanced at the birds, who seemed intent on studying Laurie. They seemed harmless, creepy in that way that birds usually were, but not dangerous. If they did attack, he could stop them. Defeating a giant dog that outweighed him was a little iffy, but he could handle a pair of ravens.

"Garm isn't attacking. He's a guard," Matt insisted from his pinned position.

"Right," Fen drawled.

Although he wasn't sure he could take on some sort of monster dog all by himself, he didn't see any other options, and he wasn't going to stand by and let it eat Matt. It wasn't because they were becoming friends or anything; Fen wouldn't let anyone get eaten by a monster. He paused. Okay, maybe Astrid. She was responsible for Baldwin's death. Fen could be on board with her being monster kibble. Not Matt, though.

"Stay out of the way," Fen told Laurie in a low whisper. "I think Thorsen's lost his mind or something."

Almost as soon as he thought *change*, Fen became a wolf. Maybe it was just because Fen was a descendant of Loki, and this world was ruled over by one of Loki's family. Whatever the reason, it was only a blink between thinking about being in his other shape and actually becoming a wolf. Fen flashed his cousin a wolfy grin, wishing he could tell her how cool that just was. She hadn't ever become a wolf, though, and even if she had, he couldn't talk to a person when he was a wolf—even if she were *wulfenkind*, which she wasn't.

He turned his attention to Garm and stalked toward

the giant dog. It might be big, but it was a dog, and wolves were tougher than dogs any day of the week. Fen figured he would just take a running leap and knock Garm off of Matt.

"Okay, puppy, let's play," Fen said.

Just as Fen was about to pounce, Garm's gaze swung to him and he said, "This is not play."

Fen skidded to a stop, claws scraping over the rough ground. "Did you *say* something?"

"I merely replied. You spoke; I replied. That is how one has a conversation," Garm said. He still had a paw on Matt, holding him in place, but his attention was on Fen now. He swept out a black tongue and licked the spittle that had been dangling from his massive jaws.

The gesture made Fen tense. "We're not kibble."

"Kibble? Who or what is kibble?" Garm tilted his head, looking like any other slightly perplexed dog, just an awfully *big* one.

"Food. We're not food."

Laurie had come up to stand beside Fen while he was focused on Garm. She leaned over, her gaze still on Garm and Matt, and said, "What are you doing?"

Fen huffed. He couldn't talk to her in this shape. *Wait. Maybe I can!* He was talking to Garm, so maybe it was a part of the magic in Hel. He looked up at her and said, "Talking."

She shook her head. "Don't yip at me!"

"They don't understand," Garm said, somewhat needlessly.

"I keep asking questions of this one"—he nudged Matt with his head, which caused Laurie to yelp—"but he doesn't answer."

Matt, despite being very close to massive, drooling dog jaws, hadn't reacted. Laurie, on the other hand, had a very familiar expression: one he'd seen on her every time she was about to leap into trouble of some sort. She squared her shoulders and went to grab a handful of small pieces of rubble. The rocks weren't that big, but they would still hurt.

"That's a bad idea." Garm's voice had a bit of a growl to it now. "I have a function, and that will not change it. It *will* anger me, though. When I am angry, I do sometimes bite."

Fen swung around and stepped in front of his cousin. Gently, he took her wrist in his mouth and held it.

"Well, if neither of you are going to do anything, that leaves me," she started.

Fen growled a little, and she dropped the rocks with a sigh. "I hope you know what you're doing."

He released her and tried to give her a comforting smile, although smiles weren't exactly a standard wolf expression. So he added a friendly lick to her already wet forearm.

"Gross." She wiped the saliva from her arm and scowled at him.

As soon as she looked at him, Fen swung his head from side to side. He couldn't talk to her, and the smile wasn't particularly effective, but maybe he could use a gesture she would understand.

She put her hands on her hips and said, "No? He has Matt, and you're standing there yipping."

The ravens swooped close to her, eliciting a small squeal as they startled her. Fen flashed his teeth at the birds, but they were gone in an instant. He turned his attention back to Laurie.

"I think Fen is talking to him," Matt said. "Right, Fen?"

The indignity of trying to communicate with them like he was a dumb beast was enough to make Fen not want to reply. Of course he was talking to Garm! What else did they think he was doing? It was insulting. Still, Fen had no way to talk to Laurie unless he shifted back, and Matt had said what Fen needed to tell Laurie, so he dipped his head to look at his feet and then up at the sky. He repeated it a second time. It was a slow movement because it was an awkward gesture for a wolf, but it was a nod.

It was hard to listen to his friends and also Garm, so although Matt and Laurie were still talking, Fen padded over to stand in front of Garm. "You ought to let him up."

"Your sort doesn't belong here," Garm growl-said.

"Kids?"

"Live people," Garm corrected with a snort. "Plus, you god sorts always end up irritating my master."

Fen tried to think of a good answer to that. This wasn't

exactly his area, though. He was more instinct and failing to think, but since he was the only one able to talk to Garm, he had no choice but to handle this situation.

"We aren't here to irritate your master," he said.

Garm huffed. "Helen doesn't like godlings."

"I don't like a lot of them, either," Fen offered, trying to be friendly. "Ray and Reyna, who didn't come, are very irritating."

Garm sort of grinned, his massive dog mouth opening slightly. "You are Father Loki's kin. Seeking silvered words to convince me to do what you want. He was like that."

Fen paused as he realized that he wasn't going to have a lot of luck conning someone who apparently had experience with the god who was Fen's ancestor. So he figured he'd try straight truth. "A friend of ours is here," Fen said. "We just want to talk to your, uhhh, master. We're not here to start a fight. Can we just see Helen?"

Garm didn't reply for a moment, and Fen thought for sure that the dog was going to refuse, but then he stepped away from Matt and said, "I will allow you to see her, but I will not guarantee your safety or her mood. Helen can be possessive of her guests. Come."

And then the giant dog turned and started toward the gates.

The gates themselves weren't particularly striking, aside from their size, but there was a creepy statue of a woman that made Fen pause. It seemed to be watching them attentively, but statues don't watch people. It was disturbing. Maybe that's why the statue was outside the gates, where it could get damaged—no one wanted it staring at them.

Laurie was rushing to Matt as he scrambled to his feet. Once Matt was up, he walked toward Fen and reached out with one hand like he was about to ruffle Fen's fur. Reflexively, Fen flashed his teeth at Matt, and within the next moment, Fen had transformed back to his human shape.

"Do I look like a house pet to you?" Fen snarled, sounding a little wolfish.

Matt held up his hands. "Whoa, I wasn't going to pet you. It was just a friendly atta-boy clap on the—"

"Don't care, Thorsen," Fen interrupted. "Just don't touch me."

Laurie and Matt exchanged another look that they probably thought he didn't see. He did. He just didn't feel like wasting time talking about it. They thought he was being a jerk, and maybe he was. Sometimes, though, Fen just wanted to be *more* than he was. Matt had already had the Hammer punch, and now he had the ice thing. In the past few days, Laurie could suddenly open portals. What did Fen have? Nothing new. Being able to turn into a wolf was the exact same thing he could do before their trip, and it was the same thing dozens of other members of his family could do. His only new thing was talking to a big dog—which might only work in Hel. It was selfish, and Fen knew it, but he wanted to be the special one for a change. If all he had was being a wolf, he wanted them to respect it, maybe even fear it a little, and being patted on the head wasn't a sign of respect.

They stood at the gates, three kids and a big dog. If not for the fact that the gates were in Hel and the dog had a spare pair of eyes, it might seem pretty normal. It wasn't, but not much had been lately. Ever since Matt had been chosen as Thor's champion and learned that Fen was Loki's stand-in for the big fight, everything in their lives had become... weird. They'd fought monsters, slept in the forest, made friends with other descendants of the gods, including a kid who was then murdered—and, oh, yeah, decided to come to Hel to get their murdered friend back. The definition of what was normal for them had changed pretty drastically. What was unchanged was that Fen still felt lost. The one person he'd trusted—his cousin Laurie—had become too chummy with Thorsen, and as much as Fen had sort of started to *like* Thorsen, he didn't like Laurie being on anyone's side but his.

"Can you, umm, tell us what Garm said?" Matt asked cautiously.

The gates opened soundlessly.

"He said that we can talk to his master, but we shouldn't be here on account of the fact that god-type people irritate her... and because we're alive." Fen shrugged as they followed Garm through the open gates. He figured that Garm had a point, or two points, really: this was a place for dead folks, and he'd never heard of any myths where the gods weren't annoying in their requests. The gods hadn't exactly *requested* that their descendants fight Ragnarök. He'd do it, but he wished he could tell off a few dead gods for the mess they'd left for their descendants to sort out.

As they walked, Garm bark-growled a couple times, and Fen debated becoming a wolf to see what he was saying, but considering the dog's pace and impatient looks when he paused for them to catch up, Fen figured it was the equivalent of *Walk faster, two-legged creatures.*

A few moments later, they walked up to a pavilion that looked like it belonged at any number of community parks—at least it did until Fen looked closer and saw that the poles supporting the roof appeared to be made of massive bones. "Maybe that's what happens to Jotunn who misbehave," he murmured to Laurie with a nod at the enormous bones.

His cousin frowned for a minute, but then he bumped his shoulder into hers and said, "Sorry."

That was all it took for her to smile at him. He wasn't always sure what he was apologizing for, but he knew that when she was unhappy, apologies helped. Today was no different. She leaned into him a little, and then rested her head on his shoulder briefly. "Grump."

"Yeah," he admitted. He nodded at Matt, who smiled at him. Fen was grateful that Matt wasn't going to push him to talk this time. It was one thing to have feelings; it was another to chat about them. Fen shuddered a little. That was one of the only benefits of not having parents: no one ever wanted to talk about feelings, or screwups, or any of that stuff. It was one of the best parts of being raised by wolves. Literally, his family turned into actual wolves. When he screwed up, he got knocked down or growled at or maybe nipped. *That* made sense to him.

From somewhere nearby, a woman's voice said, "Garm says that you are not going to irritate me."

If Fen had been in wolf form, his hair would be bristling. He looked around, not sure where the person who went with the voice was. The pavilion of bones had seemed empty when they arrived, and it still was. He glanced at Matt, and then whispered to Laurie, "Stay behind us."

The woman laughed. "Come in, godlings. I am Helen."

Fen reached back and took Laurie's hand in his, mostly to keep her from rushing into anything, but also to hold on to her in case the invisible woman decided to try anything. At the very least, by holding on to Laurie, he couldn't be separated from her.

Then, cautiously, Fen and Matt stepped into the empty pavilion. Laurie was only a step behind them. As they entered the pavilion, it went from empty to overflowing— or maybe they were transported into another building. Fen glanced over his shoulder. He could see the gates not too far away, but when he looked around him, he wasn't entirely sure that the contents of the pavilion would truly fit *inside* the space he'd seen when he was outside of it. A line of long tables stretched the length of a football field. The tables were covered with food, not the stuffy sort that he'd seen in movies, but the good stuff. Bowls overflowed with corn chips, pretzels, and what looked like potato chips in every possible flavor. Fountains of soda bubbled, and in a few cases, the soda seemed to pour out of levitating vases, the mouths of fish sculptures, and a barrel held in the arms of a monkey statue. Pizza pies were steaming on upraised platters, and mounds of hot dogs and cheeseburgers were heaped on other platters. As Fen looked farther down the tables, he could see brownies, cookies, pies, and tubs of ice cream. He was almost tempted to go to the tables, and his grumbling stomach certainly seemed to agree with that plan.

He glanced at Matt and Laurie; they seemed entranced by the feast before them, too, but then all three of the descendants noticed the extremely tall woman who watched them. She looked like she was no more alive than the monkey statue. Her skin was shiny, almost plastic, like one of those creepy dolls in the all-pink aisles of a toy store, and her eyes looked a bit like beetles. The shimmering colors in those beetle eyes made it hard to look away from her gaze— even as she stalked toward them. Despite her alien features, she was amazingly lifelike when she moved. Her dress made a swishing noise as she stopped in front of them, and Fen realized that it was covered by—or maybe *made of*—living winged insects.

The wings of her dress opened and closed rapidly as she peered down at the kids. "You amuse me so far, little godlings. What do you want so desperately that you would travel to a land filled with death?"

"We would like to take our friend home, ma'am," Matt said.

"Baldwin," Fen interjected. "Our friend Baldwin. He died by mistake, and we need—"

"Death is not a mistake, Nephew," Helen chastised. "It is many things, but not a mistake."

"Nephew?"

"Many generations apart, but..." She flicked her fingers in a small, dismissive gesture. "*Nephew* will work. My father was your long-ago ancestor, so you are my family." Helen lowered a hand onto Fen's shoulder and at the same time stroked Laurie's hair with her other hand. "Like all of the *wulfenkind*."

Laurie had tensed when Helen touched her, and Fen's first instinct was to push his "aunt" away. Her mention of the *wulfenkind* didn't do much to convince him she was trustworthy. If she turned out to be a threat, he'd have to attack.

"In the myth, one of the gods didn't mourn Balder when he died," Matt said, his voice drawing their attention and

breaking the building tension. "Loki's representative"—he pointed at Fen—"*is* mourning."

Helen's seemingly plastic face didn't change, except for a slight curve at the corners of her mouth. Fen thought it was a smile or maybe Helen's version of a laugh. The creatures out of myth that he'd met didn't exactly act like regular folks. The Valkyries were completely lacking a sense of humor; the monsters were straight out of the late-night movies that he probably shouldn't be watching; and now, the lady who ruled over the dead seemed like an animated doll—the sort that also might belong in scary movies or books. He wasn't sure what to say or do.

"We would like to take our friend home . . . Aunt Helen," Laurie said in her I'm-a-good-girl voice.

Helen laughed, a bark of noise that seemed exceedingly odd because her features remained immobile. The iridescent wings on her dress all shivered, creating a prism of color. Then, Helen looked at Laurie. "Fenrir has my father's temper, but you would mislead like Father Loki did." She shook her head. "You do not think me an aunt any more than you think yourself a hero, Niece of Mine."

Helen swept her arm to her side, and a doorway opened in the air. Baldwin stepped through the doorway, looking as alive as he had when they were in his house. On second glance, though, Fen could tell that something was different. He was a somewhat slower, paler version of himself.

Baldwin had been a nonstop blur of crazy words and hurtles into danger. Seeing him seeming so sluggish was wrong—not as wrong as seeing him dead after he'd been poisoned, but still, it sucked.

"Hey!" The dead boy grabbed Fen and Laurie in a hug and then released them and stepped away. "Man, did Astrid kill you, too? Wow. That's just not cool. I guess someone else will have to fight the big snake and the Raiders." He shook his head and looked at Matt. "Totally *un*cool for you, but I still think you'd have been great at it. It's great to see you. I mean, not *great*, but—"

"Baldwin," Helen interrupted.

"Oh, hey." He flashed her a smile. "Isn't Helen awesome? She has the best food here." He darted off and grabbed a slice of pizza.

Maybe he wasn't changed as much as Fen had thought. Still, Fen watched in shock as Baldwin shook crushed red pepper on the pizza. "Wait! What are you doing?"

"It's good," Baldwin said around a bite of pizza. "No poison on the pizza here. Plus, we're all already dead, so it's not like we can re-die."

He took another bite while they stared at him.

"We're not dead, Baldwin," Matt said carefully.

*He's not breathing.* That was the other thing that was different. It made sense and all: Baldwin *was* dead. However, he was talking, walking, and eating as if he were alive. He simply wasn't breathing. Fen found himself watching how very still Baldwin's chest was. Baldwin's death was the worst thing that had happened so far. As a rule, Fen didn't like people, but Baldwin was impossible to dislike. Fen had felt like his guts were being ripped out when Baldwin died. It was horrible. He was here now, though, and Fen hoped that Helen would let them take the murdered boy home.

"You're in Hel."

"We are," Fen agreed.

Baldwin shook his head and swallowed another bite of his food. "Shock," he said sagely. "It'll fade." He walked up to Matt and patted his back. "It's hard to accept being dead, but—"

"No," Laurie interrupted. "We're actually not dead, Baldwin. We're here to rescue you."

The boy frowned in confusion. "From what? There are monsters I can fight with, pizza, and Helen's pretty good at games. We played this one called Tafl that's like an old Viking game. Have you heard of it?"

"Sure..." Matt cleared his throat. "We'll play Tafl. At home. *After* we stop Ragnarök. Right now, though, we need you to come with us."

"I'm not sure I can," Baldwin said. "Helen, the death thing is permanent, right?"

The ruler of Hel had watched the entire exchange with the same expression, but Fen suspected that her inflexible features were just *her*, not in response to the things around her. "Typically, those who arrive here don't leave," she said, "but for my niece and nephew, I could make an exception if I chose to do so."

"You're related to Helen?" Baldwin's eyes widened. "Too cool. So do you visit her a lot?"

"No," Fen said. He took a deep breath and then locked eyes with Helen. "Thorsen says the myth is that Loki didn't weep, but I...did." Fen felt uncomfortable. Crying wasn't something anyone liked to admit to doing, but he knew that the myth said that crying was the key. In a low voice, he added, "I cried."

"Really?" Baldwin started. "That's so nice."

Laurie shushed Baldwin and then added, "We *all* wept. What Astrid did was awful."

"And clever," Helen murmured.

"She killed Baldwin. That's not clever; it's evil." Fen's hands curled into fists, discomfort ending as his temper stirred. "Baldwin is a good guy, and because some myth said his death was the start of Ragnarök, Astrid *murdered* him, and she used me as part of her sick plan."

"True," Helen said emotionlessly.

Fen wasn't sure if Helen was agreeing to the facts or that Ragnarök was starting or that Astrid was evil. It didn't matter, though. All that mattered was Baldwin's release, so he pushed his temper away as best he could and continued,

"We came. We wept. You already said you could let him go, so what's it going to be?"

Helen looked at them, her gaze assessing, and after a moment she said, "Fine. You can take him."

"Thank you, ma'am," Matt said. "Thank you very much."

But before anyone else could speak, Helen added, "There is one problem."

"Of course there is." Fen sighed. Just once it would be awesome if there weren't a problem, or a monster, or an enemy. He could see Laurie's shoulders slump and suspected she felt the same way. Thorsen, of course, was more upbeat.

"Okay," Matt said. "What is it?"

Helen looked at them each in turn, stopping last on Laurie, before saying, "The doorway that you opened, Niece, can only allow as many out of my domain as came into it."

They all stared at her in shocked silence for several moments.

"Well, if you guys aren't dead, none of you should stay," Baldwin said. "That wouldn't make any sense. I'll just stay here."

Laurie swallowed and in a very shaky voice offered, "I can open the portal, and you can all go through it, and since I'm not one of the representatives of the gods necessary for the fight, I can—"

"No!" Fen snarled. "Not. Going. To. Happen."

"Are there other ways out?" Matt asked.

Helen nodded. "One. I could give you directions."

"Okay." Matt nodded. "Laurie, you open the portal, and you three go back. I can use the other, umm, exit."

Fen's attention snapped from his cousin to Matt. "Are you cracked, Thorsen? You saw the Jotunn *and* Garm, and Baldwin says there are other monsters. He might be impervious to harm, but *you* aren't. You can't risk dying here when you're the one who needs to defeat the big snake thing!" Fen shook his head. "I'm surrounded by crazy people." He pointed at Baldwin. "You are coming back with us." Then he pointed at Laurie. "You are...just...don't you ever say something like that again. *Ever.*" Finally, he pointed at Matt. "And you're not wandering Hel by yourself. We're a team. If one of us has to stay, we *all* travel to the exit."

All three of them stared at him with expressions somewhere between shock and amusement. Fen didn't back down after his outburst. He knew he was right. They were all so eager to sacrifice themselves sometimes that no one looked at the big picture. He stared at them, braced for argument.

Instead, Baldwin grinned and said, "Huh. I thought Loki's champion would be a troublemaker, not all 'go team!'"

"Fen's right," Matt said. "We'll stick together."

Laurie bumped Fen's shoulder but said nothing.

He felt his face burning with embarrassment and forced himself not to look at his feet to hide it. Okay, maybe he liked them all a bit more than he let on, but seriously, they *were* a team: a monster-defeating, save-the-world team. Teams stuck together. With a lot more confidence than he usually felt, he looked at Helen. "So let's have it, Auntie Helen: where's the exit?"

"I'll give you a map," Helen offered, "and something you didn't ask for." She paused then, her hand absently stroking the insects of her skirt like they were pets, before adding, "Odin's child has been captured by other members of our family. They are not being kind to him."

Laurie gasped at the revelation, and Fen's stomach sank even further. He didn't know Odin's champion, but *no one* deserved to be a prisoner of the *wulfenkind*. Their *good* behavior was awful, so he didn't imagine they were treating a prisoner well at all. He wondered what other enemies were with them. It couldn't be just the wolves and Astrid, could it? Were the trolls involved? The mara? Monsters they didn't know yet? *Rescue one godling, and another is already in danger.* He stepped a little closer to Laurie.

Helen gave him the kind of smile that said she noticed and knew why. Then she handed Laurie what seemed to be hundreds of tiny wings stitched together into a parchment of sorts. As Laurie tilted it, it seemed to be transparent; the map had been drawn on the wing-paper in some sort of thick red ink. Fen wondered if this was what happened to the winged things she wore after they died. Was their fate becoming paper? He stopped himself before he could wonder what the ink was.

As Fen lifted his gaze from the map, his cousin blurted out, "Oh, wait! Can we ask which side you'll be on? In the battle, I mean?"

Instead of replying, Helen simply smiled and vanished, leaving the four kids standing in an empty pavilion.

"Right," Laurie said. "No more answers there." She took a deep breath and returned to studying the map, muttering, "We'll go home, and then try to rescue Owen, and—"

"Not try," Matt said, his tone even but firm. "We *will* rescue him."

They didn't know Owen, but he was one of them. Fen and Matt exchanged a look, and Fen saw his own resolve mirrored there.

"I hope so," Laurie said.

Fen bumped his shoulder into her. "He'll be okay. We'll go get him."

His cousin leaned into him and nodded once. Then she held up the map so they could all look at it. "It looks like we're over here, so we"—she lifted her eyes and surveyed the area—"go that way."

# THREE

# OWEN

## "THOUGHT AND MEMORY"

Owen thought he was prepared to be captured. Like his father, his grandfather, and his great-grandfathers, Owen had always known about the coming battle. They were—as their ancestor, Odin, had been—born "all-seeing," so they knew when the end of the world was going to be. It shifted, like all futures did, as people made choices. A few recent choices had brought Ragnarök forward by several years, far sooner than he'd have liked.

"Hey, god-boy!" One of the Raiders, cruel *wulfenkind* who were descendants of the god Loki, kicked him.

Owen opened his eyes. For now, he could still do that, but every day, he tried to convince himself to only open the one, to get used to losing his eye. When he was little, he'd worn an eye patch for an entire school year to practice having only one eye. The other kids called him "pirate" and "freak." He didn't tell them that he was even stranger than they thought. His family was proud of him. They called him brave. He didn't tell them that he cheated. When he was alone in his room, he would remove the patch.

"If you're so all-knowing, shouldn't you have known we would capture you?" the Raider taunted.

"Yes." Owen smiled at the boy. He'd discovered that his smile frightened them, so he smiled often. "I knew."

The boy backed up, and Owen smiled wider. He was a prisoner wearing handcuffs, but he was also a boy who was taking the place of a god in a great myth. The *wulfenkind* were just bullies. They thought that kicking him and saying mean things would make him afraid. It didn't. It reminded him when and where he was, and that helped him stay strong. Odin was a god who could see the future; Owen was a human with a god's gift. Sometimes that meant that Owen got confused on what *had* happened and what was *going to* happen. He saw everything—up until he became a participant in an event. As long as he wasn't actively a part of a mission, he could still see it. Once he started making choices about a situation, his future-sight vanished. That's why he was staying away from the others for now.

He looked forward to meeting them, though. Knowing

the future had made it really hard to make friends. In the myths, Thor and Loki were friends with Odin, and Owen really hoped that the gods' representatives would also be his friends. For now, he had only his two ravens: Thought (Huginn) and Memory (Muninn).

As if he'd summoned them, they arrived and landed on him, one on each of his shoulders. Their talons squeezed, digging into his skin. Thought and Memory told him what they had seen in Hel. He tried to listen carefully, but the voices of ravens were strange.

Owen shifted, trying to get comfortable as he listened to the ravens. They told him that Thor and Loki were still in Hel, and they cautioned that the rooster had not yet spoken.

"Maybe the rooster will stay silent, and the end won't come," he whispered.

The ravens both looked at him like he was a fool. They reminded him that Balder had been killed, and the rooster would speak. Ragnarök was beginning, and the battle was unavoidable.

"You'll stay with me?" he asked, hating that he sounded afraid. He usually hid his emotions well, but no amount of preparation would make today any easier.

"We stay now," Thought said.

"It hurt Odin," Memory added.

"It will hurt you, but we stay," Thought promised.

The Raider guarding Owen tried to shoo Huginn and

Muninn away again, but the ravens dug their talons into Owen's shoulders. They weren't leaving him. The birds cawed at the Raider, pecking at the boy's hand as he tried to make them fly away.

"Nasty birds," the Raider muttered, smearing the blood from the back of his hand onto his ripped pants.

"They are *mine*," Owen murmured. "Tell your boss that they are here. He's been waiting for this, too."

"Like *you* would know," the boy scoffed.

Owen smiled before he said, "The ravens told me. They tell me everything. I know what your boss will do next." He ·took a moment so his voice wouldn't waver, and then he finished, "And I am ready."

# FOUR

# MATT

## "BEACH OF BONES"

s soon as their feet left the stone floors of the pavilion, fog rolled in, smelling wet and rank, like swamp water. Matt peered into the fog, seeing only that thick gray blanket. The pavilion had been oddly hushed, but out here it was so silent he could hear the others breathing. The noise of it sounded strange, unnatural in this dead world. Unnatural and unwanted.

Matt took a step and his shoe crunched, making him jump back. He peered down to see sand. Or pebbles. White pebbles. That's why everything looked gray—they were walking onto a massive white beach shrouded in fog.

He continued forward. The others followed.

"Can anyone see?" Laurie had whispered it, but her voice echoed like a thunderclap.

Matt started to say no. Then he realized his eyes were adjusting. He could make out a figure ten feet away. He was no taller than Matt and thinner than Laurie but definitely a grown man, his face lined and gray. Actually *gray*—not just pale. His entire figure was that color, from his hair to his clothes to his skin to his shoes, as if he was cast in stone. He was dressed like a Viking *thrall*—an indentured servant— wearing a simple belted tunic and laced sandals.

"I think we're supposed to follow him," Matt said, pointing.

"The statue?" Fen said.

"It's one of Helen's servants."

"Um, no, it's a statue. I saw ones just like it back in the pavilion and near the gates."

Matt shook his head. "It's Ganglati, Helen's manservant. Ganglot was inside, too—she's the maidservant."

"You're losing it, Thorsen. That is a statue. Watch."

Fen broke into a lope, ignoring Laurie's cries for him to stay close. As he drew near the figure, a sheet of mist blew by, obscuring it. When the mist passed, the "statue" stood another ten feet away.

"See?" Matt said.

"That's creepy," Fen grumbled. "Statues aren't supposed to move."

49

"They're not really statues, though." Baldwin lifted a hand. "Hey, Ganglati. Thanks for the escort."

Fen turned to Baldwin. "You knew? Why didn't you say something sooner?"

"I didn't want to interrupt. That's rude. But you're right—they do look like statues. It's an easy mistake to make." Baldwin smiled, and Fen stopped grumbling.

They "followed" Ganglati. The manservant would disappear when they got close, only to reappear farther away. As they walked, the cold mist swirled around them. Matt rubbed his arms, but it didn't really help. It was so icy and wet, like a winter's rain.

*Bone-chilling cold*, his mom always called it.

*Bone-chilling.* That fit here, he supposed. So did "quiet as a tomb." The only sound was the crunch of their footsteps on the white pebbles below. As Matt tramped along, he realized his sneaker had come untied. He adjusted his shield and bent to tie his shoe. As he did, he saw the rocks. They seemed more like driftwood—bleached-white bits of varying shapes and sizes. One looked like a tiny tower, square and white with four points at the top. He poked at the piece, and the rest of it came out of the sand, a tapering white bottom. It was a tooth. A molar. Matt picked up another piece and saw the porous underside. Bone. That's what they were walking on. A beach of bones.

"Matt?" Laurie said. "What's wrong?"

"Nothing. Just fixing my shoe." He straightened and readjusted his shield. "Let's go."

After a while, the beach began to dwindle, the ground becoming soft, scattered with what were now undeniably bones—a skull here, a rib there. No one commented. They just continued on. The mist lifted, too, though occasionally Matt would feel a drip of cold water. When he looked up, he could make out roots far overhead. Yggdrasil—the world tree. Hel was under one root, earth beneath another, and the frost giants below the third.

When Matt noticed Ganglati standing to the side, he started that way, but the wraith lifted a hand, the movement so slow he seemed not to move at all. Matt continued toward him, but he vanished and reappeared farther, his hand still lifted. Very slowly, he shook his head.

"I think he's saying this is as far as he can take us," Laurie whispered.

"We're on our own after this?" Matt called.

Ganglati's head dipped in a nod. Then he vanished… and didn't reappear.

"Okay," Fen said. "So back to the map. Can you tell where we are?"

"I think so." Laurie unfolded the map and studied it for a moment. "We're looking for a river next."

"I hear running water," Baldwin said. "That way."

Matt nodded, and they continued on.

Something was following them. Matt had caught a faint noise a few minutes ago. Now it came again. It didn't sound like footsteps. More like a rustling, except…not quite. He couldn't place it and he wasn't sure he wanted to. Whatever lurked in the shadows was probably not something he cared to see. Yet it couldn't be too dangerous or his amulet would vibrate.

The sound came again, closer now.

"What is that?" Laurie asked.

"What's what?" Fen said.

"I heard something. No one else did?" She looked around at the boys, frowning.

Fen said he didn't, and Baldwin agreed. Matt thought of saying the same, just so no one would worry, but he couldn't bring himself to lie.

"I did," Matt said. "I think something's following us."

Laurie glanced over sharply. Fen spun on him, saying, "What?"

"It's probably just a ghost," Matt said. "A wraith or a *landvættir*. I hear a whispery noise, like a death shroud."

"Death shroud?" Laurie asked.

"You know, the thing they wrap corpses in. It's probably just a curious corpse following us."

"Huh," Fen said. "That's not disturbing at all."

"It *is* Hel," Matt said. "Or Niflheim. The division isn't exactly clear. There's Helen's domain, also known as Hel, and then there's Niflheim, which is—"

Something dove at Matt's head. He caught only the blur of motion coming straight at him.

"Down!" he shouted as he dropped.

The thing let out a strangled squawk and zoomed back up out of sight. As it flew away, Matt caught the beating of its wings and realized that was the noise he'd been hearing.

Another squawk and a dark shape swooped at them again.

"Take cover!" Matt said. "Over there!"

He pointed to a shadow about twenty feet away. As they ran, he could make out more shadows, domes about ten feet high, dotting the landscape. Burial mounds. He steered the group between two.

"How does this help?" Fen said as they crouched there. "It's dive-bombing us. We need to be *under* something."

"I know," Matt said. "I'm thinking." He paused as the creature squawked again. "Laurie? What does the map show? Any place to take cover?"

A rustle as she unfolded it. "It's too dark. I can't really see...."

The creature dove at them again.

"What is that thing?" Fen said. "Thorsen? You're the monster expert."

"I know; I know." Matt racked his brain to think of Norse flying beasts. There weren't many. "Maybe Hræsvelgr? He's a giant that sits at the end of the world and can take the form of an eagle."

"Or it could be a chicken," Baldwin said.

Fen laughed softly. "Yeah. I wish."

"Um, he's serious," Laurie said. "Look."

They all turned and followed Laurie's finger to see something perched on the burial mound right beside them. It was...

"A chicken?" Fen said.

Matt gazed up at the bird. It was a huge rooster, almost three feet tall and just as long from the tip of its dark red beak to the tip of its long tail feather, which was the same red, so dark it almost looked brown. *Soot red.* The words leaped to his mind, and as they did, his throat closed for a moment, breath coming hard. The rooster stayed there, balancing on the peak of the burial mound, crimson eyes fixed on his.

"'A sooty-red cock from the halls of Hel,'" he recited.

"A *what*?" Fen said.

"Cock. Rooster."

"Right. So what's with the, umm, rooster?" Fen said, his cheeks red, carefully not looking at his cousin.

"It's one of the three that will crow to signal the start of Ragnarök. The other two are in Valhalla and Jotunheim— the land of the heroes and the land of the giants."

"What if the rooster doesn't crow?" Fen said.

Fen's voice sounded odd, almost like a growl, and when Matt looked over, Fen was watching the bird the way a wolf would watch its prey.

"What?" Matt said.

"What if it doesn't crow? Would that fix things? No rooster, no Ragnarök?"

"Fen..." Laurie said, her voice low with warning.

Matt shook his head. "We've got that covered. Once we get Baldwin out of here, we've broken the myth cycle."

"We hope," Laurie murmured.

"Maybe we could use some insurance...." Fen said, eyeing the bird. "I can take down a chicken, even a giant one."

There was a definite growl in Fen's voice now, and as his hands flexed against the burial mound, they seemed to shimmer and pulse, as if about to change shape. The rooster looked right at him, head tilted. Then it turned to Matt and let out another squawk. Only this time, Matt didn't hear a squawk. He heard a word: "Soon."

The bird spread its red wings, flapped once, and lifted into the air.

"Soon," it said. "Soon."

*Soon. Ragnarök is coming soon.*

As it flew off, Matt stared after it, his stomach twisting. He dimly heard Fen make some comment, but he was too wrapped up in his thoughts to catch it.

*We got Baldwin back. We broke the cycle. We changed the myth.*

*Not yet. We still need to get him out. Then everything will be fine.*

"You don't belong here," a voice behind them said.

They all wheeled to see a huge bearded man in Viking garb. A warrior. Matt could tell by his spear and shield and helm, which—like real Viking helms—did not have horns. Otherwise, the man didn't wear any kind of armor, just a coat over his tunic.

Two other warriors stood, one on each side of him, blocking the gap between the burial mounds. All three looked—well, they looked dead. There was no other way to describe it. Their clothing was tattered, their faces gray and drooping, like they were one good beard-tug from sliding off. All three appeared to have died of old age, with graying hair, wrinkled faces, and not a full set of teeth among them.

"Viking zombies," Baldwin whispered. "That is so cool."

"Draugrs," Matt murmured back.

"What?"

"Viking zombies are called draugrs. They guard the treasures of the dead." He gazed around at the burial mounds. "But I don't think that's what they are. At least, I hope not."

As zombies went, draugrs were some of the nastiest. They weren't evil, like zombies, but if you got on their bad side, you were in trouble. Big trouble. Draugrs were the animated bodies

56

of dead Viking warriors, but they kept their human intelligence, and they could inflate to more than double their size for a fight. Plus, being already dead, they couldn't be killed.

Matt took a better look at the men. No, he was pretty sure they weren't draugrs. Just run-of-the-mill dead Vikings.

"You don't belong here," the big one said again.

"Yeah, we've already heard that," Fen muttered.

"And we completely agree," Matt said. "Which is why we're trying to leave. We'll be gone as soon as possible, and we're very sorry to have disturbed your, uh, afterlife."

"Leave?" another man said, perking up. "You can leave?"

Matt cursed himself for that one. "No, I mean, well, yes, *we* can, but only because we don't belong here, like you said. It's, uh, a special exit. For people who got here by mistake."

"Like us," the big man said. "We are here by mistake."

"You're not making this better, Thorsen," Fen muttered.

"We should be in Valhalla," the man said. "We are warriors."

"Right," Matt said slowly. "But only warriors who actually die in battle go to Valhalla, which I know is totally unfair and—"

"We died in battle."

"Little old for fighting, weren't you?" Fen muttered.

The dead man glowered at Fen and wrenched open his tunic. He pointed to a thin cut along his wrinkled breastbone. "What do you call this, boy?"

"Um, a giant paper cut?"

The dead Viking snarled and bellowed curses, calling Fen a shaggy hair, a bread nose, a half troll, and a pot licker.

As the old guy chewed Fen out, the other two men partly stripped to show equally shallow cuts. It was then that Matt realized what was going on. The problem with Valhalla was that warriors could only enter if they died in battle. Unfair, as he'd said, because if you thought about it, the rule meant you got a better afterlife if you messed up. If you were such a good warrior that you lived to die in bed? Well, then you were outta luck, like these poor guys. Matt had heard that sometimes old warriors would attempt to game the system by cutting themselves on their deathbeds, in hopes that the Valkyries would think they'd died of wounds sustained in combat. It apparently didn't work, but you couldn't blame the old guys for trying.

"You got a raw deal," Matt said finally, cutting in as Fen argued with the increasingly enraged ghosts. "I'm going to speak to someone about that."

"You?" All three dead men laughed so loud their drooping faces wobbled. "Who are you to speak for us?"

Matt pulled himself up straight. "I am Matthew Thorsen, descendant of the great god Thor. Chosen to be his representative at the battle of Ragnarök."

In a final flourish, he pulled the amulet from under his shirt. The three men stared at it. Then they burst out laughing.

"No, he's serious," Laurie said. "He's a son of Thor. And

Fen and I are..." She trailed off. "We're descendants of another great Norse god, and Baldwin here is a descendant of Balder. Everyone likes Balder, right?" She leaned over to Baldwin and whispered, "Say something."

Baldwin grinned and lifted a hand in greeting. "Hey, I'm Baldwin. I have no idea what's going on here, but you should listen to these guys. If they say they'll help, they will."

The men laughed again. Then one stopped and pointed at the map clutched in Laurie's hand.

"What is that?" he asked.

Matt tensed. If these men realized they had a map out of Hel...

"This?" Laurie held it up, but not before quickly flipping it to show them the back. "I don't know. I found it back there. Pretty, isn't it? It almost looks like it's made of insect wings."

"We really should be going," Matt said. "Like I said, I'll put in a good word for you. With the Valkyries. I know the leader. Hildar? Have you heard of her?"

As he babbled, he moved backward, subtly motioning for the others to do the same.

"That is a map," the big one said as Laurie carefully folded it while retreating.

"What?" Laurie looked down at it. "Really? Why would you think that? It just looks like shimmery paper. I thought it was pretty because, umm, girls like pretty things, right?"

"It is a map out of here," one said. "It is from Helen. No one else has paper like that."

"Really? Huh...she must have dropped it. Maybe it's a list or...notes. I bet that's it."

The dead Viking lunged. Matt grabbed Laurie's arm and whipped her behind him.

"Run!" he said.

They took off across the field, weaving in and out of the burial mounds.

"Can someone explain why we're running from old dead men?" Fen shouted as they went. "Those aren't giants, Thorsen. One good punch and they'll fall apart. We could take them."

"I don't want to," Matt called back.

"Why not?"

"Because they don't deserve it."

"Matt's right," Laurie said as they dodged a thighbone. "We can't take them out of here, but they're old warriors, so we should respect them."

"Then they should respect us, too," Fen grumbled. "We're descendants of gods. We don't run from old men."

"*Hrafnasveltir!*" one of the old Vikings bellowed. "Run, *hrafnasveltir!*"

"What's he calling us?" Fen snarled.

"Raven starvers. I'm guessing it means 'cowards'—someone who'll never fall in battle and feed the ravens."

"And that doesn't *bother* you?" Fen said.

"No, but it is kind of a cool phrase. I'll have to remember it." Matt glanced back over his shoulder. "I think we can slow down. The thing about running from old dead men? You don't have to run very far. They're way back there. Just keep walking fast and—"

Matt stumbled. Baldwin caught him before he fell, but he left his shoe behind. He looked down to see it mired in mud. Or, at least, he hoped it was mud.

"I think we found the river," Baldwin said, pointing as he retrieved Matt's shoe.

"Perfect," Matt said. "Once we're across it, we'll be past the land of the dead and on our way out." He glanced at Laurie. "Is that what the map says?"

She smiled. "It is."

Matt looked down at the boggy ground. He could make out the river about fifty feet away. Fog drifted over it, but it didn't seem to be that wide, maybe twenty feet across.

"Can everyone swim?" he asked. "It might not be that deep, but just in case."

They all said they could make it that far. They found a drier path and started across the wide bank. As they walked, the fog rolled in, licking around them, so thick they could barely see one another.

"Stay close!" Matt said. "Move slowly and make sure you can see someone else." He paused. "Better yet, let's form a line. Baldwin? Grab my shield. Laurie? Hold on to his shirt. Fen?"

"Bring up the rear," Fen muttered.

"Thanks. Let me know if you hear anything back there."

They continued forward. It was slow going. Matt didn't want to lead them into thick mud, so he felt his way with his toe, being sure to pick safe ground with each step.

"What's that noise?" Laurie called.

Matt had been paying too much attention to choosing a path to notice anything else, but when he listened, he caught a faint popping sound over the burble of water.

"The river, I guess?" Matt answered. "I think we're almost there. I smell..." He inhaled and coughed as the stench burned his nostrils.

"What *is* that?" Baldwin said.

"The river, I guess?" Matt said again.

Fen muttered something, but he was too far back for Matt to catch it.

"Stay alert," Matt said. "We should be there in just a few—"

He stopped. The fog had lifted and he could see the river now. It was wider than he'd thought, maybe forty feet across. The water came right up to the banks, but it wasn't like a beach, with shallow water stretching out to the depths. The bank seemed to drop straight off, the bone-strewn ground disappearing the moment it reached the water. Which didn't look like water at all. It was grayish-brown and weirdly thick, the consistency of stew straight from a can, gelatinous and disgusting. It even looked like stew, with dark chunks roiling through it, popping up, only to disappear again.

Also, it was bubbling.

At first Matt thought it was boiling—probably because of the stew comparison. But he couldn't feel any heat rising. Just stink. A terrible stink, like stew that'd been left out for weeks, rotting and foul. It bubbled away, popping and sputtering. When a drop hit his cheek, it hurt, and he pulled back, rubbing the spot.

"That doesn't look sanitary at all," Baldwin said.

"Or safe," Laurie said as she moved up beside them. "What is it?"

As they watched, a skull popped up. Or more of a head, really. Somewhere between the two. There was bone and there was...not bone. Hair. Skin. Teeth. Matt was happy when it dropped back under the surface.

"Whoa," Baldwin said. "I think it's like a soup. Of dead people."

"No," Matt said quickly. "That's not in the myth. It's just a river."

"A river with body parts," Fen said.

"I'll, uh, check it out," Matt said. "You guys stay here."

"No," Baldwin said. "I've got this, boss. I'm indestructible, remember?"

Baldwin edged past Matt. He took three careful steps to the river's bank. Then he dipped in his finger. When he pulled it out, Matt heard a weird fizzing noise. Smoke rose from Baldwin's finger. Matt raced forward, but by the time he got there, Baldwin was reaching another finger into the stuff. He dripped it onto his shirtsleeve. It sizzled and left a row of tiny holes where the drops fell.

"Acid, I think," Baldwin said, calmly wiping off his finger. "Huh. I liked this shirt, too."

"Acid?" Laurie said. "That's...We can't cross..."

"There must be a way," Matt said. "I think I remember something about a boat."

"I'll check the map." She did. "Okay, it looks like there's some sort of crossing. Either a boat or a bridge? It's not really clear. But it's a way across. We just need to find it."

"Then let's do that."

There *was* a boat. A longship, actually. Baldwin spotted it first, racing ahead and jumping in the beached boat, saying, "Check this out!"

It was, Matt had to admit, pretty cool. It wasn't nearly as big as a longship, of course. It wasn't even a *snekke*, which was the smallest form of longship and still about fifty feet long. This was more like a replica, ten feet from bow to stern. There were only two sets of oars. It did have the dragon on the prow. Or a serpent. It was kind of hard to tell—the two terms were often interchangeable in Norse myth, which meant he might be fighting a dragon at Ragnarök instead of a giant serpent, but he tried not to think about that.

"You need to get out of there," Fen called to Baldwin. "We can't push off otherwise."

"Sure you can." Baldwin grinned. "You've got mighty Thor. The god of battle."

"Not lately," Fen said. "More like the god of running-from-battle."

Matt looked over sharply, but Fen was smiling, and it seemed a real one. "Yeah, yeah," he said good-naturedly and waved for Baldwin to get out. Baldwin hopped over the side, and they all pushed the longship to the water's edge. Then Matt held on to it and said, "Climb in. I've got her."

Baldwin came around the stern. "Nah, you hop in. I was just kidding. I'll push her off. A little acid-wading won't hurt me."

"No, but it'll hurt your shoes, and you need them. I'll be careful."

Baldwin climbed back in the boat. He tried to take a set of oars from Laurie, but she wasn't giving them up, so he moved to the front to guide the boat. Laurie and Fen used the oars to push from the shore as Matt shoved from the back. Once it was mostly in the water, he said, "Hold her steady with the oars and I'll hop in."

Matt got one leg over the side. Then, with the other, he gave one last push off the shore. The boat shot into the water, and Matt was left hanging there for a second, straddling the side, one leg in and one out.

"Can you touch bottom with the oars?" he said. "Hold her still?"

Fen and Laurie tried, but even when they pushed their oars down as far as they could reach, they weren't touching bottom.

Matt eased his leg up carefully. Longships were known for their stability, even on rough water, but he wasn't about to take that chance when the "water" could strip the flesh from your bones.

At the thought, he moved a little too fast and had to stop, getting steady again.

"Just pull your leg inside, Thorsen," Fen said. "I know you think you're a big guy, but trust me, you're not going to flip her."

"I know. Hold on."

He pulled his leg up until it was almost on the side of the boat. Then he noticed the water burbling like a geyser right below his foot, and he started to swing over fast, but a hand shot from the middle of the geyser. It seized him by the foot. As he scrambled to grab something, anything, a whole body emerged from the river—a huge, rotting corpse, holding his foot tight in one bony hand.

Baldwin let out a cry. Fen reached for Matt. Matt caught his arm, but then the corpse wrenched with superhuman strength and Matt flew off the side of the boat, pulling Fen with him. He saw Fen's eyes go wide, and he knew it was too late to grab the boat, too late for Fen to grab the boat, and the only thing Matt could do was...

Let go.

He released Fen's arm and sailed over the river. He caught one last glimpse of the giant corpse. Then it released him, and Matt hit the water, flat on his back, arms and legs churning wildly as if he could stop his fall. He hit with a splash and watched as the acid-water closed over him.

# FIVE

## FEN

### "ZOMBIE STEW"

He just *let go!*" Fen sputtered. He stared for a split second at the spot where Matt had disappeared into the acid-water, and then, with a combination of shock and anger coursing through him, he flipped one of the oars upside down and poked the skinnier end into the water. He hoped he didn't bean Matt on the head with it, but he didn't see a whole lot of other options. He couldn't dive in: he'd end up bones and meat in minutes. He couldn't *not* try to save Matt, either.

As he sloshed the oar around in the water, he bumped into something and felt weight on the oar. He yanked it to the surface, realizing as he did so that the weight was too light but hoping that maybe Matt was swimming as Fen tugged. As he pulled the oar out of the water, he saw that the hair of a skull had tangled around the wood.

"You don't think that's..." Laurie started to ask.

Fen shook the head off the oar. It bobbed on the water, seeming to stare at them with dead eyes. It *couldn't* be Matt. Fen refused to think for a moment that it could be him. Thorsen might still get on Fen's nerves now and then, but that didn't mean that Fen wanted to see him reduced to his bones.

Quietly, Laurie asked the question she'd just left unsaid, "Is it Matt?"

"No, of course not!" Fen hoped that he wasn't lying as he put the oar back into the water and swished around, hoping Matt would grab on. It was weird that the boat and oar didn't disintegrate, but Fen figured they must be made out of something the acid-water wouldn't eat.

The remaining members of the group were scanning the water, hoping for a sight of their missing friend, when Fen realized with relief that the skull he'd pulled to the surface had stringy black hair. "It's not him!" he exclaimed. "See! Thorsen's got *red* hair. That guy"—he pointed at the skull—"had black hair."

Laurie and Baldwin both let out audible sighs, but Fen wasn't as relieved as he'd have liked to be. The current in the river was pushing the boat farther and farther from the spot where Matt had gone in, and they still couldn't see any clues of where he might be. On one hand, Fen thought that checking the spot where he'd gone in was the best idea. On the other, the current was stronger than it had seemed when they'd launched the boat; plus, there was whatever had pulled Matt into the water. If the water hadn't reduced Matt to bits of bone and meat, he was still fighting whatever had snagged him—all while under the water without air and dealing with river currents. The odds were against him. Even if none of the kids said it, they had to all be thinking it.

"Come on; come on," Fen muttered. "You're tougher than this, Thorsen."

"Fen? I'm still dead until we leave here." Baldwin pulled off his shirt and kicked off his shoes. Then he paused and glanced at Laurie. "Uh, can you close your eyes?"

"No, but I'll search on this side." Laurie turned her head so she was looking off to the other side of the boat. In a shaky but determined voice, she added, "Maybe the current pushed him this way."

Once she looked away, Baldwin unsnapped his trousers, but before Baldwin could finish stripping, Fen felt something heavy grab the oar. It felt like the biggest fish in the world, and there was no way he was going to pull it out on his own. "Wait!" he yelled. "I think I might have him...or he has me, or at least *something* does. Help me pull him up."

Baldwin and Fen tugged the oar back out of the water as

fast as they could, the boat leaning heavily to their side, and there, clinging to the oar, was Matt. His clothes were tattered, like...well, like he'd been swimming in acid-water.

Both boys reached into the water and grabbed him. The water burned to touch, but the skin wasn't sloughing off their hands like it would in real acid. Apparently, whatever was in this water destroyed fabric faster than flesh.

Laurie started to come to help, and the boat began tipping.

"Stay over there," Fen yelped. "We need to stay balanced."

"Sorry!" she squeaked.

Once Laurie returned to where she had been, the boat seemed to stabilize a bit. She leaned back, and it evened out more. It still tilted, but not so much that they'd all spill into the acid-water.

Fen looked over his shoulder and told her, "Grab that end of the oar."

Matt was clinging to it, even as Fen and Baldwin tugged at him. They had their hands on his upper arms, pulling him upward steadily. It felt like there was resistance, though, like whatever had pulled Matt in still struggled to keep him.

They weren't going to let that happen.

"Heave on three," Fen ordered.

Baldwin nodded.

"One, two, *three.*"

On three, they all yanked, and whatever had hold of

Matt lost its grip. Together they got his top half into the boat, and even in his only semiconscious state, Matt apparently knew instinctively to release the oar and grab the boat.

Laurie swayed backward as Matt released the oar, but she stayed in the boat. The momentum of her backward tilt helped offset the weight of Matt on the opposite side of the boat. It wasn't enough, though: Matt was a big guy. As the boat started to tilt again, Baldwin leaned backward, rocking in the direction opposite of the tilt.

"Go over there," Fen barked.

As Baldwin scrambled toward Laurie, Fen leaned over the side, reached in the burning water, and grabbed hold of Matt's trousers. The material ripped further, but Fen still had enough leverage to tug Matt into the boat. The semiconscious boy flopped into the boat, stretched out in an awkward position half on top of Baldwin and the oar. He looked extremely uncomfortable. His body was arched up at the upper legs, so both his torso and calves were lower than his hips. His head and one shoulder were slightly higher, too, propped on Laurie's legs. All four kids were tangled up in a mess of limbs, but they were okay.

Fen was panting from the exertion of tugging Matt free of whatever had caught him—and from the effort of pulling a person into the boat. Baldwin was grinning. Laurie was sniffling a little but smiling at the same time. Matt was...there. That was all so far.

His eyes were closed, and his whole body looked red like he had a serious case of sunburn. In a few places, it looked like he was so sunburned that he was peeling. This wasn't actually sunburn, though. Fen had seen what the water did to Baldwin's sleeve—and now to Matt's clothes, too.

"Thorsen?" Fen said, and then he cleared his throat because his voice sounded funny. He wasn't going to sniffle and sob or anything, but the death of Baldwin was still too recent. He would admit—not out loud, mind you, but to himself—that he might've been more than a little afraid and worried about Thorsen.

Baldwin prodded Matt gently. "Matt? Are you alive?"

Fen shook his head at the question. Baldwin was an odd one—or maybe not. They *were* in Hel. Maybe Matt had been drowned or killed by whatever was in the water.

*What happens if we die here?*

But then Laurie reached her hand down like she was going to touch Matt's face. She stopped just above his mouth and nose. "He's breathing."

Matt's hand darted out and pushed Laurie's hand away from his face. Eyes still closed, he sat up. Then, almost at the same time as he opened his eyes, Matt also opened his mouth. He leaned over the side of the boat and puked.

When he was done, he stared at them.

"Dead." Matt stuttered the word. He coughed, swallowed, and tried again. "Dead."

"No, you're alive, man," Baldwin assured him. He patted Matt on the shoulder.

"It's okay," Laurie added soothingly. "You're okay."

"No." Matt shook his head and coughed. "I mean the water is full of dead Vikings. *Go!*"

"Oh!" Baldwin grabbed a pair of oars and looked at Fen. "Let's get out of here."

As quickly as they could, Fen and Baldwin rowed the boat to the other shore. Laurie alternated between pounding Matt on the back as he coughed, staring at the shore, and studying the map.

A few times, Fen felt things grab at his oars, and he knew Baldwin was having the same experience because he'd hear Baldwin grunt and felt the way the boat was jerked around. It got worse and worse the closer they got to the shore. A few strokes from the bank, Baldwin looked at Fen and said, "Can we get closer?"

Fen nodded. They used the oars to dig into the sediment or bodies or whatever was hidden in the water and forced the boat still closer. It scraped against the bottom with horrible noises.

"Uh, guys?" Laurie was staring at the water behind them.

They all looked back. The dead were wading toward them, using the other bodies as ladders of a sort. Partial bodies were submerged with others standing on their shoulders or, in a few cases, on their heads. As the kids watched, the dead that apparently filled the water climbed over each other in a grotesque but determined way. They were almost silent as they trampled those around them, their focus only on the kids. The dead stared at them, some with white eyes and others with eyeless skulls. They all fixed their gazes steadily on the descendants as they climbed and struggled silently toward them.

Laurie let out a sharp sigh and then pointed to their right. Her face was paler than usual, but she sounded far less freaked out than Fen felt as she said, "We go toward those woods, and we do it as fast as we can." She glanced at the map in her hand, which was shaking and thus making the insect-wing paper shiver and shimmer. "There is a line on here that looks like a border of some sort. I'm hoping it means that if we reach it we can escape them. If not, at the least we can try to lose them in the woods." She poked the map. "There's a cave here that we need to go through to get out of Hel."

Baldwin looked in the direction Laurie had pointed and then at the shaking map in her hand. "Woods. Cave. Got it. You go first."

"*And* Matt," Fen added, still pushing the boat closer to shore. Getting into the zombie-filled waters was becoming increasingly unappealing, so he wanted to get them as near to shore as he could. "Matt, go with Laurie."

Matt opened his mouth, no doubt to object, but Fen shook his head.

"You just about drowned, Thorsen," Fen pointed out. "You're not at your peak fighting shape." He glared at Matt. "You and Laurie go first. Baldwin and I will take the rear and deal with any dead people."

For a change, Laurie hadn't objected to a plan that kept her out of danger, and Fen realized that she was as scared as he was, even if she didn't sound like it. He hoped that meant he didn't sound it, either. Matt probably wasn't alert enough to be scared, just injured and exhausted. Only Baldwin seemed truly calm, but when Fen glanced at him again, he revised that theory. Baldwin stared at the growing piles of dead people and shivered.

"Acid-water and zombies? Your Aunt Helen could've mentioned that." Baldwin pushed the oars one last time and muttered, "I hope these aren't *running* zombies."

"You and me both, brother," Fen agreed. Then he looked at Laurie. "You lead and keep Matt upright."

"I'm okay," Matt said, his voice still scratchy. "Thank you for pulling me out, but I'm fine—"

"No," Fen interrupted. "Go with Laurie."

Matt hesitated. Then he nodded.

Fen gestured to the shore. "Leap and run toward the exit."

"If we get separated, we'll wait for you at the cave," Laurie added.

"Right. We head through the woods to the cave," Fen repeated.

They jumped into the shallow water and scrambled toward the shore.

As soon as the kids' feet touched the ground, the zombies began to surge toward them. It was as if the touch of the living kids' feet on the shore had been a signal. The waters roiled as the masses of zombies tumbled over each other, pushing toward the land, trampling other zombies in the process. Fen had the brief thought that he'd stumbled into a horror movie, but then he pushed it away and yelled, "Don't look back, but run faster if you can!"

To their credit, both Matt and Laurie did as Fen asked. However, Laurie also yelled, "If you don't catch up with us, I will come back here and kick your butt, Fen!"

Baldwin grinned, but Fen knew she wasn't joking. "We're right behind you," he called out. "Just keep running!"

To Baldwin, he added in a low voice, "They need a few minutes' head start before we can follow."

"Got it," Baldwin said.

Within an instant, the dead were trying to follow Matt and Laurie.

"Not going to happen," Fen growled as he shoved one of the zombies back toward the water.

Baldwin darted to the boat, grabbed an oar, and began swinging it like it was an oversized baseball bat. Fen seized another oar but decided it was too unwieldy to use. He shifted into a wolf and charged at the zombies that were making their way onto shore. He had no expectation of being able to stop an entire troop of shambling dead, but he and Baldwin would buy Laurie and Matt enough time to get farther away. That was Fen's best plan.

Baldwin continued playing a twisted version of Whac-A-Mole with the zombies, and Fen tried not to think about how gross zombie tasted as he bit them to deter them from moving forward. His biting didn't seem to stop them, and it was exceedingly gross—so much so that he thought he might end up a vegetarian. *Zombie meat? Not so tasty.* He didn't swallow it, but the taste was hard to get out of his mouth. *And Matt swallowed mouthfuls of zombie stew with acid-water!* It was no wonder he had puked.

Fen considered shifting back to human shape, but he was faster as a wolf. He ran toward the zombies and figured he'd switch shapes when he was beside Baldwin. As Fen ran, though, he realized that the zombies had swerved out of his path. Testing his theory, he ran at them again. They turned as he came their way, several of them toppling into the water.

After that, he started herding them. It was a little lame, like being a sheepdog instead of a wolf, but it was a lot better than having to have the taste of zombie in his mouth.

*And it buys Laurie more time.* Protecting her was his number one goal in life; it had been for years, since back when Uncle Stig, her dad, asked for Fen's help in keeping an eye on her when he wasn't around. Having one clear focus had made it a lot easier to figure out the right thing to do: whatever made Laurie safest. Lately he had started adding Matt and Baldwin to his list, too. Right now, keeping them safe meant herding zombies.

Fen couldn't get all the zombies into the water, or even half of them; there were just too many. However, he drove some of them to the river in groups. At the same time, Baldwin kept thwacking them with the oar. It was a system—not the best system, but considering everything, it was a pretty decent plan—and more important, it was working.

Between rounds of shepherding the zombies back into the river of acid stew, Fen looked toward the edge of the woods where Laurie and Matt were headed. As soon as they entered the cover of trees, Fen raced back to Baldwin, scattering zombies as he ran.

When he reached Baldwin, Fen became human-shaped again.

"Whoa!" Baldwin blinked at Fen. "That was just, like, one step and then bam, you're not furry."

"It's been a lot faster switching between shapes since being in Hel," Fen answered, hoping as he said it that the change would stay like this once they reached the land of the living again. He showed his teeth to a zombie and took a menacing step toward it, experimenting with the tactic that worked as a wolf.

The zombie faltered but didn't alter its path.

"Guess that only works as a wolf," Fen said, and then he grabbed a bone that had washed up—one far too large to be from a person—and used it as a weapon to knock the zombie down. "Start toward the woods. I'll shift back and follow. I'm faster on four paws."

Baldwin knocked out two more zombies and then ran.

As soon as Baldwin was a few steps away, Fen dropped the bone and returned to wolf form. He had to charge at a few zombies that were getting too close to Baldwin, but most of the seemingly mindless dead were staying near the water. Fen ran at the ones who made it closer to the woods, and then he loped toward the woods to keep pace with Baldwin.

Fewer and fewer of the zombies pursued them, and when the two descendants reached the first trees, the zombies all started walking backward into the river as if the water was drawing the creatures back to it with invisible tethers. Fen switched back to human so he could speak to Baldwin. He nudged Baldwin's arm and said, "Look."

For a moment, they stood at the edge of the woods together, watching zombies shuffle backward toward the once-more seething river. The water bubbled and churned as the dead returned to it. If not for the fact that they were watching zombies and acid-water, it would be kind of cool. Fen shook his head. Actually, it was still kind of cool, but that didn't mean they had time to keep watching it.

"Come on," he said.

Baldwin nodded, and they headed deeper into the woods.

The path looked pretty clear, so Fen hoped that they'd catch up to Laurie and Matt shortly—and that there wasn't some other monster waiting between them and the exit from Hel. They'd run into a Jotunn, a giant multi-eyed guard dog, his creepy Aunt Helen, grumpy dead Vikings, and now acid-dwelling zombies. Fen was ready for something a little less exhausting. Somehow, though, the clear-cut path through the woods wasn't doing much to convince him that he was about to find what he wanted.

After a moment, Baldwin said, "Sorry you were sad about my dying. It's cool that you all came to get me, though. I was having an okay time, but I'm really glad I get to come back to help fight the Raiders and the big snake." He paused and looked at Fen with a very serious expression before adding, "Do you think I'll have to come back after the fight or will I stay alive? Oh! I hope I don't start rotting when we get back. I mean, I'm not going to be a zombie now, am I?"

"No," Fen said, not actually knowing if he was right but trying to be comforting. "I think you'll be as alive as I am."

Baldwin sighed. "Okay. That's good. I really don't want to be a zombie." He smiled and shuddered all at once. "That was fun and all, but they're sort of gross, right? I miss my heartbeat. And breathing. I hope I'll get those back, too."

Fen wanted to laugh. Baldwin's mood was never anything

other than cheerful for very long. His cheeriness made it hard for Fen to be grumpy around him, and that was saying something. He smiled at Baldwin before he said, "Yeah. You'll probably be just as alive as before, and you're right: they were gross. I learned something that's not in any of the movies, though."

"What?"

"Zombies taste like dirty shoes." Fen could almost gag at the memory.

Baldwin made a *blech* noise in sympathy before saying, "There they are!"

As Fen looked up, he thought he saw two black birds flying away at their approach and wondered if they were the same birds he'd seen earlier. They were leaving, though, and he wasn't going to waste time worrying about anything that wasn't attacking them.

Matt and Laurie were standing near the mouth of a cave. He was facing the darkened cave, and she was watching the path they'd traveled already. Even with everything that had happened, they were attentive to the potential risks. *Anything* could come out of that cave.

"Are the zombies still coming?" Laurie asked.

"Nope. It was like they were on rewind." Baldwin started to gesture. He shot one hand forward, fingers splayed out like a spider with not quite enough legs, and then slowly pulled it back toward him. His fingers kicked out like they

84

were struggling against some force. "The river sucked them in as soon as we hit the tree line."

Matt glanced at Fen, who nodded.

"We're done with zombies, then. Good." Matt motioned toward the cave. "Any chance you still have that lighter?"

Fen pulled it out of his pocket.

Matt peeled off the remains of his shirt, twisted it, and wrapped it around a stick that he'd apparently picked up along the walk to the cave. He knotted the ends of the shirt, and then he held the end of the stick with the shirt on it out toward Fen. "Light it up."

Fen flicked the lighter and held the tiny flame to the cloth. It blazed brightly. Evidently, zombie-filled acid-water was an accelerant.

Torch in hand, Matt led them into the dark cave. The air felt clammy after only a few steps, and it felt increasingly so the farther they went into the darkness. Without the torch, they would've been in trouble. The main path was wide enough that they could walk two across, but as they descended farther into the ground, it grew narrower.

They could hear water somewhere nearby. About ten minutes into the walk, they turned a corner and discovered why: a river of phosphorescent water raged below them.

"Whoa!" Baldwin breathed the word, dragging it out with the sort of awe reserved for the truly amazing or decidedly awful.

"Yeah," Fen agreed.

"Good thinking on the torch, Matt!" Laurie added.

Thorsen just nodded and looked around for any other threats. The ghastly light from the river below now illuminated the whole area around them; it gave everything a sickly greenish tinge. Matt's hand tightened on the torch.

As they walked, Fen wondered if their way through the cave was going to get more complicated, but aside from a few narrow passageways that required crawling through on hands and knees and some tunnels where they needed to stoop, they found no other challenges.

They were about to reach a narrow rocky ledge that crossed the glowing river. It looked like a natural bridge, created over many years when the water had worn away the stone. The bridge looked like it was only wide enough to walk in a single file, and it was a dangerous drop to the suspicious-looking water.

"I think we might be coming to the end. I feel... *better*." Baldwin sounded more excited that usual, but that made sense: for Baldwin, reaching the end of the cave meant returning to life.

"Me, too," Matt murmured. "It's like the closer we get to the world, the more energy I have."

Fen paused, realizing that Matt and Baldwin were right. He felt stronger, too. It wasn't even that he'd felt that awful before, but it suddenly seemed like he was lighter, as if he hadn't noticed how tired and heavy his body had felt in Hel until he started feeling better again.

"I think just being in Hel is depressing. It wears you out without you noticing." Laurie frowned. "Do you think we'd have died if we stayed here? Right now, I feel like *living* is seeping back into me. Does that make sense?"

Matt and Fen nodded.

"I don't know about you, but my mind is clearer. I'm *glad* you rescued me. I can't believe I considered staying here. Death is not cool," Baldwin announced.

In silent agreement, they all started walking a little faster then. Fen stopped at the bridge and motioned Baldwin forward. He was stronger than Matt right now, so he would take the lead. Fen would take his usual position at the back. The dead boy stepped onto the narrow bridge; Laurie was right behind him. Before Matt could follow, they heard a growl from their left. A low, long grumbling noise followed the first growl.

Fen and Matt both stopped and turned to face the sound. They stood side by side with their backs to Laurie and Baldwin, who were already on the bridge.

Fen could see two big yellow eyes looking out of the darkness. He muttered an ugly word that caused Laurie to gasp and Matt to say, "Yeah."

"Plans?" Baldwin asked.

"Keep moving," Matt whispered. "You and Laurie head for the exit. Fen?"

"Right here, Thorsen." Fen kept his attention on the yellow eyes. The creature hadn't come any closer yet, and Fen was wondering if it was waiting for the opportunity to charge at them. He was glad they were all feeling better, but better didn't mean that Matt was at his usual fighting ability. Fen darted a glance at him and asked, "You up to this? Or should Baldwin—"

"I can do it." Matt looked like he was thinking for a moment, and then he said, "I just need to get angry. When it tries to stop us, I'll *be* angry."

Fen let out a short sigh of relief, but he added, "This trip to Hel bites."

"No argument here," Matt said, "Are they going?"

Fen glanced behind him while Matt watched the glowing eyes. Baldwin and Laurie had gone several more feet, but they weren't yet over to the wider space on the other side of the cave bridge. He told Matt as much, and then added, "I don't want to fight over that river."

"I know. We'll hold it here," Matt said, so low that Laurie wouldn't hear. "Then once they're across, we let it follow us onto the narrow section, and I'll Hammer it."

Fen nodded. It was a good plan, even if it meant facing a monster on a bridge over presumably toxic water.

The creature started to creep out toward them, and as it did, the greenish light revealed the body that went with the eyes. It wasn't quite as big as a troll, but it was close. Mangy brown fur covered a massive body. Dirty claws clacked on the stone ground, and oversized, dripping teeth looked even grosser than they would in normal light.

Fen started, "Is that really a . . ."

"A cave bear?" Matt finished. "I think so."

"Of course. What else would be in a cave in Hel?" Fen braced himself, even as the urge to run was starting to hit him. It made no sense to stand still while a giant monstrous bear from old Icelandic sagas stalked toward them—except they had to for Matt's plan to work.

"It's almost here," Matt murmured. "Can you shift?"

"And do what?"

"Taunt it until it charges over to the narrow area, and I'll use my Hammer on the stone and push it into the water. Stay low when I blast it."

It took a lot of trust to follow Matt's plan, but Fen nodded. "Got it."

As soon as the cave bear was close enough to lunge, Fen thought he might gag. The stench of the thing was overpowering, smelling like a combination of rotting meat and an overfilled portable toilet in the hottest South Dakota summer.

*And I'm going to run toward it. . . .*

Fen shook his head at the absurdity of it, and then he shifted into a wolf and ran at the cave bear. He wasn't quite within swiping distance when it lashed out with its claws and roared. Fen turned, twisting his body so quickly that his right foreleg hurt like he'd ripped something. He ran back toward Matt.

At the same time, Thorsen had retreated onto the narrow bridge. He stood with his legs wide, bracing himself. "Crouch, Fen!" he yelled.

As Fen dropped to his belly, Matt's energy bolt smacked into the cave bear.

It roared again and kept advancing.

Matt backed up. "It needs to come closer!"

Hoping he wasn't about to take a bath in that nasty river, Fen jumped up and ran at it again, and then he darted back to Matt. Still in wolf form, Fen dropped back to his belly a few feet in front of Matt.

The cave bear followed, and Matt hit it with another burst of energy from his Hammer.

A loud *thump* was followed by a scraping noise as the cave bear scrabbled for purchase. Immediately after that came a roar and a splash. Fen looked down at the cave bear as it dragged itself toward the bank of the river far below them. It was wet, coated in green glowing goo, but otherwise uninjured. Fen let out his breath in a whoosh. Fighting *that* head-on would've been impossible.

"Let's go," Matt said. *"Now."*

Fen returned to his human shape, and they hurried after Laurie and Baldwin. Luckily, the others were at the gate to the living world. It hovered in the air, not quite on the rock wall of the cavern, but close enough to it that there was no way to reach behind it. It looked identical to the portals Laurie created, but permanent.

No more obstacles stood between them and getting out of Hel. Instead, it looked like they were actually free to go. As Fen and Matt joined the other two kids, the ground shimmered and a stack of filled backpacks appeared at their feet. Each backpack had a piece of insect-wing paper with one of their names.

"Aunt Helen seems to be making up for missed birthdays," Fen said.

Fresh, unripped clothes for all four kids spilled out of the backpacks as they opened them. Each pack somehow had a sleeping roll in it, too, despite the seeming impossibility of so much stuff fitting into small bags. As they sorted through the backpacks, they all withdrew clothes and shoes in their own sizes. Fen didn't see the need to change until he could get the dirt off of him, but both Baldwin and Matt pulled on clean shirts to replace the ones that had been destroyed in the river in Hel.

Laurie looked through her pack as the boys put on their shirts. After a moment, she withdrew an odd item from her bag: a strange bow that appeared to be made of bone and sinew. "Umm, guys?"

They all looked at the weapon she held and then checked their bags. No one else had a weapon.

"I guess I'm not the only family member who thinks you need a little distance from the fights," Fen teased.

Laurie smacked him lightly on the arm, but she was smiling. He realized he was, too. He couldn't help it: they were all together, they'd rescued Baldwin from death, and they were about to return to the land of the living. Things were looking up again. Now they just needed to rescue Owen, pick the twins back up, and get the rest of the missing items for the coming battle. Finding Thor's hammer and some feathers shouldn't be too difficult, right? They'd already *done* the impossible—rescued Baldwin from death—and they could do this, too.

Maybe they wouldn't even need to do all that. They'd changed what the myth said would happen; they weren't just trapped to repeat the myth *exactly*. Maybe rescuing Baldwin was enough to stop Ragnarök.

They were tired but smiling as they started through the portal gate that led them out of Hel. Matt stepped through first, and the rest of them followed.

# SIX

## MATT

### "HAIRY, OVERSIZED COWS"

Matt jumped from Hel into a thunderstorm. Or that's what he thought, right after his feet hit the ground and pain jabbed through his legs. As he rubbed his calves, he heard the distant roar of thunder. Still disoriented from the jump, he reached up to cover his head against the rain, only to realize it wasn't raining. The thunder kept rumbling, though, so loud it shook the ground. When he inhaled, he smelled dry earth and dust.

He looked over at the exit portal, shimmering like a heat wave. The others hadn't come through yet. When a dark shape passed overhead, he glanced up to see two birds, circling so high he couldn't make out more than black dots.

Thunder rumbled again. He glanced behind him and saw a storm coming in. A dust storm, it looked like, rolling across open ground.

They were on the prairie—the autumn grass tall and golden, dark hills in the backdrop. The sky above was blue. Bright, almost blindingly blue, scorching his eyes after the dusk and mist of Hel. The sun blazed, and there wasn't a single cloud to be seen . . . except that dust cloud on the ground, rolling closer, a whirling beige mass dotted with black—

Matt realized what he was seeing just as Fen started stepping from the exit portal. Matt lunged and hit him in the shoulders.

"What the—?" Fen began before toppling back to Hel.

Matt tried to dive in after him, but he hit the ground instead. Apparently, it was a one-way ticket out.

He lifted his head and saw the cloud of dust, and at the front of it, a line of bison. Stampeding bison.

"Laurie!" he shouted, hoping she could somehow hear him from the other side. "I could use an escape hatch here!"

He glanced around as he scrambled up, but he didn't see any sign of Laurie's door and didn't dare wait to find out if she could deliver. The bison were bearing down so fast he could smell the rank stink of their fur and hear their panicked snorts over the thunder of their hooves. He started to run, but even as he did, he knew it was too late. It wasn't just a few bison. It was a herd—a big one, at least several hundred, spread out across the land like a rolling wave of destruction, mowing down everything in their path. Including any thirteen-year-old boy who got in their way.

He still tried to escape, though. He ran as fast as he could until he knew there was no chance—no chance at all. Then he dropped into a ball and yanked the shield over his shoulder, blocking him, realizing as he did how small the shield was, how small and thin. He could see the bison through the dust. Massive, shaggy beasts. Six feet tall. Twice as long. A thousand pounds each. Huge pointed horns. Rolling, panicked eyes.

*I'm dead*, he thought. *After all this, I'm dead, and it's not trolls or demon dogs or rivers of acid. It's hairy, oversized cows.*

The herd hit, ground shuddering, dust flying into his eyes, his nose, his mouth, the sound and the smell so overwhelming that he couldn't even think. The first few bison had time to see him, and they veered past. He didn't dare look over the shield, but he knew his luck wouldn't hold. Soon there would be one that didn't see—

A hoof struck the shield with a terrible *crack*. The bison stumbled but miraculously went right over him, long belly hair brushing him as it went. The blow to the shield knocked it aside just enough for Matt to catch a glimpse of something shimmering about ten feet away. A portal door. Could he make it? He bunched his legs and braced his hands against the ground, ready to—

A figure appeared in the shimmering door. It was Baldwin, stepping through.

"No!" Matt shouted. "Stay inside!"

He shot to his feet, realizing his mistake even as he did. The bison running at him let out a snort and swerved, but the one behind it kept coming, not seeming to see him at all. Matt lifted his shield and felt his Hammer flare.

His hand shot out. The Hammer hit the charging bison. It stumbled. The one behind it barreled into the dazed bison, and they crumpled in a heap, the rest of the herd seeing the pileup and racing around it, leaving Matt standing there. He murmured an apology to the collapsed bison as they staggered to their feet. Then he spun toward the portal just as a rampaging bison, horns lowered, bore down on Baldwin.

"Baldwin!" Matt shouted.

The horns caught Baldwin. He flew into the air. The portal shimmered again, an arm coming through. Fen's arm.

"No!" Matt yelled.

He ran toward them, narrowly missing one of the giant beasts as it thundered past. He could see Baldwin now, on the ground, as the bison tried to get around him. He was off to the side, away from the portal, and Fen was stepping through.

"Fen! Get back! Don't—"

Fen walked out right in front of a charging beast. Matt slammed it with Thor's Hammer just in time to knock it off course, but now Laurie was coming through, and Fen must not have had time to even realize what was happening—it was all so fast, the shock of stepping from Hel too great.

Matt waved his arms madly, shouting at the top of his lungs, trying not only to get their attention, but to let the bison see them. Some did and veered, but one huge bull was heading right for Laurie.

"No!" Matt shouted.

There was a flash of light, and at first he thought he'd thrown the Hammer, but his hands were still at his sides as he ran. There was a tremendous *crack*, and something hit the ground right behind Laurie. Something so bright it blinded them, and Matt didn't realize what it was until he saw the black scar on the sandy ground and the dry grass around it burst into flame.

Lightning.

He looked up at the sky, but it was still blue and cloudless. He was with the others now, the bison snorting and bellowing as the smell of smoke hit them. They swerved around the scar and the small fires—and around Laurie and Fen, giving them a wide enough berth that Baldwin could get to his feet. Baldwin raced to the cousins and reached them just as Matt did . . . and just as the tiny fires went out and the bison herd started closing in again.

"Do it again!" Laurie shouted to be heard over the herd.

"What?" Matt said.

"The lightning!" Fen said.

"I didn't—"

"Thunder? Lightning? Thor?" Laurie said. "Of course you did!"

Matt stared at the herd as the bison began closing in, that gap they'd given the kids vanishing.

"Any time now, Thorsen," Fen said.

"Come on, Matt," Baldwin said. "Whatever you did, do it again. Fast. Those buffalo are a lot bigger than us."

What had he done? He had no idea. He hadn't been thinking or doing anything except panicking, and if that was enough, then there should be lightning bolts flying everywhere right now because his heart was hammering—

The Hammer. Maybe...

He clutched his amulet, and his hand shot out, but he could feel right away that it wasn't the same. There was the flash and the *bang*, but what hit the ground was just a regular Hammer blow that did absolutely nothing at all.

*I need lightning. Please, please, please, give me—*

A bison turned right into their path. Matt grabbed his shield with one hand, swinging it in front of him as he shouted, "Get behind me!" Then he launched the Hammer. It knocked the bison off course, but there was one right behind it, and there wasn't time to throw another—

A bloodcurdling scream rang out. At first, Matt thought it was Laurie. Okay, maybe he thought it was *himself*, screaming as he realized he was about to be trampled and a little wooden shield wasn't going to save him. But then he saw something coming through the dust and the herd, something huge and white. Another scream. Then an echoing whinny, and he looked up to see a woman with blue handprints on her cheeks and long red hair streaming behind her. Hildar. Leader of the Valkyries. A sight nearly as terrifying as the bison, with her painted face and her flashing sword and her snarl of battle rage as her steed ran right up alongside the bison, shouldering it off course. Matt swung his shield—

The horse swerved at the last second, and a hand grabbed the back of his shirt. He flew into the air and somehow landed on the horse, behind Hildar.

"No!" he said. "The others—"

He looked over his shoulder as three riders scooped up Laurie and Fen and Baldwin. Hildar yelled something, and he turned just in time to see a bison stumble, spooked by the horses. It collapsed in a heap, right in their path. Matt grabbed the sides of the saddle, bracing for impact. The Valkyrie shouted something, and they were about to hit the downed bison and then—

Everything went white. Bright, blinding white, and he could still hear the thunder of the herd, but they were a blur on either side. The wind rushed past and his cheeks flattened, hair whipping, eyes stinging, like flying down the biggest roller coaster imaginable and all he could do was hang on. Then the noise of the herd vanished and the blur of the bison disappeared, too. His stomach lurched, and his mouth filled with the taste of the river. The taste of the dead. Another stomach lurch. He closed his eyes fast, squeezing them tight, praying that after all that, he wasn't going to puke on a Valkyrie.

He didn't. The "ride" slowed, and he opened one eye to see thick forest. Hildar had stopped her horse in a clearing. Matt looked around, blinking to clear the dust from his eyes.

They were in the Black Hills again. Or that's what it seemed like: thick forest, the massive trees crowding in around the clearing.

"Off," she said.

Matt slid to the ground, which really wasn't easy when the saddle was about eight feet up. He hit with an *oomph*. Hildar gave him a withering look. Even her horse stamped and snorted, and Matt swore it rolled its eyes. Despite the billowing dirt, the beast managed to stay gleaming white. The only spots of color were blue handprints and swirls, like the ones on Hildar's face, which seemed to glitter in the sun as she adjusted her shield and sword.

Behind him, the other horses had arrived, and the kids were being unceremoniously ordered to dismount. Matt went to help Laurie, but Fen waved him off and helped her himself. Baldwin swung his leg over and jumped down. His clothing was ripped and filthy again, but he looked none the worse for having been nearly trampled by bison.

"Buffalo?" Hildar said, moving her horse alongside Matt. "The son of Thor is almost killed by buffalo?"

"Er, actually, they're supposed to be called bison." He caught her expression. "Never mind."

"It wasn't his fault," Laurie said. "The exit door from Hel took him right into the path of that herd."

"And you think that was accidental?"

"If you're implying Helen planned it, she didn't tell us where to exit. That was—"

"No matter," Hildar said, cutting her short, as if preferring to blame Helen. "Still, the son of Thor should have looked where he was stepping. All the descendants of the North should have."

"We just escaped Hel," Fen said. "Past fire giants and killer guard dogs and Viking zombies—"

"They're called draugrs," Baldwin whispered to Fen.

"No, actually, those weren't..." Matt trailed off as he caught Hildar's look. "Which isn't important right now. The point is that I messed up, and I accept full responsibility."

"Which would have served you well in the afterlife," Hildar said dryly. "Killed by buffalo? You would not even pass through the gates of Valhalla."

Matt could point out that this really wasn't fair—facing the bison had been at least as terrifying as any fight they'd encountered. And it was a battle of sorts. Not to mention the fact that this whole only-get-into-Valhalla-if-you-die-on-the-field thing was a crock. But it probably wasn't the time to mention any of that.

"I'm sorry," Matt said. "I messed up. Thank you for—"

"We had to rescue you. From buffalo."

Fen stepped forward. "And the fact that we messed up because we just finished rescuing Baldwin from Hel doesn't count at all? Really?"

"We are pleased with you for that, son of Loki. As we are pleased with the son of Thor for getting you all out of Hel safely."

"Um, I didn't get us out," Matt said. "It was a joint effort. I actually fell in a river of acid."

"As you should," she said. "We are pleased for that, too."

Obviously she was being sarcastic, but her expression and tone gave no sign of it.

"We all worked together," Laurie said. "I opened the door into the afterlife, and Fen convinced Helen to release Baldwin. Matt and Fen and Baldwin all fought off the zombies, and—"

"Yes, yes, you all played your parts." A dismissive wave. "But the son of Thor and the daughter of Loki need to be more careful. Each time we rescue you is considered an interference, and it will upset the balance of things. Now that we have saved you from buffalo, we will be unable to help at a more pressing time."

Ever since hearing that rooster in Hel, butterflies had taken up residence in Matt's stomach, fluttering about, whispering that this might not be over even if they got Baldwin out. As Hildar spoke, those butterflies dropped like lead pellets.

"More pressing time..." he said, barely able to get the words out. "So it's not over."

"Over?"

"We saved Baldwin. The myth has been broken. Ragnarök won't happen."

Silence. For the first time since he'd met Hildar, some of the chill went out of her blue eyes. When she spoke, he would not say her voice was kind, but it was softer. "Is that what you thought, son of Thor?"

"It's what we *all* thought," Laurie said. "Break the cycle; stop the apocalypse."

"No, children. You cannot stop Ragnarök. When you alter the course of the myth, you alter the course of the outcome. If the change is positive, such as saving Baldwin, then the odds move in your favor. That is no small thing."

Matt nodded but couldn't bring himself to speak.

"Now it is time to rest," Hildar said. "We will stand guard."

"But we can't rest," Laurie said. "Owen is out there. He's being held captive and—"

"He is free."

Laurie paused. "Is he okay?"

"Owen is as he was meant to be. No more talk. Rest. Go. Now. There is more to be done."

The Valkyries waved them farther into the clearing, and they obeyed.

# SEVEN

## LAURIE

### "GHOST ARROWS"

After the Valkyries had retreated, the kids were left standing alone in the small clearing.

"Well, that sucks," Fen muttered.

Laurie expected Matt to say something encouraging, but his head was bowed like he was as disappointed as Fen sounded. She wanted to say something to make them both cheer up, but she'd also hoped that they'd averted the end of the world by saving Baldwin. It would've been nice if they had saved the world without any more battles. She sighed.

"I knew I should've killed that stupid rooster," Fen added.

Baldwin laughed, drawing all their attention to him.

When he realized they were all staring at him, he said, "What? That was funny."

Matt started to smile a little.

"You defeated monsters to come rescue me. We survived a swarm of zombies and a cave bear, and"—Baldwin glanced at Laurie and then at Fen—"your Aunt Helen didn't kill you for showing up in Hel while you were still alive. It's been a pretty good couple days... even if you didn't stop Ragnarök." He grinned. "Or defeat a chicken."

"Hey, that wasn't just any chicken," Fen started.

Laurie giggled. "Mighty hero thwarted by Hel Chicken."

Matt sounded very serious as he added, "Sorry about the chicken, Fen." But then he laughed, too, and maybe it was just being tired or being alive, but Laurie could tell they were all starting to feel better.

Baldwin clucked, and they all lost it again.

Things felt better now that he was with them. Laurie realized that the last night when they'd all been together, Baldwin *had* died. The night before that, they'd fought the mara, and the day before that involved a fight with three trolls who had kidnapped Ray and Reyna. Laurie didn't want to point any of that out to the others, but as she thought about their prior attempts to sleep, she wasn't feeling particularly relaxed. She kept her worries to herself as the boys talked about soggy zombies and flaming trolls and giant chickens. If a stranger heard them, they might think the boys were talking about some very strange video game.

Equally strange, perhaps, was looking at the ground and seeing that the backpacks they'd been given in Hel were once more in their possession. They'd simply reappeared. Cautiously, Laurie opened hers and pulled out her sleeping roll—which was far too big to fit into the very compact and lightweight bag. "Do you all have yours?"

They did, and so they spread out their new sleeping rolls in a circle of sorts. They needed to build a fire before they rested, or the damp night would feel far too cold for them to get any real sleep. There was a small stack of wood near a fire pit that had been dug into the ground. A line of soil surrounded it, and no leaves or dry grasses were too near where the fire would be.

While Matt, Laurie, and Fen gathered more fallen wood to burn, Baldwin started building a little pyramid of twigs. "Lighter?"

Fen tossed it to him.

Baldwin ignited his tiny pyramid in the pit. "Kindling."

Fen snorted, but he brought a pile of smaller pieces of wood over to the fire pit. Baldwin nodded, but his full attention was on his task. He muttered as he sorted through the bits of wood to select the right pieces—although Laurie had no idea what the criteria were for the selection.

Once a steady blaze was going and backup wood was

piled nearby—but not *too* near, at Baldwin's insistence— they sat down to eat. The Valkyries had left them with some basic foods: a loaf of bread, a chunk of cheese, a bag of assorted apples and oranges, and some sort of dried jerky. Laurie wasn't keen on dried meat, but the rest of the food seemed okay. It was certainly better than going hungry.

She thought about the banquet in Hel that they hadn't eaten, and the meager food in their possession seemed even less appetizing. She decided to keep that thought to herself, along with thoughts of other dangers they'd faced in the dark of the night. There really wasn't much she could think of to talk about…unless she brought up the next steps in their quest or worry over Owen. No one else was talking much anymore, either, and Laurie had the overwhelming sense that it was a matter of both physical and emotional exhaustion.

She wasn't sure why Fen opened the flap of his bag, but after he did, he promptly let out a sound of surprise. "Umm, guys?"

They looked at him as he withdrew a can of soda. Frowning, he dug around inside the bag, and in short order, he'd pulled out a bag of chips, a toothbrush and toothpaste, a bottle of water, and bug spray. After he'd piled it all beside him, he said, "None of that was in there earlier."

The other kids opened their bags. Various sandwiches, bottles of juices, and snacks had appeared in their bags. Also in Laurie's was a brush, and Baldwin had wet wipes. Surprisingly, Baldwin seemed thrilled by them. He tore them open and was about to pull one out when he stopped.

"Are gifts from Helen safe?" he asked.

Levelly, Fen said, "She freed you *and* helped us get out. She didn't need to do that. She was a little strange, but..." He shrugged. "We're all wearing clothes from the bags."

No one replied to that at first, and then Matt shrugged. "My amulet doesn't react to the stuff she gave us."

"And, you know, Helen isn't evil, either," Laurie pointed out. "She's just an immortal who rules a land for the dead. It's not a place of punishment or for evil people or anything. It's just another world."

No one commented on the oddity of "just another world," but considering the things they'd seen and done lately, the existence of another world wasn't that impossible. They were silent for a moment, and then Matt said, "She's right."

Everyone looked at him.

"The myths only say that she fights on her father's side in Ragnarök, but"—Matt shot a friendly look at Fen—"Loki isn't on that side now. His representative is one of us."

"So maybe Hel's on our side, too!" Baldwin took out the wipe and cleaned his hands. When he realized the others were watching him, he said, "Zombie-filled water that burned, slimy zombies in a fight, dirt and who knows what from the buffalo, and now ashes from building the fire. I don't want to taste any of that, so I'm cleaning my hands first."

As he spoke, they seemed to realize how many gross things they'd touched, too, and everyone quickly followed Baldwin's lead.

Once their hands were clean of any possible buffalo droppings and zombie slime, they ate, consuming some of the things from their bags and from the Valkyries. They were still quiet, but it felt less weighty now that they had some food. Laurie suspected that sleep would help, too.

Not long after they ate, both Matt and Fen went to sleep. Baldwin was taking the first shift minding the fire, so he was still awake. The other two boys were snoring as soon as they closed their eyes.

Laurie was supposed to be sleeping, too. She tried—but failed. She knew they were all safe, for now at least, but she couldn't sleep. She should. There was no telling when they would next be able to do so. She knew that, too. Knowing didn't seem to erase the insomnia that she was having. Her mind kept replaying scenes from their travels—mara, zombies, trolls, buffalo—everything felt so treacherous. Everywhere they had been, there were threats waiting.

*And all I can do is open doors so we can run.*

She figured that her record was about half "open doors into trouble" and half "open doors away from trouble." Maybe she could be more useful now that the immortal being who reigned over the land of the dead, who was apparently daughter of the god who was their ancestor, had given her a weapon.

Laurie was grateful to Helen, but possession of a bow wasn't enough. The first problem, of course, was that Helen hadn't included arrows; the second problem, though, was that Laurie hadn't exactly been trained in archery. Her father was a wolf, like Fen and a lot of their family, so Stig Brekke had spent most of his only daughter's life roaming the world. Sure, he'd visited, but he didn't take her out hunting when he was in town. He hadn't even told her he was wolf. She'd only learned *that* from Fen after the first time she saw the Raiders. The fact that most of her relatives turned into wolves was still strange. Worse yet, most of them weren't *good* wolves. They worked for the other side.

"I'm going for a walk," she whispered to Baldwin.

He looked panicked. "Are you sure that Fen and Matt would be okay with that?"

"There are *Valkyries* guarding us," she pointed out.

After a moment, Baldwin nodded. There wasn't really any good argument against that. The warrior women had said they were safe, so that was enough assurance for Laurie. Baldwin apparently agreed enough not to insist she check with the others.

Quietly, so as not to wake either of the sleeping boys— who might not be as reasonable as Baldwin—she pulled the bow out of her bag and crept toward the edge of their camp-site. She didn't have arrows, but she could at least practice drawing the string back and figure out how to hold the bow. Maybe she could try to see how one aimed a bow.

It looked simple enough: a curved bone and string meant to fire projectiles. She ran her hand over it, a little grossed out by the bone and trying very hard not to wonder about the string. Somehow, after seeing Helen's dress and the pavil-ion of bone, Laurie didn't think Helen would string it with anything common—or maybe this *was* common for her. She was in charge of the dead, so her sense of the ordinary was probably a little different from what a thirteen-year-old liv-ing girl's was.

Of course, Laurie also wasn't sure she should have a bow. Maybe it wasn't really meant for her. Maybe it'd be better to give the bow to Fen. She held it in her hand, feeling fool-ish. He was the champion, the warrior. She was a girl who opened doors. Even as she told herself she should give it away, an insistent thought intruded: *It's mine.*

Her hand tightened on the curve of the bone, and she decided that—no matter how silly she felt—she was going to figure out how to use it. She was going to help keep the champions safe so they could fight in the final battle and save the world. Now she just needed arrows. *Which are made of wood.* She smiled to herself. Maybe she could make some sort of basic arrows.

As she looked for a tree branch to break off for a potential arrow, a flash of blue hair caught her attention.

"Owen!"

He walked toward her, looking a bit less confident than he had in Blackwell.

"I'm sorry that...you..." Her words faltered as she saw that one of his eyes was missing. The skin around it was still red. She gasped, and then she clamped a hand over her mouth. *Owen is as he was meant to be.* The words of the Valkyries came back to her, and she understood with sickening clarity what they'd meant: he was destined to lose an eye.

"I'm so sorry," she whispered.

"Some things are unavoidable." Owen shrugged like it didn't bother him, but she *knew* it did. She didn't know him, not really, but most of the friends she grew up with were boys. A lot of boys acted like things were okay when they were really, really not. There was no way he wasn't upset about losing an eye.

"This had to happen," he added quietly.

"No!" She shook her head. "It's not *fair.* Baldwin died, but he came back. If we were just acting out the myth, he'd still be dead."

"Not everything can be changed. We aren't trapped by the myths completely; we aren't *really* the gods. We're their stand-ins, so we have some of their gifts and some of their fates, but not all. Matt can call the storms; you and Fenrir have some of Loki's skills. Baldwin is nearly impossible to kill." Owen shook his head. "And yet he died, as in the myth. Loki's descendants wept this time, and unlike the myth, Balder lives again." He paused and smiled sadly at her before continuing, "But I am still the one-eyed god. This is a better path than Baldwin staying dead."

They stood there silently for a few moments. She felt like there were so many things she had to say that she couldn't figure out how to say any of them. She settled on, "We were coming back from Hel to rescue you, but when we got here, the Valkyries said you were free."

"I escaped. It wasn't time for any of you to face my captor." He shook his head. "I wish you didn't *ever* have to, but I can't see any future where it's avoidable."

"Any future?"

"There isn't one set future. When we make choices, there are different possible futures that result from them. As long as I'm not involved in the choices, I can see the possible outcomes."

Laurie tried to remember what she knew of Odin from her mythology lessons. She wasn't a bad student, but mythology wasn't one of the things she'd loved. Of course, she'd never realized just how important myth would be in her life or she would've studied it a lot more. She tried to remember what she knew about Odin, but couldn't remember anything other than the fact that he was supposed to be the wisest of the gods, the All-Father.

He held out a hand for her bow. "Can I try?"

She gave it to him.

As if they hadn't just been discussing Baldwin's death, Owen's lost eye, and the end of the world, he calmly pulled the string back and demonstrated how to hold the bow. "You need to be steady. The arrows will fly true, but you need to trust yourself."

She took the bow back from him and tried to imitate his posture.

Owen gestured to her feet. "Widen your stance."

She stepped so she had her feet farther apart. "What else?"

"Think of your body like the letter *t*. You'll want your bow arm straight and steady, directly out, and your string arm should be straight and in line with the bow arm." Owen demonstrated with his body, as if he held an invisible bow. "Spine straight. Neck straight. Imagine arrows lining your spine and arms to make them straight and strong."

She tried to do as he directed. As she did, she realized that he'd said something odd. "You said 'captor.' Do you mean the Raiders?"

"In part," Owen murmured. "When you grasp the bow, keep your wrist straight and steady, not curling."

"What do you mean, 'in part'?" She continued to position herself as he suggested. The straightness of her form made everything feel more in control. "Was someone else with the Raiders? That Astrid girl? She said she was your girlfriend, and then she killed Baldwin."

"She isn't my girlfriend." He put one of his hands on Laurie's, and he showed her how to draw back the string. "Straight back, so your hand goes under your chin."

As he demonstrated, she could swear that she felt not only the tension in the sinew-string, but a whisper of a feather and shaft as if an arrow were there. "Owen, who was with the R—"

"Focus, Laurie," he interrupted. "Aim at the tree. Release the tension, and let the arrow fly."

She dropped her question for the moment and concentrated on his instructions. She released the string as if there were an arrow. It was a surprisingly natural process. She couldn't swear she'd be able to do it quickly any time soon, but once she had arrows, she could . . . try.

*Thwack.*

"Good," Owen murmured.

As she stared at the spot she'd targeted, she saw a white arrow sticking out of the tree. Silently, she lowered the bow so it hung loosely in her hand, and she walked to the tree. Cautiously, she lifted one hand. Her fingertips slid down the arrow that was stuck in the tree. The arrow was real: she could touch it.

Owen had followed her. He moved almost as silently

as her wolfy cousin. Unlike Fen, however, Owen was very patient. He simply stood waiting for her to speak.

"You knew there were arrows," Laurie half accused.

"Without them, it was no use to you as a weapon." Owen tugged the arrow from the tree. As soon as he had pulled it free, it vanished as if it hadn't existed at all. He touched one fingertip to the cut in the bark. "The wound is as if by the strongest of arrows. The arrows, though, are only ghosts."

"Ghost arrows?" she echoed.

He nodded. "An endless supply of lethal arrows that exists only when fired by your hands." He caught her gaze. "Loki's daughter has chosen her side in the coming fight. Helen stands with *you*. She answered that question when she gave you this. It won't work for anyone else."

At that, Laurie didn't know what to say. She'd been given a warrior's weapon, one that would only work for her, if Owen was right, but she hadn't even been sure she could convince Fen and Matt to let her help in the final battle. Helen had given her the means to do so.

And now Owen was with the rest of the descendants, too.

"Thank you," she told him. "I'll keep practicing. Maybe I can do that while you talk to the others. You can at least tell them about your captors, and then we can figure out where to find Mjölnir." She remembered what she'd been trying to think of earlier. "Ravens! Odin had ravens. That was how he knew things. Do you have ravens?"

"Always thinking, aren't you?" Owen smiled at her. "I used to think that part of Odin's story was weird. I've always just *known* things, but I didn't have ravens."

"Maybe we can help you find them," she suggested. "There was a pair of giant black birds in Hel. They could've been ravens. I'm not quite sure the difference between ravens and crows." She shuddered. "I didn't look at them too closely anyhow. I'm not a bird lover."

Owen nodded but didn't speak.

Impulsively, Laurie threw her arms around Owen and hugged him. She whispered, "I'm so sorry about your eye."

"It was meant to be," he said, his words sounding sad enough that she knew he wasn't as at peace with it as he was pretending to be.

"That doesn't change anything!" She squeezed him tighter. "It had to have hurt. You must have been so scared."

Owen held on to her, but he didn't speak at first. After several moments had passed, he admitted, "I *was* afraid. I thought knowing would mean I wasn't going to be scared when the time came. I was so...wrong."

"We're all scared." Laurie squeezed him once more, and then she pulled away. "Baldwin died. The twins bailed. Matt is supposed to die fighting a giant snake, and Fen is to turn evil or something. We've been fighting monsters nonstop, and...I don't think we're going to win every fight. We *can't*."

"I wish I could tell you," Owen murmured. "I wish

I could tell you everything I see, but the Norns and the Valkyries and so many others would all stop me. All I can do is tell you that I will fight at your side when the time comes."

"They'll be relieved! We—"

"Not them, Laurie," Owen interrupted. "I will fight at *your* side." He paused and stared down at her. "I wish I could stay, but I shouldn't be here."

When she said nothing, he kissed her cheek, and then he turned and walked away. She had the urge to chase after him, to force him to tell her something more, but she knew that Owen would say only what he thought he should—and there was nothing else he was willing to say now.

*I'll be at the fight.*

*Owen will be at the fight.*

*A boy just kissed me.*

She wasn't going to share that third thing with Matt and Fen. She knew Owen was a good guy; he was part of their team. The problem was that Fen took his overprotective-brother role very seriously, and although he and Matt were her two closest friends, they were boys. They would either not care that Owen kissed her or they would threaten him for doing so. Neither response was one she liked; she'd keep that detail to herself.

Laurie walked back to camp and stretched out to sleep. In the morning, she could tell them that Owen was planning to be at the fight—and that he said she would be there, too. For now, she would sleep.

# EIGHT

## MATT

### "GETTING HIS GOAT"

Matt pretended to sleep until he heard Laurie leave. Then he slipped away and walked in the opposite direction. Right now, he just wanted some time to himself to think about what Hildar had said: that they hadn't averted the apocalypse.

He didn't get very far before he heard footsteps. He turned fast, his hand going to his amulet. It was Hildar.

"I'm not running away," he said.

"I know." She drew up alongside him, her shield glimmering as the moonlight caught it. "You are disappointed."

*Yeah, that's one way of putting it.*

She glanced his way as they walked. "If you had known it

would change nothing, would you still have gone to Hel for the son of Balder?"

"Of course."

"Now that you know nothing will stop Ragnarök from coming, do you wish we could find a new Champion of Thor?"

"No."

"Good." She moved in front of him, turning to face him, making him stop walking and look up at her. "Because you are the only choice, Matthew Thorsen. There are other descendants who could take your place, but you are *Vingthor*. They are not."

"*Vingthor?*" Matt repeated. "Battle Thor? No, I'm definitely not. If you're trying to make me feel better—"

"I would not." Her words were sharp now, chin jerking up, as if insulted. "I am a warrior, not a chieftain. I do not need to tell pretty lies. I speak only truth, and if I say you are *Vingthor*, then you are. It was prophesied, and you have proven it."

Matt hesitated, then looked at her. "So what does that mean? That I'm the Champion of Thor?"

"More."

"The chosen representative of—?"

"More."

Now he really hesitated, taking at least ten seconds before he dared to say, "The reincarnation of—?"

"Less."

He sputtered a laugh. He couldn't help it. As he laughed, he began to relax. "All right, then. What does it mean? I know we're supposed to be the living embodiment of the gods, but I'm not sure I even get what *that* means. So explain."

Hildar stared at him, and Matt had to bite his cheek to keep from laughing again. She looked like the head quarterback, expecting to be asked for his game play and instead told to recite the periodic table of elements.

"You are *Vingthor*," she said after a moment.

"Which means..."

"You are the god born anew. In mortal form."

"But not reincarnated?"

She seemed to struggle to find the right words. "Gods are more than people. They are ideas. They are whatever their people need them to be. There was Thor. There can be another Thor, with his blood and his powers and everything that he was. That is *Vingthor*. You are *Vingthor*."

"Okay."

He smiled as she let out a soft breath of relief.

"You understand, then?" she asked.

"I do."

Now she went still, her eyes searching his. "But you do not believe."

Matt shrugged. "I'm flattered—"

That stiffening again, her chin lifting. "I do not wish to flatter."

"I know. Sorry. I just..."

"You do not believe."

No, he did not. It'd taken him long enough to accept he was the Champion of Thor. Now Hildar called him *Vingthor*? Said he was all that Thor had been? Absolutely not. He could tell by her face that wasn't what she wanted to hear. Nor could he lie.

"I will be whatever I need to be," he said.

"That is all we ask. Now, walk a little more with me. Then you are going to sleep."

A slow smile. "Whether I want to or not?"

"Yes."

Matt did sleep. Maybe there was magic in that. Or maybe he was just too exhausted to lie awake thinking of all that had happened.

He woke at dawn. Everyone else was asleep. Weird. Weren't they supposed to be taking turns watching the fire? Maybe the Valkyrie offered to cover a shift. He pulled himself up and sat there, staring through the trees at the distant sunrise. He'd dreamed of the serpent again, of the nightmare the mara had sent him, the one where the serpent devoured his family.

"You have doubts," a voice whispered behind him.

He turned sharply to see a Valkyrie. This one wasn't much older than him. She wore a blue dress with a laced scale breastplate. Her blond hair was mostly pulled back in a band, wild loose pieces framing her face. When he stared at her, her blue eyes glittered and she smiled.

*I didn't know they* could *smile.*

He could see the other Valkyries through the trees. They ringed the camp, sitting astride their horses, gazes fixed, faces expressionless. None of them glanced over as he rose to greet the young one. When he started to say something, though, she motioned him to silence and beckoned him into the forest. He followed until they were in a clearing.

"You have doubts, son of Thor," she murmured.

"N-no. Just…" He shook his head. "I had a nightmare." He pulled himself up straight. "But I'm fine."

A faint smile. "Of course you are. You're always fine, Matt."

He blinked at the use of his name. She laughed, the sound rippling around him, light and teasing and…familiar?

"I'm sorry," she said. She cleared her throat and lowered her voice. "You are fine, son of mighty Thor. Is that better?" A roll of her eyes. "They know your name. They're just playing their part. The drill sergeants. Training the young warrior with harsh lessons and insults. You're the one who should be insulted. You deserve their respect. You are the mighty Thor. You know that, don't you? The incarnation of the great god."

He shook his head. "I'm the representative—"

"No, you *are* Thor," she whispered, moving closer, breath against his ear. "You know it. You feel it. The others?" Contempt dripped from her voice. "They are mere representatives, and poor ones at that."

He stepped back sharply and when he looked at her face, he still saw the young blond Valkyrie, smiling at him, but he knew it wasn't a Valkyrie at all. And as soon as he thought that, his amulet started to vibrate.

"Astrid," he said.

Her smile grew. "Matt." She leaned toward him. "Did you miss me?"

He jumped back, hand flying out, the Hammer knocking her off her feet. As she hit the ground, she threw back her head and laughed.

"That seems like a yes," she said.

She slowly pushed up. Then, suddenly, she lunged, her lip curled back, her eyes glittering. Matt swung his shield arm up and, to his shock, the shield was there. Astrid hit it and Matt flew backward, landing flat on his back. He leaped up and—

Matt fell on his side, sleeping bag wrapped around his legs. He stopped. He looked around and saw Baldwin and Laurie still asleep in their bags. Fen was awake, tossing twigs into the fire, but he said nothing when he saw Matt wake.

"Son of Thor?" a voice said.

He twisted, expecting to see Astrid, but it was Hildar, moving her horse into the clearing.

"You are disturbed," she said.

"Just a...bad dream."

"About what?"

He paused before answering. "A girl. Her name's Astrid. I think she works with the Raiders."

Hildar frowned. "I do not know an Astrid."

"She killed Baldwin."

A nod. "Yes, she must work with the *wulfenkind*, then. You ought not to think of her."

"Believe me, I wasn't trying," he muttered.

He sat there, still in his sleeping bag, staring out into the night, as he had been in the dream, which made him shift and rub his face, trying to forget it.

"You are disturbed," Hildar said.

"I'm just tired."

"You want to sleep."

Matt shook his head. "No, I want..."

*I want normal back. And I know I can't have that. I can probably never have that.*

"You want..." Hildar prompted.

"Nothing," Matt said. "I want nothing."

"Then I will give you something. A reward. You have done well, and it is permitted. Rouse the others. We ride."

It took a while to get the others up. Once they were awake enough, Baldwin asked Hildar where they were going.

"We have a gift for the son of Thor," she said.

"Of course you do," Fen muttered, rubbing his eyes. "And the rest of us?"

"You do not require our gifts," she said. "What you need, we cannot give you."

"So what does Matt get?" Baldwin asked. "Wait! Is it Odin? I know we're supposed to find Odin or Owen or whatever his name is."

"Not yet," Laurie said. "He's . . . I'll explain later."

"The daughter of Loki is correct," Hildar said. "You are not ready for Owen, and he is not ready for you. This is a gift for the son of Thor. One that will prove essential in the battle to come."

"Mjölnir?" Matt perked up for the first time since the Astrid dream. "Thor's hammer. The real one. Is that it?"

"No, you must retrieve Mjölnir yourself. That is another quest. Another trial you must overcome."

"Of course it is," Fen grumbled.

Hildar ignored him. "What we have for you is just as important as Mjölnir. A great and mighty tool."

Matt grinned. "Is it the gloves, Járngreipr? The belt, Megingjörð?"

"You will not need those to fight the serpent. They are other tools for other quests. No more questions." She reached down. "Come. We ride."

She caught Matt's hand and swung him easily up behind her.

"Are you prepared?" she asked when the other Valkyries had their passengers in place.

"Sure," Matt said. "But we could use a soundtrack this time. Maybe a little Wagner. Da-da-da DUM dum."

Hildar looked back at him blankly.

"Wagner? *Ride of the Valkyries*? Da-da-da... Er, never mind."

"Oh!" Baldwin said. "I know that one!"

"Don't feed the geek," Fen muttered.

"Hey," Matt said. "I'm not a—"

"Oh, yeah, you are, Thorsen. You really are," Fen said in a voice that might have been teasing.

"Both of you, cut it out," Laurie said. "Let's go get Matt his present."

The Valkyries took them on another breakneck ride. When they stopped, they were up in the hills, in a rocky open area.

"Hey, look! Donkeys!" Baldwin said as they climbed from the horses.

They followed his finger to see a half-dozen wild burros foraging on the long grass. Across the clearing was another herd, this one of goats. They looked kind of like mountain goats, but not quite. They had long, shaggy fur—some all white, some black and white, and others brown. Both the goats and the burros seemed unperturbed by the horses or the people.

"This is cool," Laurie said. "I've never seen wild goats this close, and I've never seen wild donkeys at all."

"So," Matt said, looking around. "Where...um, I mean..."

"He wants his present," Fen said.

"It is there." Hildar pointed at the goat herd.

"Behind the goats?" Baldwin said.

Hildar turned to Matt. "Son of Thor...?"

All through the ride, Matt had been running through the myths, wondering what gift the Valkyries had for him, thinking of the all the amazing possibilities—all the cool weapons in the old sagas. He hadn't felt like that since he was a kid, waiting impatiently for his parents to get up on Christmas morning. Now, as he stared out at the field, that excitement fizzled in his gut.

"Son of Thor?" Hildar prompted.

"It's the goats," he said, his voice low.

"The *what?*" Fen said.

"The, uh, goats. Thor...in the myths...Thor has goats."

Fen pressed his lips together, but after only a moment, he sputtered a laugh. Baldwin joined in. Even Laurie seemed to be trying to hold one back. Matt's cheeks heated.

"Seriously? Goats?" Fen said. "That is awesome."

"They're magical goats," Matt said.

"Magical..." Fen couldn't even manage the rest without choking on his laughter.

"Do not mock the son of Thor," Hildar said. "The goats are very important. It is an aspect of the great god. *Oku-Thor.*"

"*Oku-Thor?*" Fen said.

"Lord of Goats," Hildar said.

All three burst out laughing, even Laurie. Matt tried to explain that wasn't the real translation—it meant "Driver Thor," referring to the goat cart he drove, not the actual goats, but no one was listening to him. The damage was done.

"Look, I appreciate the, uh, goats," Matt said to Hildar. "But I really don't think they'll work out. Maybe I could have..."

He looked around the field. As his gaze passed over the burros, Hildar frowned.

"You would prefer a donkey?" she said.

"Oh, yeah," Fen said, sputtering between laughs. "Matt would really rather be Thor, Lord of—"

"No!" Matt said. "I would not. I don't want a donkey or a goat or anything like that." He looked up at Hildar. "I understand that the real Thor had goats, and they were very important in his travels as a source of food."

Laurie screwed up her face. "Thor *ate* his pet goats?"

"They came back. He'd eat them for dinner, and they'd resurrect before he needed them again."

"That's disgusting," Laurie said.

"But kinda smart, too," Baldwin said.

Matt turned back to Hildar. "We already have food, from Helen's bag. So the goats . . . well, we don't need them."

"You will. These are your goats, son of Thor. They have lived here for centuries, waiting for you."

He looked at the herd of about thirty goats. "All of them? I thought there were just two."

"Two are special. They are your cart-bearers. But they are all yours to command. You speak. They will obey."

"Matt Thorsen, goat whisperer," Fen said.

Matt glowered at him.

"Call your goats, son of Thor," Hildar said "Do you know their names?"

"Tanngrisnir and Tanngnjóstr."

"No," Fen deadpanned. "You're not a geek, Thorsen. Not at all."

Laurie hushed him and stepped up beside Matt. "Go ahead," she whispered. "Hildar wants you to, and who knows, they might come in handy." She gave him a slight smile. "Just don't ask me to eat them."

Matt hesitated. Then he called the names. He did, admittedly, not call them very loudly, hoping maybe the goats wouldn't hear, and Hildar would decide he didn't have the power after all. But as soon as the words left his mouth, two goats broke from the herd and galloped over at full speed. They stopped short right in front of Matt. They were the biggest ones in the herd, both snow white, with long flowing hair and huge yellow-brown horns; they seemed to glitter like gold in the morning sun.

"They're gorgeous," Laurie said, reaching to pat one.

"They're *goats*," Fen said.

"Still..." Laurie ran her hands through the long hair at one's neck. "It's like silk."

The goats pressed closer to Matt and nuzzled him. When he awkwardly patted one, it rubbed its head against him, like a cat.

"I think she likes you," Fen said.

"It's a he. The horns mean—" Matt stopped before he got the geek comment again. "So, um, which one is Tanngrisnir—?"

The goat on his left bleated. Unlike its brother, it had black dots under each eye.

"They're...nice," Matt said, being careful not to offend the beasts as they nuzzled him. "But I'm not really sure what to do with them. I can't ride around South Dakota in a chariot, and I'm sure not going to eat them."

"They have their role to play," Hildar said.

"Which is...?"

"You will know."

"But I don't."

"You will. When you need them, call them. They will come. We must leave. You are ready to find Mjölnir."

"Will the goats help me find—?"

"No. You will find Mjölnir in the kirkyard of Saint Agnes."

"Kirkyard?" Matt said. "You mean cemetery, right?"

"The old Saint Agnes cemetery outside Blackwell?" Laurie asked.

"That is the one," Hildar said.

"It's not a small place," Matt said. "Where exactly in there do we find it?"

"Your amulet will lead you. Good-bye, son of Thor."

"Wait!"

They were already riding away, leaving Matt with his goats.

# NINE

## LAURIE

## "WORSE THAN MONSTERS"

Laurie tried to keep from laughing at the adoring gazes of the goats, but there was something undeniably funny about a gift of goats. *How did the Valkyries think goats were a great gift?* Hildar had gone on like this was a useful tool, an asset to the coming fight, but instead she'd presented Matt with livestock. Maybe if they were living in another age, having a goat to slaughter and reslaughter every night for dinner would be a great advantage, but the idea of slaughtering a goat even once made Laurie feel queasy. Food definitely had been an issue on their trip, but now Helen's bags of many surprises were delivering up far more palatable foods. Bag of chips? Juice? Sandwich? That was the sort of food that worked. Killing and skinning a goat? That was just gross. Killing a *nice* goat was even worse! That would be mean *and* gross.

"We should head out," Baldwin said, drawing everyone's attention away from the goats.

One of the two named goats—and Laurie had no idea which one it was—bleated again, and Matt looked back at it.

"Matt?" Laurie prompted. She wasn't sure if it was the goats or the thought of returning to the Blackwell area that had him so distracted. There were APBs out on both Laurie and Matt. The Thorsens were a very close family, and Laurie missed her mom and brother a lot. Fen was the only one who didn't have a reason to want to go back. She shook the thoughts of home away before she missed her brother, Jordie, even more.

*Save the world first, and then go home.*

"Matt!" she repeated, louder this time.

Matt scowled at the goat. It bleated again, and Matt turned away. "Baldwin's right. We should go."

He didn't seem too thrilled with his gift of goats, and Fen wasn't helping matters. His sense of humor wasn't always kind, and Laurie saw Matt's expression of hurt when Fen said things that he didn't mean to be insensitive. She might need to talk to him about trying to make it clearer when he was just teasing. Fen wasn't exactly gifted in dealing with non-Brekkes, as he made very clear in the next moment.

"Any idea where we're going to store your troops, O mighty goat lord?" Fen said.

Matt looked at the goats. "They'll, uh, stay here."

As Matt spoke, one of the goats came up behind Fen, and they all heard a loud *rrrrrrip*. Fen jumped forward, one hand raised in a fist while the other reached for his backside. "Hey!"

Now it was Matt trying not to laugh. His cheeks half bulged out like a fish's as he swallowed the sound and tried to make it sound like a cough or something. Laurie clamped her hand to her mouth. Maybe she didn't need to talk to Fen. The goat had handled him.

Fen stared helplessly at the pocket that *had* been on his jeans and now was dangling half out of the goat's mouth. "It bit me!"

"Nooo," Laurie corrected. "It bit your jeans."

Fen looked over his shoulder where his boxers were now exposed for any and all to see. Considering where they stood—utterly surrounded by goats—any and all was pretty much three other descendants of the North and a herd of goats.

Matt grinned. "You might not want to walk around like that."

"I think I have a . . . skirt in my bag." Laurie couldn't even finish the sentence without laughing. Her words were broken up by giggles.

Fen's expression was somewhere between horrified and furious. "Thanks," he said sarcastically.

"Scots wore kilts," Baldwin pointed out, "and some guys like skirts—"

"No," Fen interrupted. "I'm not 'some guys'...or Scottish." He rummaged in his backpack and pulled out a flannel shirt. Instead of putting it on, he tied it around his hips so the shirt hung down over his backside.

"All fixed," Fen pronounced with a smug smile...which lasted all of a moment before several goats started trying to nibble the dangling shirt.

"I'm not sure if I should help or laugh," Matt said.

Laurie was laughing so much that she hiccuped. "Laugh," she suggested. "Definitely laugh. It's the Brekke way."

But Matt was a Thorsen, not a descendant of Loki. He shook his head and said to Fen, "I'm sorry about your clothes."

"Whatever, goat lord." Fen shrugged it off, and the four descendants made their way across the rock-strewn field. They had a destination of sorts, and Laurie could portal them into the general area where they needed to be. What they needed to do first was to get away from the goats. Unfortunately, the two named goats were following them, and the rest of the herd was following those two goats.

"I don't know if I can portal us fast enough to keep the goats from following," Laurie admitted to the boys. "I'm getting much better at this, but it's not as simple as opening a door and darting through it."

"Then we'll just keep walking," Matt said. "They'll give up soon enough."

Unfortunately, the goats weren't taking the hint. They continued to follow the kids through the field, not doing anything really but trailing them. Still, it was oddly unnerving to be stalked by goats.

"Maybe the goats decided to eat *us*," Fen muttered. "They're watching us like we might be a possible meal."

Laurie shook her head. "They're not going to eat us."

"Says you." Fen stepped closer to her so he was between her and the goats. "Do something about your troops, Thorsen. They're creepy."

"Believe me, if I knew how to get rid of them—temporarily—I would," Matt said.

None of them had a plan, so Laurie said, "I'll try to open a doorway, and you guys just have to be quick." She paused before adding, "Look, Matt. Maybe you don't understand the goats, but they keep bleating at you like they think they're talking to you, and I don't think the one that bit Fen did it on accident."

Fen scowled again at the trouser-eating goat, and Matt pressed his lips together in an I'm-not-admitting-anything way. *Boys!* Laurie shook her head at both of them, and then she said, "Just tell them they can't follow us right now. It can't hurt to try that, right?"

"Tanngrisnir and Tanngnjóstr," Matt said, "I need you to stay here."

The goats really did seem to be listening. It was hard to tell for sure because goats didn't have a lot of facial expressions, plus, well, they had *already* been watching Matt pretty intently. Laurie hoped they were listening to him, though; portaling goats with them when they were going to break into a cemetery seemed like a bad idea.

Matt stared at the two goats and then at the rest of the herd. "You guys can't come with me right now. Maybe later. I'm sure we'll need your, um, help at some point and I appreciate your, uh, enthusiasm."

"Geez, Thorsen, just say 'stay' and—" Fen dodged the snapping teeth of a goat that had crept up behind him.

"The goats at least understand tone," Baldwin said, nodding in a sage way. He glanced at Fen and added, "You're not making any goat friends, man."

Laurie giggled as she prepared to open the portal to the old Church of Saint Agnes outside the edges of Blackwell. She was aiming for a wooded area not too far from the original settlement that had moved and become Blackwell. The area where the cemetery was, commonly called Old Blackwell, was still far too close to the sheriff, the Raiders, and her family, but that was where the Valkyries had said to go, so that's where they were headed.

They stepped out of the portal a mile or so from Saint Agnes, far enough that they could duck through the forest and approach the church from the rear. Laurie was glad that Old Blackwell was several miles outside of the actual town, tucked into a heavily wooded area that seemed to almost hide the ruined church and graves. The path was covered by thick pine needles, muffling their footsteps, and the trees around them were so thick that it almost felt like night, although it was still the afternoon.

The shadowy forest hid them. That didn't, however, erase the sensation of being in danger. If anything, being in the quiet of the woods made Laurie feel more nervous. Trolls lived in the woods. They'd already encountered them there once. Who knew what else was waiting in the shadows? It seemed like every creature out of the old myths was on the side of the enemy, and Laurie was getting tired of being attacked by monsters all the time.

She suspected that Fen either noticed her anxiety or felt the same way. He came to walk at her side and casually bumped his shoulder into her. She smiled reflexively at the usual Brekke way of communicating affection.

Baldwin noticed. "Is that a dog or wolf thing? My uncle's dog is like that, too. She's a German shepherd, and she runs into him and leans on him. You both do it when one of you is uncomfortable."

Fen flushed. "Yeah, I guess."

"This, too." Laurie butted her head against Fen's shoulder. "I didn't know other families weren't like ours until I was older, and I didn't know about Fen being a wolf until right before we met you." She paused, realizing how much they didn't know about each other. "I just know that it makes me feel a lot better when he does it because it means he's here or understands or that everything is okay."

"Yeah, what she said, I guess." Fen looked uncomfortable, but when Baldwin said or asked anything, Fen seemed to try extra hard to be...nice. Laurie knew that for him that wasn't always easy.

Matt was quiet as they walked, scanning the shadows of the woods as if he expected trouble to hop out any minute.

"I don't think any goats came through," she said.

"I know," Matt said. "I just have a bad feeling."

At that, Fen stopped and looked at Matt. "Bad feeling as in *I don't like being goat master* or bad feeling like *My amulet's buzzing?*"

They all waited as Matt thought.

"My amulet isn't doing anything, but...just stay alert."

They resumed walking. Instead of continuing to razz Matt about the goats, Fen turned to Laurie and said,

"We should've asked the Valkyries for some pointers on your bow."

"I'm feeling pretty good, actually. Owen showed me some—"

"What?" Fen interrupted.

Suddenly all three boys stopped walking and turned to stare at her.

"*Owen?* You saw Owen?" Fen folded his arms and scowled at her, suddenly seeming more like her dad than her cousin, and asked, "When—between returning from Hel with the bow and ending up in a field of pants-chewing goats—did you have time to see him?"

Laurie winced. "Right. Well, I sort of went for a walk last night."

"Alone?" Fen turned to Baldwin. "You were up with the fire for the first shift; did you doze?"

"No." Baldwin looked a little sheepish. "The Valkyries were guarding the camp, and then she was back before you took your shift with the fire, so I didn't say anything."

At the contrite tone in Baldwin's voice, Laurie felt even worse. "Don't blame him," she interjected. Then she resumed walking, figuring they'd follow her, before continuing, "I was going to tell you, but we were distracted by the information on where to look for Mjölnir and then by the goats."

She quickly filled them in on everything—well, *almost*

146

everything; the kiss wasn't any of their business—about her late-night encounter with Owen. Fen looked like he was about to start flashing his teeth as if he were a wolf, and Matt just looked thoughtful. When neither of them said anything, Baldwin prompted, "Are we sure Owen's a good guy?"

"In the myths, he's the All-Father. He knows things, and he works for the good of the gods and the world, so yes, he's definitely a good guy. Like Thor." Matt didn't say aloud that the god who was iffy was Loki, but they all knew that already. "In some stories, Loki and Odin are close. They say the two were bonded as blood brothers, and they traveled together—often with Thor. Loki also"—Matt glanced at Fen—"um, he was the mother of Sleipnir, Odin's eight-legged horse."

"Don't you mean the father?" Laurie asked.

"No," Fen said. He sighed and then said really quickly, "Our great-whatever-granddad took the form of a female horse and had a baby."

No one said much for a minute, and then Baldwin said, "So Owen is friendly with one of Loki's descendants, but it's not Fen?" He shrugged. "I can see that. I like Fen, but sometimes he's a little mean...not to me, but to most everyone." He shot an apologetic look at Fen. "You *are*."

Fen shrugged. "Whatever. I just don't think you should be wandering around in the dark with some strange guy just because he *says* he's Odin. Astrid said she was his girlfriend and one of us. Look where that got us. Baldwin dead, and us going to Hel to get him back."

Laurie growled, sounding a bit less human than she ever had before. "Astrid was a *liar* who obviously works with our enemies, Fen. Owen lost an *eye*. You don't think that's proof enough that he's Odin?"

"Nope." Fen glared at her. "If you want to see him, he needs to talk to you when I'm there or Thorsen is. Period. I'm not going to tell Uncle Stig that you got yourself killed or captured when you trusted some guy just because he only had one eye."

"You're being a jerk." Laurie poked him in the shoulder.

"Yeah, well, at least I'm not being careless. You should have—"

"Umm, guys?" Baldwin interrupted. "Did you hear something?" Fen opened his mouth, but Baldwin continued, "No, really. I heard something. You can argue later."

They all stopped walking and listened.

"Maybe the goats did get through the portal," Matt said, "or they followed us."

"This far?" Fen scoffed. "How fast do you think goats run, Thorsen?"

Laurie was tired of Fen's attitude just then, so she said, "They *are* magic goats."

"Whatever." Fen scowled at her, and she suspected that

she wasn't going to be forgiven right away for the Owen thing or for standing up for Matt. She loved her cousin, but when he got surly, she'd learned just to ignore him until his mood improved.

That was exactly what she did, and everyone else seemed to follow her lead. They walked the rest of the way to Old Blackwell in silence. There wasn't enough of the original settlement left to call it a ghost town, but there were enough stories about the things that lived out here to create ghost stories aplenty. She used to ignore the stories about creatures scuttling around in the dark, dead walking, and wolves prowling. Today, she had to wonder if some of those stories might actually be true.

"Be careful," Matt said. "We don't know what's out here."

Matt and Fen always seemed to get along best when there was a potential threat, so they easily slipped from boys who were bickering to a team as they scanned the area. Baldwin followed their lead, as did Laurie.

Saint Agnes was in pretty good shape for having been abandoned a few hundred years ago. The cemetery was still kept up, too: no vandalism, broken stones, or overgrown weeds here. Of course, that also meant that they had an obstacle to getting into the graveyard. A tall iron fence surrounded it, and the gate was held shut by a shiny silver chain and padlock.

"I can scale it," Baldwin offered.

They looked for another option, but short of blasting the lock, they weren't going to get in. Fen tested the bars, looking for a loose one that they could slide to the side and slip behind. He didn't find one, but even if he had, Laurie wasn't sure anyone other than her or Fen would fit through such a narrow space.

Baldwin grabbed the iron fence and, in moments, he'd pulled himself up and dropped to the other side. Once he was through, they handed him their packs. Most of what was in them was soft enough that they could probably just toss them over, but no one really knew when one of Helen's surprise presents could appear. Plus, Laurie's bow and Matt's shield didn't seem like the sort of things to throw over fences carelessly.

After Baldwin had their things, Fen and Matt acted like ladders to help Laurie hoist herself up. With a hand on either boy's shoulder, she looked down at them where they were crouched at her feet. Matt cupped his hands, and Fen did the same.

"Step in our hands," Matt said.

Once she did, balancing herself with one hand on each of their heads, they stood and lifted her higher. It was wobbly, but she could almost reach the top rail of the fence.

"A little higher," Baldwin said from inside the graveyard.

Her fingers grazed it, but she still couldn't grasp the rail.

"Just about..." She felt the boys pushing her up. Matt had sort of stepped away as Laurie stepped on Fen's shoulders.

Her cousin stayed still as she wrapped her hands around the bar—and hung there. She was able to handle a lot of things, but she didn't have the upper-body strength to pull herself to the top of the fence. She had both hands gripping the top bar of the fence, but even with Matt and Fen pushing her, she wasn't able to pull herself up like Baldwin had. The fence was too high.

"You can do it," Matt said.

"I'm not so sure."

"Shhh!" Baldwin whispered loudly. "I *know* I heard something that time."

Matt and Fen looked back toward the woods, and Laurie tried again to pull herself up and over the fence so that Fen was free to fight if necessary.

"Hide," she told Baldwin. "Take the supplies."

As she managed to pull herself up a bit more, she was able to get one foot up on the bar, not quite enough to use it as an aid to get to the top and over to the other side, but closer. Her arms burned, and she considered dropping back to the ground beside Matt and Fen. Her only weapon was inside the graveyard, though.

"Can you see anything?" she whispered. She looked from the shadows to Matt and Fen.

"No." Matt was watching for movement. This close to Blackwell it could be the police or Raiders. Of course, it could also be some monster they hadn't encountered yet. "Fen, you're next."

"Like I'm leaving you on the ground alone. If it's anything other than goats, you'll need help, and the only weapon I have is me. Turning into a wolf won't be any use with a fence between me and the bad guys. You go up and help her the rest of the way over. Your Hammer works at a distance."

Matt started, "I don't think—" His words ended abruptly, and he crumpled to the ground.

Laurie looked toward the woods, expecting to see any manner of enemy—a troll, a mara, a zombie even—but what she saw was utterly unexpected. A red-haired man in ragged camouflage clothes stood with a gun in his hands.

"You *shot* him!" She dangled from the top rail, neither able to go over or come down. At her feet, Fen was growling so loudly that she expected him to be furry. On the other side of the fence, crouched behind a tombstone, was Baldwin. She looked in his direction and mouthed, *Stay there.*

"It's just a tranq." The man scowled up at her like she was some sort of vermin and scoffed, "Like I'd shoot a Thorsen." He lowered his gaze from her down to Fen. "But a Brekke... especially one that turns into a dirty wolf, well, we'll see. Do you want a running start, wolf?"

"Fen," Laurie warned.

He didn't look at her, and she wasn't sure what he'd do. He was facing off with a man who was aiming a gun right at him. For all of Fen's flaws, he was fiercely loyal. He wasn't going to run, not even if she tried telling him to do so. Matt was unconscious, and she was weaponless. Baldwin could fight, but if he came out of hiding and tried to scale the fence to jump into any fight Fen started, he'd be tranquilized before he cleared the fence. Laurie dropped to the ground, stumbling a little as her ankle rolled under her.

She could open a portal, shove Fen in, and try to dive through, but that didn't help Matt. Even if Matt were conscious, she wasn't sure she could open one fast enough, and there was no way they were leaving him behind.

"Lift him," the hunter said.

Fen glared at the man. "You shot him; you lift him."

"Don't try me, boy." The hunter shifted slightly so the gun was aimed at Laurie. "These were for Matt, and he's twice her weight. Should I see what they do to her?"

With a familiar reckless expression on his face, Fen stepped in front of her. She couldn't see his face now that he was blocking her body with his own, so she wasn't sure if he would charge the hunter. He had done less intelligent things in their lives, and she knew that he wasn't likely to be okay with going anywhere with the hunter. Maybe it was a wolf thing, but Fen didn't always do well with enclosed spaces. The man who had tranquilized Matt was either going to cage them or hurt them. Neither option was great.

Laurie leaned closer to Fen's back and said, "We don't have any choice. I can't get us out of here, and we can't leave Matt."

Fen growled, but she knew it was frustration, not anger at her.

"It'll be okay," she said. "Just help me with Matt."

Fen turned to face her.

Then she crouched down beside Matt, ducking her head to hide her expression from the hunter as she tried to pass a message to her cousin and the hidden boy. "All three of us will just have to go with him. He'll probably turn us in to the cops or the Raiders, whichever one he's working for, and we'll figure out a plan."

Fen squatted down beside her; his side was to the hunter, so his expression was partially hidden by his hair when he lowered his head slightly. "Get help," he mouthed in the general direction of Baldwin, all while he made a show of trying to find Matt's pulse to check it and feel his head to make sure it wasn't swelling. "You're making a mistake trying to arrest us or whatever."

The man snorted. "Can you carry him or not? I can't carry three people, and I'm not going to get in trouble because I left witnesses."

Fen and Laurie exchanged a look, and she knew he was

trying to stay calm—and still think of a plan. She was, too. "It'll be okay," she said, trying to sound positive, and then she raised her voice. "We can carry him."

Fen looked like he was ready to bite someone, but he nodded at her and together they hauled Matt into their arms. Not only were they captives, but they were being made to carry one of their group off to wherever the hunter was taking them. Monsters suddenly seemed much easier to face than humans.

# TEN

# MATT

## "HEAP OF TROUBLE"

Matt opened his eyes. He was staring at a rough wood board dotted with green and gray lichen. There was another plank above it. He rubbed his eyes and looked down. He was lying on an old blanket stretched out on a wooden floor.

*A cabin*, he thought. *I'm in an old cabin. Is this where we spent the night?*

No, he remembered sleeping bags on cold ground. Then something about goats? And Astrid? Was that a dream? His thoughts were muddled and distorted.

Mjölnir. They'd been looking for Mjölnir. Did they get the hammer and then find a cabin for the night—?

He bolted upright. As he did, his stomach lurched, his brain lurching, too, and he bent over, gagging. Someone shoved a bucket under him.

"Easy, son. Take it easy."

Matt looked up, struggling to focus. The first thing he saw was Thor's Hammer. Not Mjölnir. An amulet, hanging around a neck. His fingers flew to his own throat and touched the metal there. He could see the other one wasn't his now, too. The design was different. Yet it was definitely a Thor's Hammer amulet. He tried to lift his head to look at the man's face, but his stomach and head lurched again and his gaze dropped to the arm holding the bucket. A thick, brawny arm covered in fine reddish hair. Finally, he managed to look up at the man himself. He was as tall as Matt's dad, with even wider shoulders, a broad face, and a red beard.

The man was a Thorsen. He had to be, a big guy with red hair and that amulet.

"Whaaa..." Matt's throat wouldn't open to form the rest of the words. It felt like he'd swallowed acid again. Or maybe dust. Sand, even. His throat was parched.

The man handed him a bottle of water. "Drink slowly, son."

Matt racked his brain to pull up the last thing he remembered. They'd been going after Mjölnir....

Blackwell. They'd been in Old Blackwell.

Matt's gaze shot up to the man's face, ignoring the

pounding surf in his head as he struggled to focus on the man's features. He had a leathery face and a slight squint in one blue eye. A scar bisected his cheek. He wasn't anyone Matt recognized. That meant he wasn't a Thorsen from Blackwell.

What *had* happened? *Come on, Matty. Think.*

Goats. The goats had been following him. Thor's goats. Tanngrisnir and Tanngnjóstr. He'd been trying to give them the slip, but they just kept following until...

Until the portal. It had seemed as if Matt left the goats behind there, but then they'd heard something following them again and thought it was the goats. They'd reached the cemetery and Baldwin had gone over the fence and Matt had passed his shield through and...

And then what?

And then he woke up in this cabin, with this man.

"How...? Where...?" He looked around. "My friends. I was with—"

"If you mean the Brekkes, they're not your friends, son. But they're safe." The man said it with a slight twist of his lips as if he'd rather it was otherwise. "Now, you've caused a heap of trouble for your folks, Matthew Thorsen, but I know you didn't mean to. You're a good boy. Things just got confusing, didn't they? Those Brekke brats steered you wrong, but your grandpa understands that."

"G-Granddad?" Matt scrambled up now, looking around wildly. "Where am I?"

"'Bout two miles outside Blackwell." The man paused. "What were you doing busting into that graveyard, son?"

Matt blinked, feigning confusion as he tried to think of an excuse fast. His muddled brain wouldn't cooperate, and he could only say, "I...I don't remember."

"Were you looking for something?"

Now he really fixed on the confused look. "Looking for something? In a graveyard?"

The man seemed to buy it. "Never mind about that, then. Tell me—"

"Who are you?" Matt cut in. "I know you're a Thorsen, and you seem to know my grandfather, but I don't know you. I'm not sure I should be talking to you."

Again, the man bought it. Either he thought Matt wasn't too bright, or he didn't know enough about thirteen-year-olds to realize they were past the age of refusing to speak to strangers.

"Rusty Thorsen," he said. "Out of Sioux Falls. No, we've never met, son. I know your grandpa, and he asked me to come find you. I'm a tracker. I help folks find big game." A broad smile. "And it seems that works just as well on finding young fellas who run away from home. I—" A rap at the door interrupted him. "Well, now, I think that's your grandpa."

As Rusty strolled out, Matt tensed, waiting until he'd passed through the open doorway. Then he pushed up, looking around as he did, ready to run . . .

Nowhere. There wasn't anyplace for him to go. He was in a bare room with no windows and only one door—the way Rusty just walked out.

Matt crept toward the door, but even as he drew near, he knew it was useless. He could hear Rusty's voice right outside it. Then he heard another voice. A familiar one. His grandfather. His knees wobbled, and all he could think was, *I'm home.*

When Hildar said he had to return to Blackwell, he'd been sure he couldn't do it. Getting that close to home would be too much, the temptation to run back to his parents and tell them everything and hope—pray—they didn't know his grandfather's plan, and that they would help him.

He hadn't run home, obviously. Even when he'd seen the familiar landscape, he'd stayed on mission. Get Mjölnir. Move on to the next quest. Keep training. Keep preparing.

He'd been proud of himself for that. He wasn't a child anymore, dashing home when things got tough.

Yet now, as he heard Granddad's voice . . .

Matt sucked in a breath and squeezed his eyes shut.

*Gonna run home now, Matty? Run to be saved by Granddad? Run back to the guy who wants to sacrifice you to a giant serpent? To sacrifice most of humanity?*

No. Of course not. He was a leader, a fighter, a winner. He might not believe what Hildar had said about him being the god reborn, but he was still a son of Thor, a true descendant of the North.

Maybe it didn't have to be like that, though. He wasn't the same messed-up kid he'd been when the runes chose him. He'd been tested, and he'd passed those tests. Yes, his grandfather had told the elders that the world needed Ragnarök, but Matt was sure he didn't really believe that. He'd been saying what they needed to hear. Putting the best possible spin on the worst possible situation. Ragnarök was coming, and there was no way a bunch of kids could train fast enough to defeat the greatest monsters in Norse legends. Blackwell had to prepare and, as mayor, Granddad had to help them through it, as much as he might wish he didn't have to.

*What if you're wrong? What if he really does want you to fail?*

The doorway darkened. Matt looked up and there was his grandfather, his lined face drawn with worry. His blue eyes lit on Matt, and he let out an audible sigh of relief and in three long strides, he crossed the floor and caught Matt up in a hug so tight his ribs crackled in protest.

"Matty," his grandfather whispered, his voice catching. "I was so worried."

"I'm sorry." Matt didn't mean to say that, but he couldn't help it. He saw his grandfather's face, and there was no question. Granddad loved him. Whatever he'd said to the elders, he hadn't really planned to let Matt die. He hadn't planned to let the world end. The thought was so stupid that Matt's cheeks flushed with shame for ever believing it.

Yes, Granddad had doubted him. He might have even thought they didn't stand a chance. But now Matt could tell him about the Norns and the Valkyries and the shield and their new powers, and he'd understand that they could do this. They really could.

"I'm going to fix this, Matty," his grandfather murmured, still hugging him. "I know you've been through a lot. I know you've tried so hard to be a champion. You *are* a champion. But you've been misled, and things have gone wrong."

"What? No. We've—"

Granddad moved back, hands going to Matt's shoulders, gaze locking with his. "I know what happened, Matt, and I know it wasn't your fault. You thought you could change fate. You thought you could stop Loki from killing Balder, and you couldn't, and you must feel terribly guilty about that—"

"Fen didn't kill—"

"I know what happened, Matt. I know the boy died, and I know Fen Brekke killed him. That was the prophecy, and that's what happened, and it isn't your fault."

"No, Baldwin—"

Another knock, this time at the front door. Matt tried to

blurt out the truth, that someone else killed Baldwin, a girl working for the Raiders, a girl named Astrid, that they'd brought Baldwin back and he was alive again. He only got the first part out, and his grandfather didn't even seem to hear that. He was already heading out to answer the knock, pulling the door shut behind him, and Rusty was pushing Matt back into the room, keeping him from running after his grandfather, telling him to relax, it was okay, it would all be okay.

He heard the door open. He heard a man's voice, one he didn't recognize.

"You have the boy here, sir?" the man asked.

"I do. Thank you for coming, Officer. This is a terrible situation, I know. One boy dead at the hands of another. A horrible thing. Justice will be served, though. The killer is here, in the next room. A boy from my own town. Fen Brekke."

"No!" Matt said, wrenching wildly against Rusty. But the big man held him easily, one huge hand slapping over Matt's mouth as his grandfather led the police into the next room to arrest Fen for Baldwin's murder.

# ELEVEN

## FEN

### "FALSELY ACCUSED"

As the officer led Fen into the main room of the cabin, Mayor Thorsen smiled at Fen. It was the sort of smile that wasn't really friendly. Fen growled.

He knew that Matt was behind the door that had slammed shut, and he wanted to attack the hunter for drugging Matt with that dart. They might not have been friends before they decided to work together to save the world, but they were a team now. Not knowing how to rescue Matt was awful; knowing that the hunter was on the other side of that closed door, probably restraining Matt *right now*, was even worse. Matt was a captive of a man who'd shot him with a tranquilizer, and Fen and Laurie were facing an officer with a gun, one with real bullets in it, most likely.

*Would he shoot a kid?*

Fen looked around the room for some sort of weapon. There was a small table and a beat-up sofa, but they weren't going to be much use. Beyond that was the closed door to the room where Matt was. This was not a good situation in any way.

Laurie trailed behind Fen. She could run. The hunter must be in the room with Matt. Mayor Thorsen and the officer were focused on him. Laurie, at least, could get to safety.

Fen turned and whispered to her, "If you can, make a break for it."

She rolled her eyes. "As if."

"What did you say?" the officer demanded.

"Nothing." Fen huffed out a breath. He wanted to argue with Laurie, but he also wasn't sure what the officer would do if she did run. The thought of her being arrested made him feel sick—not that the thought of *him* being arrested was much better.

"You're making a mistake," Laurie told the officer.

"Thorsen?" Fen called out to Matt. "You keep her safe if they take me."

Although Matt didn't answer, Fen had to hope he'd heard, that he was conscious, and that he would find a way to get Laurie to safety.

"Was she a part of this, too?" the mayor asked, glancing at Laurie. "Did you help him, young lady?"

Laurie grabbed Fen's hand. "No one did anything wrong...except the man who shot Matt."

"No one shot my grandson," the mayor scoffed. "The lies children tell these days. It's absurd that they think they can get away with lying—and worse. It starts with the parents, of course."

The officer nodded and said, "Broken homes. Bad influences. Lack of discipline." He sounded sad as he spoke, like he genuinely felt sorry for the kids. His forehead furrowed. "Bad parenting ruins so many young people's lives."

Fen almost felt sorry for the man. *He* was the one being lied to, and he really seemed like he might be a nice enough guy. Still, he was there to arrest them. That decreased Fen's sympathy a fair amount. When the officer had arrived, Fen had heard the muted conversation from inside the room where he and Laurie had been locked up. It was ridiculous that he was about to be arrested for a murder that he didn't commit—especially now that he'd been one of the people who had brought Baldwin back from the dead. Unfortunately, it wasn't that surprising that Fen was unjustly accused. The police in Blackwell had a longstanding habit of assuming that the Brekkes committed most crimes in the area. Okay, admittedly, his family regularly broke more than a few laws, but that didn't mean that they were at fault for *everything*. Case in point: Fen did not kill Baldwin.

"Just tell us what happened," the officer said in a reasonable voice. "We know you killed the boy, but we need to know why."

"*Why?*" Fen repeated, staring at the officer who had just accused him of murder. It felt different hearing it said to his face than through a locked door.

"Why did you kill Baldwin Osgood?" The officer held out a picture of Baldwin.

"You honestly think I *killed* someone?" Fen half growled the words, which probably didn't help the situation, but he wasn't exactly at his calmest. They'd been kidnapped; Matt had been shot with some sort of tranquilizer. Now the mayor had called in an officer to arrest Fen for a murder he hadn't committed, all of this after he and the others had gone to the afterlife to rescue Baldwin... which hadn't been exactly easy, what with dealing with a sea of zombies, the stinky cave bear, and creepy Aunt Helen. Oh, yeah, and a flaming two-headed giant. He couldn't even tell them all that he'd gone through to rescue the kid they thought he'd killed. Adults just didn't *listen* half the time.

Laurie stayed beside him; she clutched his hand in hers, and he wasn't sure if it was to keep him from doing something stupid or because she was afraid. The more he thought about it, the more he wanted to do something crazy. They'd been captured, forced to carry Thorsen to this cabin, and then locked in a tiny room with only a sagging bed and a battered dresser. He'd been pacing, plotting, and coming up with only ridiculous plans—ones that would result in someone getting shot. He hoped Baldwin was having better luck at mounting a rescue, but he wasn't sure that Baldwin could even find them, much less rescue them on his own. Being the embodiment of a cheerful god wasn't going to be quite enough of a skill for Baldwin to get them out of this.

"Fen didn't kill anyone," Laurie said finally. "I'm not sure why you think—"

"The mayor called us, Miss Brekke." The officer gave her the sort of look that would've scared Laurie into silence last week, the kind that adults always give kids when they think they know everything. After a swarm of zombies and a stampede of buffalo, it obviously didn't frighten her like it once would have. His cousin simply glared at the officer.

"Baldwin isn't even *dead*." Fen shook his head. "You're arresting me for something that didn—"

"We have witnesses, boy," the mayor interrupted.

"Witnesses to a crime that didn't happen," Fen scoffed.

"They're obviously lying," Laurie said.

The mayor shook his head and turned to the officer, "Fen Brekke has been a vandal and troublemaker as long as he's been old enough to walk into town. And all the Brekkes are liars."

Neither Fen nor Laurie replied.

The officer stared at Fen. "You said this was Eddy Brekke's boy, didn't you?"

Mayor Thorsen nodded.

The officer shook his head. "The apple certainly didn't fall very far from that tree, did it?"

Laurie squeezed Fen's hand, and he forced himself to remain silent. He wasn't like his dad, not really. Sure, he had screwed up here and there, but he was trying to be a good guy. He was *trying* to be a hero. Maybe they could see that if he tried to explain—not the monsters part or the going to Hel or the turning into a wolf—but the part they *should* understand.

"Baldwin isn't dead," Fen repeated. "I told you that. He's not dead. I didn't kill him. Seriously, if he's dead, where's the body?"

"You tell us, young man," the mayor said.

The officer apparently had run out of patience. He pulled out a pair of handcuffs and took a step toward Fen. The mayor was behind the officer, and Fen and Laurie faced him. There was no way the odds were fair, but they hadn't been fair in the fights against the other monsters—the not-human ones—either. Heroes didn't give up. It was in the rule book or something.

Fen growled, sounding nothing like a person but unable to stop himself. He wasn't going into a cage. He had no idea how he'd get out of that, and he *had* to so he could keep Laurie safe, rescue Matt, defeat the bad guys, and maybe save the world. He didn't have time to be arrested, especially for something he hadn't done.

"Fen," Laurie started, but she didn't say more. She looked at him sort of helplessly and then stepped in front of him. Fen winced. She was a girl, and she was trying to protect him like he was weak. Fen's job was to protect *her*.

"Move," he said in a low voice. His eyes met the mayor's over her shoulder.

"Look," the officer said. "I don't have time for this. I'm going to put these on." He tried to reach past Laurie, and she backed up, pushing Fen backward with her body.

"No, you're not." Her chin went up as she said it. "Whoever told the mayor that they were witnesses has to be confused. Baldwin is alive. Fen said so. You have no reason to arrest my cousin." She put her arms out on either side of her, and then she stepped back again. "He's not going with you. He's not an *animal*. Right, Fen?"

At that, Fen felt stupid. He could tell he was to get some message out of that last bit, but he had no idea whether she was telling him to change or not to change. All he knew was that her message was about being a wolf.

"I could be," he murmured.

"No!" she yelled.

He sighed. That wasn't the answer he was hoping to hear.

In another minute, it didn't matter, though, because the officer pushed Laurie aside and grabbed Fen.

Fen tried to jerk away, and the officer shoved him onto the table.

"Wait!" Laurie yelled. She shot the officer a smug grin. "Now you'll see. Just answer the door."

"It's about time," Fen muttered. The officer's hand was in the middle of Fen's back, holding him so he was facedown on the table with his arms pulled behind him. All Fen could do was stand there with his cheek flat to the table and his arms restrained behind him. The officer cuffed him. It was humiliating, but his cousin's words eased that feeling tremendously. She could sense the descendants; she *knew* who was at the door.

Laurie darted over and yanked it open. There, grinning in that way that he had before every bit of trouble they'd faced, was Baldwin.

"Someone said you thought I was dead," Baldwin said as he came into the cabin. He left the door open and gestured behind him, where a group of about ten kids waited. "My friends here helped me reach you so I could see if you really thought that, but I think they're teasing or something. I'm pretty sure I'm not dead. Anyone can see that."

The officer looked from Baldwin to Fen to the mayor. He removed his hand from Fen's back but didn't remove the cuffs.

Fen straightened up, rolled his shoulders, and cracked his neck.

"Told you," Fen muttered.

Frowning, the officer lifted the photograph he had of Baldwin, looked at it, and looked back to the boy who stood watching them with a friendly smile. When the officer looked back at the photo again, Fen caught Baldwin's eye and mouthed, *Get Laurie out.*

The expression on the boy's face didn't change, but he stepped farther inside the cabin, moving toward Laurie. The people outside were all watching.

"Close the door," the mayor said.

"It's okay. They're with my friend *Odin.*" Laurie glanced at the mayor. "Do you know Odin, Mayor Thorsen?"

"She's not under arrest, is she?" Fen asked.

The officer looked confused. "You're Baldwin Osgood?"

Baldwin nodded as he walked over to the picture. "Yeah. That's me. Not a great picture, though, is it?" He pointed at the image. It was undeniably him, but whatever likability Baldwin had seemed to kick in more as he spoke. "I couldn't get the trick I was doing that day. Broke my board trying." He laughed. "That's why I look so grumpy in the picture."

The officer nodded. He was swayed by Baldwin's persuasive presence just like everyone else. He smiled at the boy. "My son's like that."

"Hey, do you mind if my friends come in?"

"I don't think that's necessary," the mayor interjected.

For a moment, the officer paused. He frowned as if trying to think if there was a reason it was a bad idea to let them inside the house.

Baldwin added, "It's getting darker, and you know how many dangers are out there, right? I mean, you thought someone had *killed* me. Thanks for caring about that, by the way. It's cool of you."

The officer smiled. "You kids, come on in."

The strangers outside—ones Laurie said were with Odin—started to fill the cabin. Several of them surrounded Laurie, and after she whispered something in the ear of the one closest to her, others moved toward the door that led to Matt and the hidden hunter.

"Can you uncuff my friend, Officer...? What's your name?" Baldwin sat and looked up at the officer.

"Davison. Officer Davison," he said as he uncuffed Fen.

Calmly, Mayor Thorsen said, "Well, I guess there was a misunderstanding. Thank you for your time." He gestured toward the still-open door. "Sorry for the inconvenience."

Fen rubbed his wrists and immediately went to stand by Laurie.

The officer looked around at them, clearly not sure what was going on. He folded his arms. "Why don't I just stay until we get this sorted out?" It wasn't really a question, even though he'd said it like it was. He might be influenced by

Baldwin's persuasiveness, but he was still able to notice that something was very wrong here.

"No, no," the mayor insisted. "These kids can all go along home. I'll take my grandson home to his parents."

"We can't leave Matt here," Laurie whispered as she hugged Fen tightly to her.

"I know." Fen looked toward the closed door.

The mayor was looking around at the crowd of kids.

"Why don't you go ahead home," Baldwin suggested. He put his hand on Officer Davison's sleeve. "There's no one here to arrest. The mayor's here, so you don't have to worry about unsupervised kids."

Officer Davison glanced at the mayor, who nodded and said, "The boy's right. I can handle this."

After a moment's pause, Officer Davison left. One of the kids stopped the door from closing. It was quiet as the officer got in his car and left.

Then, one of the kids bowed to Laurie and said, "Odin sends his regards." He turned to Fen, nodded at him, and added, "He thought you might need a bit of help, so we're at your command tonight."

Fen grinned. They wouldn't be going to jail, and with this kind of help, even the hunter on the other side of the door wasn't going to be able to stop them from getting out of here and getting back to Saint Agnes. Things were about to get better.

# TWELVE

## MATT

### "HARD TRUTH"

S top," Rusty said as Matt tensed.

"I wasn't—"

"You were getting ready to make a run for that door. Your granddad wanted you to wait here, and I need to make sure you do. I don't want to hurt you, son."

"You already did."

Matt hated the note of shock still in his voice. He sounded like a little kid, stunned that a grown-up had struck him. He was supposed to be Thor's champion. A fighter. The old rules didn't count. Except it felt like they did. He touched his sore jaw and winced, as much at the pain as the lingering surprise that Rusty had hit him.

He'd tried to go after Granddad. To explain that Baldwin wasn't dead. But Rusty had grabbed him and when he'd broken free, Rusty had smacked him, the blow knocking him clean off his feet.

It wasn't just the fact Rusty had done it that shocked Matt. It was the *way* he had, matter-of-fact, no anger. No apology, either. He'd sent Matt flying, then given him another shot of tranquilizer. This one didn't knock him out.

"It's just to keep you calm, son," Rusty had said. "While your grandpa handles this."

It kept Matt calm, all right. So calm he could barely move. It was like getting gas at the dentist, except this kind didn't make him happy—it made his head fuzzy and his limbs heavy, practically pinning him to the chair.

He'd tried to explain to Rusty that Baldwin wasn't dead. But the man had only smiled, like Matt was a little kid telling stories—and not very good at it. So Matt sat there, struggling to listen to the conversation in the next room. But he couldn't catch more than the murmur of voices through the thick wood walls.

He had to get out. He had to explain.

Matt had focused on the door and on gathering his strength to jump up and race out and . . .

He'd barely tensed when Rusty had said, "Stop," knowing exactly what he planned.

"Relax, son. It'll be over soon and you can go back to

your folks. They're mighty worried about you. What I hear, your dad's been out every night, searching. All day and all night. Your brothers, too. Your poor mama waiting at home, hoping you're going to walk through that door any minute now. And you will. In just a couple of hours. You'll see them, and everything will be okay."

"Fen didn't kill—"

"The courts will decide that. If he didn't, he'll be fine."

"My dad's a sheriff. I know Fen won't be fine. He'll be arrested, and he'll be charged, and if he gets bail, he'll go to a group home, but he almost definitely won't get bail, because they think he killed someone, meaning he's in jail until—"

"Juvenile detention, not jail. From what I hear, the boy could use it."

"Fen—"

The door opened. Granddad stood in the opening. Matt leaped up and when he did, his weak legs gave way and he almost fell, catching himself on the chair just before he did.

Granddad didn't make a move to help Matt recover. Rusty did, but Matt brushed him off and turned to his grandfather, who stood there, a distant look in his eyes, as if he hadn't noticed Matt stumble.

"It seems there's been a mistake," he said. "Balder— Baldwin—is still alive."

"So Fen…The police didn't take Fen?" Matt asked.

"No."

Matt crumpled into the chair and exhaled. His head was still fuzzy and his arms and legs felt like they were weighed down with stones, but he managed to find his voice.

"I know about the plan, Granddad," he said. "I know you don't expect me to win against the Midgard Serpent."

Granddad lowered himself into a chair. He didn't look shocked. Just tired. Really tired. Sad, too, his gaze down, his hands folded on his lap as he leaned forward, elbows on his knees.

"I thought you might," Granddad said finally. "You were there at the community center. When I was talking to the other elders. You listened in."

"No! I mean, yes, but I wasn't eavesdropping. There was this girl—or I thought she was a girl—and I chased her in and—"

"Do you really think I'm going to give you trouble for listening in, Matty?" Granddad gave a wry, sad smile. "You overheard me say that I didn't expect you to survive the battle. That I expected you to lose. To die. I can't imagine how that must have felt."

Matt remembered how it felt. Like the worst thing that ever happened to him. His hands started to tremble, and he clenched his fists.

"You're angry," Granddad said.

"No, I'm not—" He lifted his head and met his grandfather's blue eyes. "Yes, I'm angry. I've never been more angry or more—" He bit the words off with a sharp shake of his head.

"You thought I didn't believe in you. That I didn't think you could do it."

Matt shrugged. "Can't blame you. If I screwed up everything else, you'd figure I was going to screw up that, too."

Granddad frowned. "Everything else? When have you screwed up?" He paused and nodded. "If you mean running away with the Brekkes—"

"No, I mean before that. At Jolablot, when I messed up my reading. At the science fair, when I didn't win like my brothers. Everything."

A soft laugh. "Those aren't 'everything,' Matt. They're a couple of stumbles and, considering you got an honorable mention at the science fair, that's hardly a 'screwup.' Your brothers excel at what they excel at, and you excel at what you excel at. You have As—in English and history. You have trophies—in wrestling and boxing. These may not be traditional areas of expertise for a Thorsen, but that's what's made you something your brothers can never be. The Champion of Thor. His chosen representative."

"Chosen to die, according to you."

Granddad blinked, as if surprised by Matt's tone. Matt resisted the urge to apologize.

"No, not according to me, Matt. According to the runes. According to the Seer. You heard me say that, because that's what the runes say and if I argue, I sound like a sentimental old man. Blackwell doesn't need a sentimental old man right now. It needs a leader. One who is willing to accept hard facts. The hardest, most unpleasant facts, like the death of his favorite grandchild. You know that, don't you, Matty? That you are my favorite?"

Matt squirmed. He didn't want to hear that, not now. He needed to be a leader here, and that meant thinking clearly, not letting his feelings get the better of him.

Granddad murmured something to Rusty. The other man nodded and left. Then Granddad moved his chair toward Matt's, stopping so close their knees brushed.

"I don't want you to die, Matt. I will do everything in my power to make sure you don't, no matter what I say to others. I have ideas. Plans. I don't think the serpent needs to kill you."

"But you think Ragnarök needs to come. I heard you say that to the others."

Granddad sighed. "I tell them what they need to hear, because it *is* coming and raging against it won't help. It's easier if we believe it's for the best, and we prepare for it." He met Matt's gaze. "You cannot defeat the serpent, Matthew, and that's not because you aren't strong enough or clever enough or powerful enough. You cannot win, because you are fated to lose. The prophecies say—"

"The prophecies are wrong."

"I know you'd like to believe that, but—"

"They are." Matt got to his feet. "Fen didn't kill Baldwin. This girl named Astrid did. She's a witch with no connection to Loki. She killed Baldwin and tried to steal my shield, but I got it back, and we went to the afterlife and we talked to Helen, and she gave us Baldwin back."

Granddad stared. "You went to—?"

"Yes. Just like in the stories. Except in the stories, Helen doesn't give Balder back, because Loki doesn't grieve. This *isn't* the stories. Loki didn't kill Balder. Loki did grieve. Helen gave Baldwin back. That means the prophecies—"

Granddad rose and cut Matt short with a hand on his shoulder. "Someone has done something to you, Matty. Maybe given you some kind of drugs. I don't know. There's a lot of magic out there, and someone has worked it on you. There's no way Baldwin died and came back, and there's certainly no way you went to Hel and—"

Matt yanked back. "I did. *We* did. I can tell you everything we've done, if you'll listen. We found the twins. We fought trolls. We fought Raiders who turn to wolves. We've talked to Norns. We've ridden with the Valkyries. I have my shield. I know where to find Mjölnir."

"You—you've…" His grandfather seemed beyond words.

"Yes. All of that. Let me explain, and you'll see that we can win this."

His grandfather put his hand on Matt's shoulder. "Yes, I think you should explain everything, Matt. Tell me everything you've done. Everything you've seen. And we'll get Mjölnir together—"

The door burst open. It was a kid Matt had never seen before. He was about sixteen, maybe seventeen. Matt's height but thinner. Blond hair in braids, tied back, with black feathers hanging from them. Laurie stood beside him, looking anxious.

"Matt Thorsen," the kid with the braids said, "if you're done talking to your grandfather, I think you guys better hit the road."

"Who—?" Matt began.

"His name is Vance," Laurie said. "He's a Berserker. They're like Owen's personal army. They're going to escort us out of here." She cast a worried look up at his grandfather. "Hopefully without any trouble."

Matt shook his head. "I've explained things to Granddad. He understands. He's going to help—"

"Help you find Mjölnir?" the Berserker said. "Is that what I heard? I don't think you want him doing that. In fact, I'm pretty sure you don't. Come on, Matt. Let's get you out of here."

Matt looked at Laurie. She nodded, her eyes imploring him to come and come quickly. Behind her, he could see Fen and Baldwin and when he leaned to see them, their faces urged him out, too.

"You've had your chat with your grandson, old man," the Berserker said. "Now we need to have ours. About you." He paused and gave a humorless grin. "Or do you want to be the one to break it to him?"

"Break what to me?" Matt said.

He looked over. His grandfather's face was expressionless. One big hand reached for Matt, but Matt stumbled back.

"Break *what* to me?"

Another teenage guy raced in, pushing forward to stand by the other one. "Vance," he said, "we've got trouble. He must have called in reinforcements."

"Who?" Matt said.

The new guy motioned at Matt's grandfather. "He didn't want a chat with Thor's champion. He wanted time for his troops to arrive. We're surrounded."

"Troops?" Matt said. "What troops?" He paused. "You mean the Thorsens?"

When no one answered, Matt raced out the door, pushing past Vance and Laurie, past Rusty, standing in the next room, surrounded by Berserkers. He ran to the nearest window and looked out. There were kids out there. Dozens of kids, brandishing sticks and knives. And wolves. There were wolves.

Matt remembered what he'd told Astrid: that he thought someone else was in charge of the monsters. Someone leading Skull and the Raiders. Matt had wanted to question a captured Raider, but the guy had escaped. So Matt never got his answer.

He had it now. He knew who was leading the enemy team. His grandfather.

# THIRTEEN

## MATT

### "THE SERPENT RISES"

**M**att turned from the window. The cabin was packed with Berserkers, but he didn't notice anything more than that they were in his way and he had to step to the side to see his grandfather.

"I don't understand," he said.

Granddad didn't seem to notice the Berserkers, either. Or he didn't care. He was in a room with at least fifteen legendary fighters against him and Rusty, and he didn't bat an eye. He just walked forward as if they were alone.

"I don't understand," Matt said. "I just don't—" He stopped himself. He sounded stupid, repeating the same thing, but that was all he heard, looping through his head.

He'd just discovered that his grandfather was in charge of the Raiders. The *Raiders*. Which meant he was in charge of Astrid and all the forces that would align against him and Fen and Laurie at Ragnarök.

That was not possible. A Thorsen, leading the monsters. Leading them against Thor's champion. Leading them against *Matt*, his grandson.

*I do not understand.*

Somehow this was worse than at the community center, hearing that his grandfather expected him to die.

No, not *somehow*. Matt knew why it was worse. Because at least before, as much as it hurt, he'd trusted that his grandfather believed he had no choice. Believed Matt would die. Believed it was for the best. For the Thorsens. For Blackwell.

But this? *This?*

"Blackwell," he said finally. "The Thorsens. All the Thorsens. Our town. You're going to let them—"

"Let them live," Granddad said, still walking toward him. "Help them live. Lead them into a new world. A better world. Everything I said is true, Matt. You can't win this. They"—he motioned at the Raiders beyond the window—"they can't win this. I'm not choosing a side. I'm on yours, and I'm on theirs. Ragnarök will come, and no one will win the battle. Both sets of champions will die—for a better world. A reborn world. Yes, most people will perish, and that's a terrible tragedy. But the Thorsens will live on, under my leadership. The Raiders will help. They've trained for this for generations. Trained to survive anything. Even the end of the world. They'll teach us that."

"And me?"

His grandfather hesitated. "I still hope to save you, Matt. If there is a way—"

"Liar!" Matt roared. The word came out as loud as thunder, blasting against his skull and echoing through the room, and some of the Berserkers stumbled back, as if he'd hit them with his Hammer.

Granddad didn't even blink. "Matty, you need to calm—"

"Calm down? You lied. You're lying now. You've been lying to me my entire life!"

He advanced on his grandfather. As he did, he was shaking so hard it seemed as if the floor quavered under his feet. He felt something on his cheeks, something hot and wet, and he realized they were tears, and shame shot through him, and the shame fed the rage, whirling in his gut, his Hammer burning so hot it hurt, his head hurting, too, pounding, the rage building.

His grandfather stood his ground, his face hardening. "Matthew—"

"Your favorite grandson? Your favorite *sacrifice. That's* what I am. The one stupid enough to fall for it."

"No, Matt, that's not true. You are my fav—"

"Liar!" Matt screamed, and he felt the Hammer fly from

him. He didn't even need to reach out his hand. The wave of energy seemed to shoot from his entire body with a blinding flash and a deafening *crack*.

The Hammer hit his grandfather like a lightning bolt, sending him flying into the wall, the Berserkers scrambling out of the way, some knocked down by the reverberation.

The floor shook beneath Matt's feet.

*Not the floor. I'm shaking. Because of him. Of what he did.*

Rage whipped through him, and he swore he heard it crackle, swore he saw blue sparks flying off his skin. He kept going, advancing on his grandfather, now on the floor.

"You lied—"

Granddad leaped up and threw his own Hammer, knocking Matt back a step. "Matthew Robert Thorsen," he said, his voice low, his face hard. "You calm down right now or—"

"Or what?" Matt said. "You'll sacrifice me to a giant *serpent?*"

He roared the last word, and when he did, he heard another *crack* and he felt the floor shake. Around him, Berserkers stumbled and grabbed walls, their eyes going wide.

"Um, guys?" Baldwin said.

Matt dimly saw Baldwin pointing at something, but he kept moving forward. His grandfather was on his feet, braced, his blue eyes blazing, fingers out.

"Are you going to take me down?" Matt said. "Throw your Hammer? Teach me a lesson?"

"No, Matt. I would never hurt—"

"You already did!"

The cabin rumbled all around them, like thunder rolling through.

"Matt!"

It was Laurie, grabbing his arm. He shook her off, but she caught him again, directing his attention up to a crack in the wall, daylight shining through it.

*Why is there a crack...?*

The floor slammed up into his feet, setting him staggering forward, and when he turned, he was staring at a floorboard, popped straight up now and cracked right in half, splintered ends still quivering. As he stared, another board shot up, ripping free, nails flying. Then another and another—

"Everyone out!" Vance shouted.

Matt didn't move. He stood there, watching the floorboards burst and fly free, as if something was under them, pushing up, pushing free—

Fen grabbed his arm. "Move it, Thorsen! This place is going to—"

A thunderous *crack*, right under their feet, boards giving way. His grandfather raced out the door. Fen yanked Matt, dragging him across the room as the boards collapsed behind them, dropping into—

A hole. The boards were dropping into a hole. A gaping crater, opening up right under—

"Out!" Matt shouted, twisting and pushing Fen toward the door. "Everyone out now!"

Most were already running, but a few of the younger Berserkers just stood there, staring in horror as the floor vanished under their feet. The older ones realized they weren't following and began dragging them out. As Matt pushed one to safety, he heard another *crack* and looked up to see the fissure in the wall zooming down it, like a giant zipper opening, the cabin breaking in two, beams falling from the roof.

"Thorsen!" Fen shouted. "Get your—"

Boards crashed onto the floor, cutting Fen short. Matt looked around, but all he could see was debris falling and dust flying up and the cabin collapsing. He started for the door.

"Baldwin!" he heard Fen shout. "Where's—?"

Again, the thunderous chaos cut him short. Matt turned, blinking and peering into the dust until...

He saw Baldwin across the cabin. Standing against the wall. Matt raced over to him as the floor continued giving way. He made it across, and as the swirling dirt cleared for a second, he could see Baldwin staring into the abyss growing at their feet.

"There's something down there," Baldwin whispered.

Matt turned. The hole was still growing, but slowly now. At first, that's all he saw—the hole. It was almost as big as the cabin floor, a dark pit with pipes and roots sticking out like quills, leading down into darkness. Endless darkness.

A dank, sour smell wafted up, and from the depths he could hear a strange dry, whispery sound.

"We need to go," he said.

"No, I saw something," Baldwin said. "There's—"

The earth shook and dirt rained down from the sides of the hole, and for a moment that was all Matt saw, but then the dirt cleared and—

Something flashed in the dark depths. Something long and pale, twisting in and out of sight so fast that Matt caught only a glimpse. He kept staring, but that was it. A single glimpse of—

The ground shook again and a smell billowed out, a horrible rank stink that made him reel back. The dirt rained again and the thing appeared again, and this time Matt saw it. He saw scales, huge scales on a huge body, twisting and roiling in the hole, rasping against the roots, the earth shaking as it moved. He saw that, and he knew what it was.

"The serpent," he whispered. "I woke the—"

The floor bucked under their feet, the serpent bucking under the earth, the floorboards screaming as they tore free, leaping up like matchsticks as huge chunks of earth fell into the hole. As the hole grew. Right under their feet.

"Let's go!"

Matt shouted to be heard over the noise. He twisted to

go back the way he came, and as he did, the floor crumbled into the void. The entire strip disappeared, right up to the wall, swallowing their escape route. Matt swung around to go out the other way, but the floor was already gone.

They were standing on two boards. Two remaining boards. Trapped between the hole and the wall. As the Midgard Serpent twisted and roiled and set the earth trembling, set the earth *crumbling*, right under their feet. Everything around them fell into a gaping hole, and them with it.

# FOURTEEN

## FEN

## "WHEN GOATS ATTACK"

Fen and Laurie had escaped the collapsing house. Fen looked back at it: pieces of wood and stone were jutted up at odd angles, and the air was cloudy from the dust and dirt that had been stirred by the fall. *It isn't a complete catastrophe*, he thought. The house was, but the situation was better than he'd expected. He paused. *When houses falling through the earth is a* better *outcome, what does that mean?* He shook his head and continued surveying the wreckage.

The Berserkers—Owen's little personal army—had begun fighting against the Raiders. Individuals and small groups were fighting all around the newly created cavern in the ground. Mayor Thorsen and the hunter seemed to be standing back.

The hunter had his gun held out, and he stood like a guard protecting the mayor.

"Baldwin," Fen said, scanning the crowd as best he could with the dirt-thick air obscuring everything. "Where's Baldwin?"

Laurie shook her head. "I don't know. Where's *Matt?*"

An uneasy weight settled on Fen. They'd just rescued Baldwin from Hel, and they'd just pulled Matt out of the river of zombie stew. Now both boys were missing again. Fen was awfully glad he hadn't gone to jail, but this wasn't any better.

"How are we to even get to the battle at the end of the world if everyone keeps getting injured, dying, or going missing?" Fen grumbled. He gave his cousin a warning glare and ordered, "Stay with me."

"Obviously," she said with an eye roll.

"Thorsen! Where are you?" He dodged a punch from a Raider still in human form, and then he spared a grin as a Berserker tackled the Raider in some sort of running flip-kick move. They had such an odd fighting style; it was like martial arts meets extreme sports meets parkour.

The Berserkers were keeping a perimeter of sorts around the house, giving the descendants of the North space to get out of the wreckage. From the looks of the Berserkers who unexpectedly went flying, Mayor Thorsen was doing much the same with his amulet. Both sides of the fight were keeping the other from getting too close to the crater where the house had been.

Fen was surprised that the mayor didn't stop them as he and Laurie went toward the hole, where he assumed Matt still was. He wished he had something like Matt's Hammer or Laurie's bow or Ray and Reyna's magic. If the mayor used his Hammer against Fen and Laurie, they were defenseless. Maybe Mayor Thorsen didn't know where they were headed, or maybe he wanted someone to rescue Matt...which made sense but was also a little weird.

As Fen and Laurie eased closer to the crater, he could see Baldwin and Matt standing on a ledge in the ruins of the house. Beneath them was a gaping darkness.

"Don't move," Fen called.

Matt said, "Believe me, I don't intend to."

Baldwin, on the other hand, replied, "We *have* to unless we want to go down to whatever monster is in the hole."

Almost as if he couldn't resist looking into the darkness, Matt dropped his gaze. His face was tight, and he swallowed visibly. All he said, though, was, "Baldwin says he brought your bags. Maybe something useful will appear in them."

"They're over by the tree, under a hedge of some sort. Yellow flowers, I think," Baldwin offered helpfully.

Fen had a general idea of where Baldwin meant. Unfortunately, it was on the other side of a brawl. The air wasn't clearing very quickly, so a gray haze hung like a gritty fog all around them. "Of course the bags are over *there*," he muttered.

Laurie and Fen exchanged a look.

"Maybe there are ropes or vines or something over here," Laurie said as she started to pace away from Fen.

He grabbed her forearm.

He stomped his foot a little, testing the ground. "This seems stable-ish. Stay here. Right here."

"So the plan is that I hope I don't fall to my doom while you face a pack of wolves?" Laurie muttered.

"Pretty much."

Matt's voice came from the hole in the ground. "Umm... guys? Not to rush you, but..."

When Fen looked down again, he could see how exhausted and haggard Matt looked. He'd been through a lot. They all had. Of course, poor Matt had been drugged, and he'd just gotten the shock of discovering that his family wasn't as perfect as he'd thought. Not only did the old man think that it was fine for Matt to get eaten by a snake, he also seemed to be working with the Raiders. Fen's own relatives weren't looking quite as bad in comparison. On the other hand, a lot of the Raiders who were here fighting for the mayor were also Fen's relatives. Not everyone in a family was always *good*, but the descendants of the North—his friends, the *heroes*—were good. Fen wasn't going to let them down the way their families had let him and Matt down.

"Keep him safe," Fen told Baldwin.

And then he was shifting into another form, a furrier one capable of darting through the crowd. With a happy growl, Fen realized that his transformation was faster than it had been before visiting Hel. It wasn't quite as instantaneous as it had been in Helen's domain, but it was faster than that of any *wulfenkind* he knew.

Unfortunately, once he was a wolf, he was just…himself. He didn't seem to have any extra speed or sharper teeth. He was just Fen. He was quickly intercepted by an almost-white wolf. It was Hattie, Skull's sister and second-in-command of his pack. She offered what looked like a menacing smile. It wasn't, not really, but the brain inside Fen was still human, and his human mind translated the wolf expression to the human words.

Fen growled and pulled his lips back, baring his teeth at her.

Hattie didn't seem to have even noticed. He was going to have to charge her; it was the only way he could see to get past her and to the bags. Hopefully, whatever magic had made the bags deliver up clothes and sandwiches would also deliver up ropes to use to pull Matt and Baldwin up to safety.

Fen threw himself at Hattie. It wasn't a graceful tackle, but fighting wasn't about points and prettiness. It was about ferocity. That's why Fen couldn't ever do the wrestling or boxing stuff Matt did. It was too orderly. Fen fought because he had to, and his only trophies were bragging rights and survival.

As Fen landed half atop Hattie, she threw herself to the side, dislodging him after a few moments of him somewhat precariously clinging to her fur. He didn't even have his feet under him before she spun and tried for his throat. It was a predictable move, though, and he darted away.

Hattie stalked toward him, not attacking but intimidating. She moved steadily closer, feinting bites that were only to frighten, not to hurt—at least not yet. She'd always liked to play with her kills. It was a cruel tendency that was far more human than wolf.

Fen charged again, aiming for her front left leg. He collided with her, and she wavered on her feet. He leaned down and bit her leg, not hard enough to truly hurt her but enough to startle her. She went down, falling in an awkward move like she was kneeling.

That moment of distraction was what he'd wanted. He kept moving, fleeing past her toward the hedge where the bags were hidden. It wasn't a great plan, but he was half hoping that Hattie would get knocked out by one of the Berserkers. What he needed was to get back to Matt, to get him and Baldwin to safety, and to get Laurie out of the area.

Fen tore through the fight, dodging wolves and Berserkers, darting under feet, leaping over fighters who were rolling on the ground trying to wound each other. He didn't look back, but he heard Hattie growling as she pursued him.

He dove under the hedge, bit the bags with his teeth— and realized that they were peculiarly light. Fen hoped that was because they were magic. He didn't have time to check. *Focus.* He spun around and realized that he couldn't get past Hattie. She was standing right there, feet planted and ready to attack.

With a wash of disappointment at his failure, he dropped the bags and prepared to fight her. He had to defeat her in order to reach his friends because he couldn't have her following him back to the cave-in. They stared at each other, both looking for the weakness that would enable a successful attack.

Then she let out a high-pitched yip as she was suddenly propelled backward, away from Fen, by an invisible force.

*Thorsen?* Fen thought, looking around for the red-haired boy. Maybe Laurie had found a rope and pulled him out. Fen's jaw dropped open as he saw the mayor looking at him. It *had* been Thorsen's Hammer thing, just not the Thorsen he'd expected. The mayor, the man who had only a short while ago tried to have Fen arrested for murder, had just attacked one of his own Raiders.

"Save Matt," Mayor Thorsen yelled.

The mayor *had* been keeping them all away from where Matt was trapped. Fen was still confused why the same person who'd ordered Matt's capture now wanted to save him, but Fen wasn't going to waste any more time trying to figure it out. He grabbed the bags again with his teeth and raced back toward his trapped friends.

It was a little easier getting through the fighting area this time. Fen wasn't sure if that was because the Berserkers were winning or if it was because Hattie wasn't pursuing him. Either way, he ran toward Laurie with the bags clenched tightly between his teeth. When he was almost at the edge of the giant hole, he slowed from a run to a lope to a cautious walk so he didn't drop the bags—or careen into the cavern.

He released his grip on the bags, and they tumbled to the ground beside Laurie. Almost absently, she patted his head, ruffling the fur on his neck like he was a pet. If anyone else had done that, he would've bitten them, but she was his best friend and cousin. Fen rarely expected her to follow the same rules as everyone else in the world.

In the brief time it took for him to shift back into his human shape, Laurie had already opened her bag.

"Aha!" she crowed. She reached into the bag and withdrew a length of sturdy rope. It looked new, looped up and wrapped as if it had just been measured out at a hardware store.

"Thank you, Aunt Helen," Laurie murmured. She looked pointedly at Fen.

He grumbled, "Right. Thanks, Auntie H."

Laurie rolled her eyes at him, and at the same time, she began to unwind the rope and lower an end to Baldwin and Matt. She called, "We have it! Here. Grab this."

Now, Fen wasn't ready to start another round of I-can-do-everything-you-can with Laurie, so he didn't even bother taking it from her and pointing out that there was no way she could pull Baldwin and Matt up, especially since the truth was that he wasn't sure *he* could pull Matt up, either. Thorsen wasn't exactly a little guy. Fen could probably pull Baldwin out, and maybe together they could get Matt up.

"Baldwin first," Fen suggested, still trying to think of a good way to deal with her without fighting. "I'll take the rope."

"Fen?"

He thought she somehow knew that they were going to have an argument, but then he realized that she was looking behind him. He glanced over his shoulder and saw a Raider running toward them. The boy was about Fen's size, probably one of the younger *wulfenkind*.

"I got it," he said, but Laurie just handed him the rope.

"No," she said. "You get Baldwin and Matt."

"What the—"

"Bow," she announced as she grabbed up her bag and opened it. In mere moments, she had her arrowless bow in her hand. She didn't look at Fen as she added, "I'm not as strong as you."

He turned away, trying to force himself not to watch her, concentrating on swinging the rope to Baldwin.

"Got it," Baldwin said.

Behind Fen, he heard a yip, and then Laurie muttered, "Got you."

He didn't look back. He dug his heels into the ground, hoped it didn't fall away under his feet like the house had, and tried to hold on tightly as Baldwin climbed up. He wasn't sure he could've pulled him, but Baldwin was scaling the rope like a happy monkey.

In a few quick minutes, Baldwin was standing beside Fen.

"There are more," Laurie said.

He glanced at her and saw her draw back the bowstring again. Then, under the ground, he heard a rumble and felt the earth tremble. He half threw, half swung the rope to Matt, and together with Baldwin, they heaved Matt upward. Pulling him out was a bit more of a struggle. Unlike Baldwin, Matt wasn't a great wall climber, but he was strong, and he was trying.

As Matt started to ascend out of the hole, he glanced behind him a few times, and when Fen followed his gaze and saw what looked to be scales glistening in the darkness below, he understood why Matt looked so tense. Whatever monster writhed in the distance had to be immense. The shaking of the ground or house explosion or whatever must have disturbed its lair.

"Faster," Laurie urged. "The ground is shaking again."

Fen didn't tell her what he saw; he just pulled harder on the rope. In what seemed like several minutes, but was probably much faster, Matt was crawling out of the pit and onto the ground beside them. He crawled a little farther from the edge before he stood.

Fen glanced into the darkness below, and whatever monster he'd seen was gone. He didn't mention it to Baldwin or Laurie, but he caught Matt's eye and said, "It's gone."

Matt nodded, and then he said, "Let's get out of here."

"No argument from me." Fen grabbed both his bag and Laurie's and slung them over his shoulder.

Baldwin grabbed his bag, too, and then told Matt, "I left yours somewhere safe because of the shield."

Laurie kept her bow in one hand, and she held out the other for her bag. "I can carry mine."

Fen handed it over, and together the four of them ran toward the woods on the far side of the fighting, where the Berserkers were holding a line of defense. The Berserkers seemed to be struggling a little as the Raiders surged as one toward them. While the Berserkers had style and creativity in their fighting, the *wulfenkind* had an all-out ferocity that gave them an edge when it came to charging.

"We should help them," Matt said.

"Laurie, you and Matt can stay back here. You have weapons that can work from a distance," Fen started.

"I can come," Laurie objected.

"I need you to protect Matt," Fen whispered. "He's not looking too great right now." Then he turned to Baldwin and said, "You take any that get past me."

Matt was uncharacteristically quiet, and Fen worried that maybe his plan was stupid. He didn't *want* to dive into yet another fight, but he couldn't do anything from a distance—and both Matt and Baldwin looked tired. Laurie, of course, wasn't ever someone he wanted to send into battle.

"Tanngrisnir and Tanngnjóstr," Matt suddenly said in a strained voice.

"What?" Fen looked in the direction Matt was now pointing.

The two biggest goats led the herd, their snow-white hair standing out in the darkness, and their heads angled so their huge yellow-brown horns could connect with the Raiders and *wulfenkind*.

"When goats attack," Baldwin said in awe. "Sweet!"

No one spoke for a moment. Matt was staring at his goat army in shock, and Laurie was already firing arrows at the enemy. Baldwin was grinning like a madman at the sight of a raging herd of goats. *It's like a strange circus.* The acrobatic fighting of the Berserkers and the angry charging of bleating goats were the weirdest things Fen had ever seen.

"They actually came," Matt said, sounding a little awed.

Then one of the Berserkers motioned for them to keep moving. She called, "We have this. Start toward the camp."

*The camp?*

"New plan, then," Baldwin said. He took the lead, so obviously at least one of them knew where they were headed.

With one last look at the wolves who were being defeated by the increasingly large group of goats, Fen followed the boy who used to be dead, his cousin with her invisible arrows, and their leader—whose grandfather led the enemies. *Nothing strange here*, Fen thought.

*Yeah, right.*

# FIFTEEN

## LAURIE

### "FIGHTING EVERYONE"

Laurie could see the wolves and kids fighting, wolves and goats fighting, but she also saw kids fighting kids. Seeing kids fighting kids seemed somehow different, *worse* than most fights. Maybe it was because they'd become used to fighting monsters. These weren't monsters; they were simply kids who seemed to believe the end of the world was a good idea—or maybe they didn't *know* that the descendants of the North were trying to stop Ragnarök. That thought gave her hope.

Of course, it didn't change how awful today had been. Fen had almost been arrested, Matt had been shot, and there was a horrible moment when she thought they would all die as the cabin started crumbling around and under them. She almost preferred fighting trolls. At least there, the good guys and bad guys were a little clearer.

The Berserkers surged and moved through the trees and around one another like acrobats in a routine. The mayor was using his Thor's Hammer against them, but the Berserkers used the energy shoves as if they were discovering invisible trampolines in the air. They were pushing off of trees, wolves, and other Berserkers when they could, and landing in fluid rolls and flips when they were unable to find surfaces in the air for leverage. In the midst of the fight—turning the tide—were the goats. The sharp horns rammed into wolf after wolf. With the goats' arrival, the heroes outnumbered their enemies.

Laurie shook her head at the joy the Berserkers seemed to be taking in the chaos of the fight, and all the while, she kept her bow at the ready. She had Baldwin, Fen, and Matt—three of the heroes necessary for the big final fight—and she wasn't going to let anyone or anything take the boys away.

Since the Berserkers and goats were keeping the Raiders occupied, their small group was getting through the fight zone relatively easily. Matt looked rattled, but she didn't know if it was because of his grandfather or the tranquilizer or maybe even the cabin collapsing. Baldwin was... Baldwin. He smiled and walked along, looking willing to jump into the fight but also happy to be with his friends. Fen kept darting glances in every direction, and in his typical way, hovering very close to her.

She knew he had to be shaken up by his near-arrest. He'd looked positively humiliated when he'd been cuffed, and while she wasn't going to tell him that she'd noticed, she *had* heard the fear in his voice. Baldwin's death had been hard on them—as had his rescue from Hel—but Fen felt guilty for not saving Baldwin, and he'd been accused of murdering the boy once already by Astrid.

"Astrid," Laurie blurted.

Matt tensed and looked around. "Where?"

"No. I mean she's the only one who could've been a witness to Baldwin's murder," Laurie clarified.

The boys were quiet for a moment as they moved farther into the woods, leaving the fighting behind finally. Then a crashing sound behind them made all three boys tense up even more. Instinctively, all four of them arranged themselves back to back so they were in a small circle, each looking out in a different direction. In a blur of legs and arms, two Berserkers somersaulted into the path.

"That was more fun than I expected," one announced.

"Odin should be waiting," the other added with a grin. "Let's go."

Now that there were strangers among them, the descendants stopped talking about their potential enemies. The

Berserkers might be Owen's private fighting force, but they weren't descendants of the North.

When they reached the campsite a little while later, Laurie was glad that this was a well-maintained campground surrounded by a small wooded area. She was sick of making camp. The campground was perfect: it had running water, and it appeared to be mostly deserted. No RVs or tents were in sight. The only people there were a few Berserkers and one familiar boy with blue hair and an eye patch.

Laurie felt an odd sort of happiness at seeing Owen waiting there. He smiled and walked toward her. She would've gone to him, but Fen stepped in front of her.

"That's *Owen*," she said from behind her cousin.

Owen continued walking as if Fen weren't standing between them.

"Thanks for lending me your Berserkers." Baldwin walked right up to Owen as if he'd known him forever and held out a hand. That was Baldwin, though. He would probably walk right up to the Raiders if no one was throwing punches...or maybe even if they were.

Bemused, Owen shook his hand. "I'm glad you're safe."

Fen still didn't move.

Owen folded his arms over his chest and stared at them. "Hello, Fenrir."

Silently, Fen stared at Owen. After a moment, Owen

shrugged and said, "I think you should know that I won't hurt Laurie...not like you will."

Before Laurie could react, Fen threw himself bodily at Owen. He landed only one punch before Baldwin and Matt grabbed him and pulled him back. "Stay away from my cousin," Fen snarled.

Oddly, Owen was smiling at Fen, as if he approved of his actions. "Good. Perhaps now that we have our fight out of the way, things will be better in the future." Owen nodded once, and then he looked over at Matt. "I'm sorry about your grandfather. It's hard when family disappoints you." His gaze slipped to Laurie as he said the last bit. He smiled sadly at her and then turned his attention to Baldwin. "It is good that you're not dead anymore. If you'd stayed dead, we'd have had fewer options for rescuing Matt." He frowned. "And Fenrir would have been unhappy in jail. I think he's avoided jail entirely now. I see no option where that changes."

"My name is *Fen*, not Fenrir." Her cousin growled and shrugged out of Matt's and Baldwin's grips. "Just Fen."

"You are not *just* anything, Fen. None of us are." Owen shook his head.

Two ravens swooped down and landed on his shoulders. They were enormous black birds, but Owen didn't seem to even notice them.

"I *have* seen them before." Laurie stared at the ravens and then leveled a glare at Owen. "I thought you said you didn't have ravens like Odin did."

"I didn't until recently," Owen said. He looked guilty, though, and she wondered *how* recently they had been with him. As nervous as he suddenly looked, she was fairly certain that they were with him before their conversation the night with her bow.

"I saw them in Hel," Matt said. "When we were with Garm."

"And with the zombies," Baldwin added. "Remember, Fen?"

"Yeah, I remember." Fen stalked up to stand beside Laurie, not quite in front of her but nearly so. "Why are your birds following us? If you want to watch us, why don't you travel with us?"

Owen glanced at him with genuine approval. "Memory and Thought go where I can't...or when I can't. I couldn't go to Hel. I had to stay here and lose my eye." He flipped up the eye patch so they could all see his injury.

Fen's anger seemed to fade as he stared at the red skin where Owen had been injured. He opened his mouth but said nothing. He stayed beside Laurie, though. She wasn't sure what to say. She'd already told him how sorry she was when he showed her how to hold her bow.

"That bites, man. The eye thing," Baldwin interjected into the silence.

Owen's lips twitched in a cross between a laugh and a smile, but all he said was, "It does."

The birds began making horrible noises, sounding like neither ravens nor people but some unnatural combination of the two. Their sharp beaks were so close to Owen's face that Laurie was worried for him. She knew that the birds were his—extensions of him, according to the fragments of myth she'd managed to remember—but they were still scary creatures with talons and beaks that could cut like knives.

"I need to leave now," Owen announced. "I'd hoped that if Fenr—if *Fen* hit me sooner, it would be enough of a difference in what comes next. I couldn't change the larger details, but I'd hoped this would be enough. . . . I wanted to stay." He stepped forward to move around Fen and get closer to Laurie.

Fen growled.

As one, the ravens swiveled their heads to glare at Fen.

"Stop it," Laurie snapped at her cousin as she pushed him to the side. "I'm not in danger."

"The ravens won't hurt either of you," Owen assured her with a small smile. "There is a time that they startle you, but that will only happen if I live through Ragnarök."

The birds were still watching Fen, but Owen wasn't

doing anything other than watching her. It all felt far tenser than she would like.

"Can I talk to you? Alone?" Owen asked.

"No," Fen snapped.

"Okay," Laurie said at the same time. She put a hand on Fen's arm and squeezed. "I'm safe with him. Trust me?"

Fen frowned a little, but he didn't stop her when she walked away.

Once they were a little farther from the others, but still in sight, Owen said, "I want to go to Saint Agnes with you, but the twins will die if I do. The ravens tell me I need to go right now."

No one else could hear him, and she wondered if he wasn't supposed to tell her. She was pretty sure she wasn't to tell anyone, or else he wouldn't be pulling her away and whispering. She glanced at the birds warily. It wasn't that she hated birds, not really, but they always seemed more frightening than she wanted to admit to anyone. She'd read that they were supposed to be descended from dinosaurs— which didn't help ease her fears at all. Thought and Memory, Owen's ravens, were staring at her; they'd been watching the descendants for who knows how long.

"You shouldn't lie to me anymore," Laurie whispered to Owen. She glanced pointedly at the ravens. "You didn't want us to know we were being watched. I don't know why, but secrets are why they don't trust you."

"Do *you* trust me?"

Laurie paused. She wasn't sure why, but she *did*.

"What's he saying?" Fen demanded.

Laurie's gaze drifted to the ravens' sharp beaks and talons.

"Cool it, Fen." Matt sounded exhausted. "Please?"

The birds watched her.

"For now," she told Owen. "I'll trust you for now. No more secrets, though."

"When I return, I'll tell you what I can, but I can't tell you everything. There are rules."

She nodded, and Owen smiled.

"For now, try to make peace with your cousin. I provoked him so he *would* hit me. Don't be angry with him because of today."

Laurie blinked at him. Owen's request to her was to patch things up with Fen. It was unnecessary. They always made peace. They were too much alike to avoid fights, though, and he was too protective of her, but after their tempers faded, they were fine again. "Fen and I are okay. We always are."

"I hope so," Owen said.

Laurie panicked a little at that. Owen saw the future. His tone made her think that he saw a future where she and Fen *weren't* fine. That wasn't going to happen. She wouldn't let it.

Owen raised one arm in a signal of some sort and started to walk toward the shadowed trees. Every Berserker who was in the camp started following him, moving around him like ripples spreading out from a center. Owen was their center.

"Hey, wait!" Matt called. "We need to find Mjölnir, and we could use a few of them—"

"No," Owen said. "I have to go somewhere. You four should go after the hammer."

"Okay," Laurie said.

"Now, wait a minute!" Fen ran forward and grabbed Owen's arm, yanking him to a stop. "You have your birds follow us. You talk to my cousin away from all of us alone *twice* now—back in Blackwell and in the Black Hills. Now, when you know we need help, and you have all of these kids helping you, you *leave*? Thorsen needs his hammer, and the bad guys knew where we were, so they probably know where *it* is."

"You should probably go now, then," Owen said mildly. "I have something else I need to do."

"He's the All-Father, Fen," Matt started. "Whatever he sees must be imp—"

"Not more important than this," Fen interrupted.

"You *are* impulsive like Loki. You forget there are consequences until after it's too late," Owen said musingly.

"So?" The flash of teeth that Fen showed Owen would've

caused most people to hesitate or at least pull away. Owen, however, acted as if Fen weren't threatening him. He stood perfectly calm and relaxed, waiting.

Fen said, "Matt was knocked out. We fought monsters. What we should do is get some sleep, and you all come help us with Mjölnir in the morning." His voice was more growl than words. "They need to be safe, and Thorsen needs his hammer."

Owen smiled at Fen. "I see the future, Fenrir. I *know* what's going to happen, and I'm not going to be with you at Saint Agnes."

"Fen, let go of him," Laurie said.

Matt and Baldwin might have said something else, too, but Fen wasn't listening to them. He stared at Owen, ignoring the ravens and the Berserkers, and added, "You could help us."

"If I weren't helping you, you'd be in jail right now, and Baldwin would be dead. I need to be in Hot Springs now. Not here."

Fen shoved Owen away. "Whatever."

"You probably should go *now*," Owen told them, and then he started running. The Berserkers closed around him, and they all took off into the darkness.

Laurie watched them vanish before looking at the boys. "Okay, then. Which way to Saint Agnes?"

Mouth open, Fen stared at her like she was cracked.

"Seriously? That's all you have to say? 'Which way'?" He crossed his arms over his chest.

"He sees the future," Matt said simply. Then he looked up at the sky. "We're west of Saint Agnes, so we need to go that way."

Baldwin shrugged. "Okay."

"Nice of you to help reason with him," Fen said bitterly to Laurie. "He might have actually listened to *you*." Then he walked away from her, following Matt and Baldwin.

"Fen," she started, but he waved his hand at her in a go-away gesture.

She understood that Fen was angry with her for agreeing with Owen, but the Berserkers were *his* followers. If he said they were to go with him, they would. She wasn't sure what they could've done differently.

They all stayed quiet for a while until Fen dropped back beside her. She figured that his temper must have calmed, but when he started to speak, it wasn't the apology she expected.

"You take everyone's side but mine lately," he said quietly as they walked toward Saint Agnes. "Do you ever think I might be right? Or is it just Thorsen and Owen you trust to make decisions?"

Laurie stared at him in shock. "You're such a...arrrgh. How could you think that? I trust you, Fen. After everything, how could you doubt that?"

He shrugged, and Laurie didn't know what to say. She could list all the times she'd done what he wanted, when she'd followed him into disastrous plan after dangerous idea *before* this whole the-world-could-end trip. Somehow, she didn't think that would help.

"We're a team, Fen." She bumped her shoulder into his. "I listen to what *all* of you say."

He didn't bump her shoulder back like he usually would. Instead, he muttered, "So you listen and then decide I'm always wrong? Great. Thanks for that."

"I love you, but you're being ridiculous," she said. It made her feel wretched that he was hurt, but until he calmed down, there was no sense talking to him. She shook her head and pressed her lips together, and they walked the rest of the way to Saint Agnes in silence. Even angry, he stayed by her side. She couldn't imagine what her life would be like without him, and she really didn't want to.

# SIXTEEN

## MATT

## "GRAVE SITUATION"

Back to the cemetery. Back to Blackwell. It was different now. Before, it just felt like passing by, and Matt had been able to forget everything else. Now...?
Now he wanted to be anyplace else on earth.

Matt had lost all hope and all faith in the one person who'd always believed in him. He wanted to talk to someone about that, but when he looked at the others...He liked them. He trusted them. But could he talk to any of them about something so personal? They weren't like his best friend Cody or his brother Josh. Maybe they could be, someday, but right now it felt like there was no one he could really talk to.

He was angry that he'd been deceived. Furious, even—furious enough to call up the Midgard Serpent, apparently. But there was more than that. The serpent was his sworn enemy, and it had no reason to wake just because he was angry.

No, the serpent had sensed weakness. Despair—that was the right word. Mix that hurt and that despair and that fury, and he'd been vulnerable, his powers raging beyond control. That's what the serpent had sensed, and even if it wasn't time yet, if it wasn't Ragnarök, it had responded. Writhing in glee as Matt showed exactly how much of a child he was, throwing a temper tantrum because his granddaddy had hurt him.

The whole trip to Saint Agnes, he tried to snap out of it. Granddad wanted him to be the sacrificial goat? Too bad. He was the chosen champion of the greatest Norse god ever. He would not lie down and die obligingly. He would fight. He would win.

The others left Matt alone on that walk. Which meant that maybe, just maybe, they did understand what he was going through after all.

"Okay," he said as they approached the cemetery. "This time, we're taking precautions. My grandfather might know we'll head back here. He might even have figured out this is where I expected to find Mjölnir. So let's be extra careful. Baldwin? You'll come over the fence with me. We need my amulet to find the hammer and, if there's trouble, your invulnerability will help."

"Invulnerability?" Baldwin grinned. "That's a good word. I have to remember that."

"Don't encourage him," Fen grumbled.

"I think it's great he knows lots of stuff," Baldwin said. "The stories always say Thor is just a big, dumb guy with lots of muscles. Matt's not, and that's cool, right?"

Matt managed a smile for Baldwin. "Thanks. So I'll take you over. Fen and Laurie, I'd like you two to stand watch, one from either side, if you're okay with splitting up."

"We can do that," Laurie said.

"Oh, no, we can't," Fen said. "We aren't separating. Not if we're expecting trouble."

"Fine." Matt lifted his hands against their argument. "You two work it out. But remember, Laurie has her bow, and I think it's okay to leave her on her own. Fen? If you could change into a wolf, that would be great."

"I can change, but I'm *not* letting Laurie out of my sight." He glanced at his cousin. "Not happening, Laurie. The last time we were here, Thorsen got *shot*."

"Matt has a good plan," Laurie said. "We can stand watch without being too far apart. Now let's get going before someone *does* show up to try to stop us."

Again, Matt knew this was just to make him feel better. Baldwin complimenting him on his brains. Laurie quickly supporting his plan. Little pats on the back to say everything was okay and Matt could get past what happened and move forward. It helped. Fen didn't seem to realize that and cast a scowl Matt's way. Probably still upset about nearly being arrested for murder.

Probably? That almost made Matt laugh. Of course Fen would still be upset. Who wouldn't? He'd had a scare. A bad one. It obviously had made him even *more* overprotective of Laurie, and Owen's visit hadn't helped matters. He just wasn't feeling himself. Matt had to understand that and not take offense if he snarled and growled.

They discussed the signals they'd use for communicating. Then Matt said, "All set? Let's move out."

Saint Agnes Cemetery. It wasn't the first time Matt had been inside the graveyard. He hadn't said so to the others earlier, because they might have expected him to know a secret way in, and he didn't. He always scaled the fence.

The first time he came out with Cody, they'd been nine. They'd poked around the cemetery, scaring each other with ghost stories. Cody had wanted to bring other kids back on Halloween, to do the same, but Matt had a better idea. As much fun as it would be to camp out in a graveyard and tell ghost stories, not many kids would turn down bags of candy for a cold night in a cemetery. So Matt came up with his own tradition, based on his research into the cemetery's patron saint herself. Saint Agnes actually had her own eve, like Halloween. The eve of Saint Agnes was January 20, when girls were supposed to sneak out at night and go into the field, where at midnight, they would see…their future husband. Yeah, a perfectly good setup, totally wasted with a boring resolution. So Matt changed it.

There were actually four historical Saint Agneses. Or maybe five. He never bothered to keep track. He just made up his own version, where Saint Agnes had been a noblewoman accused of kidnapping and slaughtering young girls, which naturally meant she was a vampire. She'd been staked to death and her corpse beheaded. Only later did the townspeople discover that she'd actually been rescuing girls from horrible situations and sending them off to the convent for schooling. So they made her a saint. Yet, because of how she died, she would forever be associated with vampires and the undead, so on Saint Agnes Eve, if you went to a cemetery and invoked her name, you might see those very undead—vampires or zombies or ghosts.

That was a much better story. Their friends certainly liked it. So every January 20, they'd gather sleeping bags and tell their parents they were staying at a friend's—and they'd troop off to Saint Agnes and start a bonfire and wrap themselves in their sleeping bags and tell ghost stories as they waited for the dead to rise. Of course the dead never obliged, but it was too much fun to cancel for a simple lack of actual ghosts.

There was another reason Matt hadn't told the others he'd been here before. Because Fen and Laurie had never been invited to those nights. By last January, almost their entire class had been in the cemetery, and not one kid had ever said, *Hey, how about we invite the Brekkes?* Matt never even considered it, and he'd been the one who always suggested bringing the new kids and the shy kids, making them part of the secret. While he was sure Fen would have mocked the whole idea and certainly never joined in, he should have been invited. Laurie, too.

Matt thought about that as they went over the fence, while he tried to keep his focus on his surroundings so he didn't get caught off guard again.

They slipped into the graveyard. It looked more like a proper cemetery than Deadwood's, with its rolling hills and headstones spread everywhere. Here the graves were crammed together and you knew, with each step, that you were treading on the long-dry bones of some long-dead person.

People from town still visited. There were flowers dotting the kirkyard, weirdly bright bursts of color on weathered gray stones and dry brown grass. Matt noticed a bright spray of red near one of the mausoleums. Roses, it looked like, as he turned—

His amulet seemed to . . . move. Not vibrate so much as jump once, as if to say *This way.* Matt clutched it.

230

"Got a signal?" Baldwin whispered.

Matt nodded. They'd been keeping quiet, even though there was no sign of anyone here. Cemeteries did that to you.

"Let's get it and go," Baldwin said. "This place gives me the creeps."

Matt looked around. He didn't see creepy. He saw spooky…in a good, spine-tingling way. When he was younger, he used to imagine all the dead warriors here, now dining in Valhalla. As he got older, he'd realized most of them were probably farmers and traders who'd only ever held a blade to cut down corn or carve up meat, but it didn't change the feeling of being surrounded by greatness. Thorsens who belonged in Valhalla, even if they'd never swung a sword.

Matt took a few steps to the left. His amulet stopped vibrating. It started up again when he went back to where he'd been, only to stop as he headed right. He turned and faced the mausoleum. Three careful steps toward it and…

The amulet buzzed against his chest.

"It's in there," he said, pointing.

"Of course it is," Baldwin said with a shudder.

"Hey, would you rather it was in one of those?" Matt pointed at the graves beneath them.

"Good point."

As he headed for the mausoleum, Matt heard a piercing birdcall. It was just Baldwin, giving the signal to tell Fen and

Laurie that they were about to retrieve Mjölnir, meaning if there was any sign of trouble, let them know now. Fen replied first with a double whistle. Laurie repeated it. All clear.

Matt walked to the mausoleum. It looked like the oldest one in the cemetery, but it was impossible to tell because there wasn't any date on it. Made of rough-cut gray stones, it wasn't as fancy as some of the others. In fact, it might be the plainest one in Saint Agnes. Just a dull gray stone block without even an arched doorway—only a simple rectangular door with a big gray block over it. Carved in that block was one word: THORSEN.

"Cool," Baldwin said. "I guess that means we're in the right place."

Matt didn't tell him he'd find the same name on half the gravestones around them. Yet with all the others there were names and dates and a few words. Even the mausoleums, which usually held a bunch of people, would have a plaque outside listing who was in them. There was nothing like that here. Just the name. Thorsen.

"Now we just need to figure out how to open it," Baldwin said.

That was indeed the problem. Matt and his friends had tried a few mausoleum doors in the past, to see if they could get in. They'd all been locked. Cody had wanted to break in to one, but Matt said no. If the door was open, that was fine, but breaking in was disrespectful.

Now as he looked at the door, he realized he had a very big problem. There was no lock. No handle, even. It was a solid stone slab.

He stepped up and pushed. Nothing happened. He ran his hands over the door, in case there was a secret latch. It was sealed shut.

"I'll have to get Laurie," he whispered. "See if she can open a gate."

"Or you could just use that."

He looked over to see Baldwin pointing at Matt's amulet. Matt could feel it buzzing. When he looked down, it started to glow.

"I think it wants to help you get in," Baldwin said.

Breaking in with his Hammer? That seemed even more disrespectful than picking a lock.

"Even if I could, I'm not sure I should...." he said.

"Why not? Mjölnir is in there. And your other Hammer is there." Baldwin pointed at the amulet again. "One should help you get the other, right?"

That made sense, Matt supposed. So he stepped back, set down his shield, focused, and shot his hand up, fingers out. He didn't expect anything. He wasn't angry or anything that would launch the Hammer. But a bolt flew from his fingers, making him stumble back in surprise. The door groaned, and it opened, just a crack, dust swirling out. Something else billowed out, too.

"What is that smell?" Baldwin exclaimed, hands flying to cover his nose and mouth.

"Dead people."

Baldwin looked a little green, and Matt wished he hadn't said that quite so bluntly. Baldwin probably felt different about the dead after having spent some time among them, in the afterlife.

"You can wait out here," Matt said.

"No, I'm good."

Matt pushed on the door. At first, it didn't budge, but then he put his weight behind it, shoulder against it, and it groaned again and began to open with a grating noise that set his teeth on edge. It was hard work, and he stopped as soon as the opening was big enough to get through. It was also big enough to let out a whole lot more of that stink.

"Um, maybe I could stand guard?" Baldwin said.

"Good idea. I'll be right back."

Matt turned sideways and eased through the opening. Inside, the mausoleum was pitch-black. His amulet still glowed, but it didn't seem to give off any actual light, as if smothered by the darkness. Even the light from the open door didn't penetrate more than a few inches inside. Matt peered through, and his heart beat faster at the thought of stepping in there.

*It's only darkness. It can't hurt me. Just take it slow. Let the amulet lead the way, like it did with the shield.*

He got through the doorway and took one step into the mausoleum. The amulet began heating up.

*If only it would glow a little brighter, that would be much more useful.*

Matt put one foot out, sweeping the way, then doing the same with his hand, checking for obstacles before he—

A papery whisper sounded deep inside the mausoleum. Matt froze. It came again, like something moving over the stone.

Rats. Or snakes, holed up for the winter. A brown snake or a bull snake. No problem.

Matt chuckled to himself. A few weeks ago, the thought of a snake might have stopped him in his tracks, but compared to the Midgard Serpent, he wasn't even sure a rattler would faze him.

Matt took another step—

The air whistled. He caught a faint blur of motion. Then something hit him in the jaw, right where Rusty had smacked him, and he slammed backward into the stone wall.

# SEVENTEEN

# OWEN

## "DEADLY WATER SPORTS"

Owen worried the entire trip to Hot Springs. He worried about Laurie, Fen, Matt, and Baldwin. He worried that he had changed too much or not enough or that by inviting Fen's anger, the wrong details of the future would alter. Whatever the consequences, he now had blank spots in his knowledge of the future. He was involved, and that changed how much he could see.

Since he wasn't yet involved in the fight at Hot Springs, he could see the twins. Right now, they wouldn't survive the attack. This time, he knew what to do. He had to intervene, even though it would end his ability to see what happened next. When the others were in Hel, he'd watched. He'd sent the ravens. Every time they made a major choice, he'd been poised to intervene, but they hadn't needed him, so he'd stayed away. The presence of his ravens wasn't the same as *his* presence, so it didn't count as involvement. It didn't mean he'd stop being able to see their futures.

He'd stayed back, watching through the ravens and looking at the possible futures for the descendants of the North. Right now, they wouldn't all survive Ragnarök. He kept seeking that one choice that could change that outcome. So far, he'd had no luck, and now he was on the verge of being so involved that his vision would be limited. He hadn't told them his reasons. He wasn't ever sure how much was too much to reveal, and it wasn't something he'd had much experience with. His family hadn't liked trusting him alone around people after an incident with some lottery numbers when he was a kid. But, really, how was he to know it was a big secret what the winning numbers were going to be? She seemed like a nice woman, and she'd asked him what they were. It turned out she'd been joking, humoring a kid in line as far as she knew. Then she won, and on every interview, she talked about him: *Some kid in line just told me what numbers to pick.* Owen's mother still brought that up when she lectured him.

He hadn't said much to Laurie and Fen about what they'd learn soon, but he'd had to say something, to offer a *clue* so she could try to prepare. If she lost Fen while they weren't speaking to one another, it would hurt her too much.

Owen wasn't able to stay silent this time. He'd followed the rules his family had taught him even though it cost his eye. Sometimes, a person just had to break the rules—and he figured that if he pushed *too* far, the Norns or Valkyries or someone would show up and warn him.

Owen hoped that the others would make the smart choices at Saint Agnes. The twins certainly hadn't made the right choices, or he wouldn't have ended up here today to rescue them and convince them to join the rest of the team. The reason Owen was gifted with being all-knowing—or in reality, *mostly* knowing—was so he could help keep things on the right track when possible. Today, that meant returning Ray and Reyna to the path they should've been on.

One of the Berserkers, Vance, stepped in front of him. They had reached Evan's Plunge. It was really just a swimming pool that used the natural mineral waters of Hot Springs, South Dakota, but since it was the oldest tourist attraction in the Black Hills, pretty much everyone in this part of the state had been there at least once. More impressively, since it had opened way back in the 1800s, their parents *and* grandparents had been there, too.

Vance opened the door to the building, and they poured inside the lobby. Two of the Berserkers stepped forward to pay the admission fees.

Owen didn't have time for waiting in line, so he instructed Vance, "Give me a distraction. Follow soon."

At Vance's signal, the Berserkers started doing flips and tumbles. Two ran at the wall and used it for leverage, half walking up it and flipping back. Their movements were often mistaken for parkour. It wasn't truly PK, although it was a mix of the sport and several different martial arts. The Berserkers had used their unusual style for as long as Owen could remember, and he knew that generation after generation of athletic fighters trained and lived in preparation for the battle that *this* generation would soon fight.

As the others created some harmless chaos, the young woman on duty looked away, and Owen darted past the counter.

Once he reached the pool area, which looked a lot like most community pools but with slides and gymnastic rings, he slowed to a complete stop. He saw the missing descendants safe in the water. He wasn't too late yet!

The twins were fair-haired and pale, pretty in a way that probably caused them more attention than they liked. They were clearly trying to look scary. They had multiple piercings and black fingernail polish. Reyna wore a one-piece skull-covered swimsuit; her brother had a pair of black trunks. Most important, they were both still alive.

If this had been a regular water park, they'd have been safer, but the water here was from a natural hot spring. In the past, it had been claimed by at least two different Native American tribes, the Cheyenne and the Sioux. Back then, in the late 1800s, the water had been thought a cure for a variety of ailments. Now it was harnessed and used for recreation. The one unchanging fact, however, was that the water was natural. It flowed from the earth as springs did all over the world, and in such rivers, deadly creatures like nykurs could thrive.

Even as he thought about the threat, one of the nykurs lifted its massive gray head from the water beside Reyna. Owen hadn't ever seen one so close. They were much larger than he'd thought. Like the nykurs of legend, this one was made of water and was allover gray with its ears aimed the wrong direction. He couldn't see them, but he had heard that their knees bent in the wrong direction, too.

"Another monster, Ray!" Reyna yelled, and then she struck out, swimming quickly to the edge of the pool where her twin reached down and yanked her out of the water. Most of the other swimmers stayed in the water, staring at the nykur that had just risen in the middle of the pool.

Then one little girl yelled, "Horsey!"

Her father scooped her up, and they hurried out of the water.

"Get out," Reyna shouted at the people in the pool.

Some of them looked at the nykur as if it were a trick or an illusion. It was as if they were in shock. Horses didn't appear in the middle of pools, and they certainly weren't made of water.

"Get out of the water!" Ray yelled. "Now! Out. Out. Out."

Then the enormous horselike water monster moved under a girl who looked to be about fourteen. Once she touched its back, it rolled, flipping her under the water and holding her there. The water frothed around the struggling girl as people rushed to the edges of the pool to get to safety. One man with an obvious military haircut tried to reach the drowning girl.

At the edge of the pool, the twins stepped closer together and clasped hands.

"Show them that you are not so easily frightened," Owen said, although they couldn't hear him. He was used to speaking when no one was near him. It was a way to pretend he was connected to people, feel invested in them, one that his father had taught him when he was a small child crying over his loneliness.

The twins acted as if they were one being divided into two bodies. Their free hands lifted to either side. Their palms were open as if they were cupping something that no one else could see, and then at the same time, they flipped their hands upward so they were palms-out in a "halt" gesture.

As they did so, the water lifted like a wall in front of the nykur.

"Help the others escape," Owen told the Berserkers. "Wait outside the building."

He dove into the water and swam to the girl who was

under the water still. He knew the wall the twins had erected wouldn't hold long, but he couldn't spare the time to look for the nykur, either.

As quickly as he could, he grabbed the girl's hand, yanked her away from the nykur, and pulled her to the surface. The man who'd tried to help her joined him, and together they tugged her to the edge of the pool. Once there, a Berserker heaved her out of the water, and others pulled him and the man out. Owen felt the nykur's teeth snap in the air near him, not quite grazing him, but close enough that it made him jump. The man carried the unconscious girl out of the pool room.

Owen stayed where he was and watched the water, knowing that the threat wouldn't be easily contained but unable to know any more than that. Being involved in a situation made the knowing fade away. All he had were straggling details. If he hadn't gotten involved, he'd see more clearly—but the girl would have drowned.

On either side of the nykur, another just like it lifted its head from the warm mineral water. All three of the monstrous water horses watched the Freitag twins.

"You need to—" His words were cut off by a towering wave as the nykurs drew untold amounts of water from the springs outside. The wave fell over everyone still inside, including the twins, sweeping all of them violently off their feet and into the pool, which now flowed over the sides and partway up the walls.

He could see three of his Berserkers struggling to swim to him. Another was trying to reach the twins—who were trying to reach each other.

Owen started to swim toward the door, hoping to open it and release some of the water.

Two of the nykurs were after the twins, and the third was bearing down on him. He took a deep breath, preparing for the inevitable, and closed his eyes as it pulled him under the surface. His hands gripped the nykur's mane, and he tried to use the creature's body as leverage to pull himself to the surface. After several chest-tightening moments, he managed to climb atop its back—which it *really* didn't like. It immediately began bucking, trying to throw him off, and from the force of it, he realized that if it did throw him, he could break a lot of bones on impact. The upside, though, was that as it bucked, it pushed him out of the water. He was able to gasp a quick breath before it rolled again.

Owen clung to its back, hoping the others were faring better.

This time when it surfaced, Owen saw Huginn and Muninn, his ravens, swooping into the building, making straight for him. Huginn dived for the nykur's eye, clawing and beating his enormous wings while Muninn called to Owen, "Look up!"

Above his head, Owen finally saw his escape route: rings

hanging from the ceiling. They were the same kind that every boy used in basic gymnastics. Luckily, because of his time with the Berserkers, Owen's training was a bit more intense than that of the usual kid in gymnastics class.

When the nykur bucked again, Owen leaped, pushed against the nykur with both feet on its back, and stretched out his arms to grasp the rings. He only caught one, but after a brief struggle, he managed to grip a second ring.

Underneath him, the nykur bared its teeth and leaped after him, leaving the water briefly, vaulting higher than should be possible for such a large creature. The nykur was sluggish outside the water, though, and Owen hoped that would be enough to keep him safe. He swung his legs up, tucking himself into a ball, and hoped it couldn't reach even higher.

It seemed like only a moment between the nykur returning to the water and leaping a second time. This time, it seemed to pull the water underneath it like a platform to allow extra leverage.

Again, Owen folded himself up to the rings. He wasn't sure he could get high enough to be out of reach.

Then Huginn and Muninn flew toward the nykur's face, talons outstretched and beaks open.

"Ours!"

"Vile beast!"

"Pluck your eyes!"

"Gouge your throat!"

He wasn't sure if other mythic beasts could understand the words his ravens cried out, but the nykur's attention flickered to them, so Owen took his chance and started to move across the rings. As he swung from ring to ring, his ravens darted at the nykurs and cawed threats.

The nykur dropped back down to the pool again. As it watched him, he worked his way across the row of rings. A quick glance down showed him that his Berserkers were with the twins, and they were slowly working their way up the slide that snaked down to the pool. Another of his Berserkers was atop the catwalk above that spanned the length of the building.

As the twins reached the top platform of the slide, they joined hands, and in a shaky voice, Reyna murmured words Owen couldn't understand. In a matter of moments, a gash appeared in the side of the building and the waters poured out in a rush.

The nykurs let out loud screams of protest and began to kick against the pull of the water. It frothed as their hooves churned it, but the pressure of the water escaping created a current that was too much to resist. They started moving toward the opening in the wall.

Reyna leaned against her brother and watched as the bodies of the thrce nykurs dissipated into the water. There was no way to tell if they returned to where they originated or if the flow pulled them apart. Either way, they were gone.

Owen flipped from where he still hung on the rings toward the now-vacant edge of the pool, slipping along the tile as he landed and tearing his trousers. Blood turned his already wet jeans darker, but it was only a cut. He'd avoided broken bones, and the Freitag twins were both alive.

The Berserkers helped the twins down from the slide, and a few moments later they joined the rest of the confused crowd outside. Huginn and Muninn had left again. He felt grateful, and more than a little surprised, that they'd come to his aid. His ravens weren't meant to be creatures that entered into battles. They watched. They brought him knowledge.

"I'm Odin," he said to the twins when they reached him. "It's time for us to leave."

Reyna's eyes narrowed. "And exactly why should we trust you?"

Ray said quietly, "Maybe—"

"Your girlfriend killed Baldwin." Reyna spoke over her brother. "When Astrid showed up at Baldwin's house, she actually *brought* monsters with her. Now you show up here, and more monsters appear?"

"Astrid is not my anything. A stranger arrives and lies about me, and you hold me responsible? I showed up to *help* you. . . . Also, Baldwin is alive. Fenrir, Laurie, and Matthew retrieved him from Hel." Owen accepted a shirt from one of the Berserkers, ripped it, and wrapped it around the cut in his leg like a bandage. "They're expecting us."

Reyna eyed him. "So you say. Let me repeat: why would we trust you?"

As much as Owen understood her doubt, he didn't have the patience for it today. "Your grandmother gave you a cloak of feathers when you were a small child, Freya. It will work now."

She opened her mouth and closed it without speaking.

"Her name is Reyna," Ray muttered.

Owen nodded. He did forget sometimes that they all weren't as accustomed as he was to thinking of themselves as their other identities.

"Only Ray knows about the cloak," Reyna said.

For a moment, Owen saw the twins as they were: kids like him, but also kids who were afraid. He was, too, but he had learned to hide that most of the time. They didn't have time for fear. Ragnarök was coming.

"As I said, I am Odin. I am all-seeing." He shrugged. "We should collect your cloak before we join the others. Your father's driver will take us to Blackwell when you tell him you won tickets to a concert by a band he's never heard of. If the other descendants aren't there, you can turn around and return to fighting monsters on your own."

The twins exchanged a look, and then Reyna nodded.

"But your acrobat guys aren't coming with us," Reyna said.

"I know. They'll meet us at camp." Owen smiled. Now he just had to hope that the others were holding up well with the surprise waiting for them at Saint Agnes.

# EIGHTEEN

# MATT

## "MJÖLNIR"

Matt recovered from the blow and raced out the mausoleum door. Well, it was more like "race and then squeeze out the door as fast as possible," but that was the basic idea. He couldn't fight something he couldn't see. So he got out of there, stumbling into the light, blinking.

"Where's the hammer?" Baldwin asked.

"There's something in there," Matt said. "Something alive. It punched me."

"Punched you?" Baldwin's face screwed up. "Are you sure a bat didn't fly into you? I bet there are a few in there."

Matt rubbed his tender jaw. "Unless its name is Bruce Wayne, that wasn't a bat."

At a noise from the mausoleum, he spun, fists going up.

"There *is* something in there," Baldwin said.

"Yep."

Baldwin inched toward the door. "Could be a homeless guy."

"How would he get inside?"

"A tunnel?"

Matt shook his head and walked back toward the door.

"What?" Baldwin said, inching away. "You're going back in?"

"Nope. I'm going to get this door open so I can see him. Better yet, try to flush him out." He turned to Baldwin. "Are you okay with that? If you want, you can switch off with Fen."

Baldwin squared his shoulders. "I'm fine. Sorry. This place just weirds me out."

Matt imagined it would, considering Baldwin himself had been dead just a day ago. He might still be fearless about most things, but apparently, that experience hadn't left his confidence quite as unshaken as he pretended.

Matt walked to the door and put his shoulder against it. "Give me a hand here?"

"Right. Sure."

Baldwin took up position on the side farthest from the

opening. He did give it his all, though, and with both of them pushing, the door slowly scraped open until it was as far as it could go, hitting a stone pillar inside. Then they looked inside and saw...

The light only extended about a foot beyond the door.

"Whoa," Baldwin said. "Now, *that's* dark."

Something whispered and shuffled inside. Baldwin staggered and caught himself. He looked sheepishly over at Matt.

"Sorry."

"It's okay."

"So what do we do now? Find a flashlight?"

Matt had a feeling that wouldn't help. The gloom inside the mausoleum wasn't a natural darkness.

"I have an idea," he said.

He motioned Baldwin back and whispered his plan. He knew Baldwin wouldn't be thrilled with it, so he offered again to call in Fen, but Baldwin insisted he'd play his role.

"I'll go find a lantern or something," Matt called loudly. "You wait here. And whatever you do, don't go inside."

"Got it!"

It was a trick, of course—to get whatever was inside to venture out. It wasn't the best ruse in the world, but the monsters they'd run into so far hadn't exactly been rocket scientists. Matt walked a little ways, veered left, and then zipped back alongside the tomb. He crept along the wall until he was beside the door, hidden out of sight. Once Matt was in place, Baldwin started for the mausoleum door.

"I don't see what the big deal is," Baldwin muttered. "It's probably just a bat. I bet I can find that hammer before he even gets back."

Baldwin stepped into the entrance and peered inside as Matt watched.

"Huh. It's really dark," Baldwin said, "but it can't be far. This place isn't that big."

Baldwin took another step, and Matt heard that whisper again. He saw a blur of motion and raced forward, grabbing for it just as Baldwin did, too. They both caught the thing and heaved, yanking backward, trying to drag it out of the—

It was like pulling a cork from a bottle. One minute they were heaving with all their might. The next they were sailing backward with the force of their pull, prize clutched in their hands. They both lost their balance and fell together, right outside the door, still holding—

Baldwin let out a yelp and rolled away, leaving Matt clutching...

An arm. He was holding an arm. Only it didn't look like an actual limb. Not really. He could see fingers and skin, but the fingers were long and curved and the skin was gray and leathery, and there was bone sticking out from the skin, and the smell—

The smell.

Matt dropped the arm and staggered back. His hand shot up to cover his nose. Except it was the hand that had been holding the arm, and the smell—

Matt swallowed, trying not to puke. He stared down at the mummified arm, now lying in the grass.

"When you said you needed a hand..." Baldwin began.

"Not what I meant."

Baldwin let out a laugh, but it was a nervous, sputtering laugh. Matt bent to look at the hand. It was from a dead body. A *long*-dead body. Had someone hit them with that? Using a corpse as a weapon?

That was the only explanation he could think of.

Actually, no. There was one other thing—

Something barreled from the mausoleum darkness. It stopped in the lit doorway, threw back its head, and let out a bloodcurdling roar. At least as big as Matt's father, it was dressed in a moldering leather tunic and leggings, with huge boots and a rusted metal helmet. With tangled reddish-yellow hair and a long matted beard, it was clearly a man. Or it used to be. When it was alive. Now it was rotted, with bits of leathery flesh hanging off it, bones showing beneath the holes. One side of its face was gone, leaving only skull.

Also, it was missing a hand.

Before Matt or Baldwin could react, the thing rushed out. It snatched up the discarded arm and stuck it back on. Then it bellowed, jaw stretching, showing a few remaining yellowed teeth. Its one eye rolled upward and its chest collapsed, as if it was taking a mighty breath. Then, as it released the breath, its whole body expanded, growing until it was taller than the mausoleum behind it. It roared again and the very earth quaked under their feet.

"Um, you know those guys we met in the afterlife?" Matt said. "And I told you they weren't Viking zombies?"

"Uh-huh..."

"This is."

The draugr charged Baldwin. Matt flew at it, knowing the Hammer was too risky. Apparently, so was tackling the rotting undead. He slammed into its arm and only took off a big chunk of dried-out flesh. The draugr hit Baldwin with a massive fist. Baldwin flew into the nearest gravestone. Matt tried not to wince at the impact, but Baldwin just bounced back, saying, "Hey, ugly! Want a piece of me? We already got a piece of you."

Baldwin dodged the draugr's next blow and tore past him. One problem with being rotted is that, apparently, your joints don't work so well, and the draugr turned awkwardly, stiffly, before charging Baldwin again.

Baldwin kept taunting it as Matt snatched the shield, then prepared his Hammer, focusing on getting mad. That wasn't hard—this thing was standing between him and Mjölnir, and the hammer was rightfully his. Plus, he'd had a really bad day. So he found that core of anger and lashed out, and the Hammer flew, stronger and straighter than it ever had before. A concentrated ball of pure power.

It hit the draugr in the side and for a second, Matt thought they were going to be dealing with two draugrs. Or at least two halves of one. But the draugr toppled, still intact. When it tried to rise again, Matt held out his fingers, glowing now, and the draugr stopped.

"Do you speak English?" Matt said.

"Um, it's a zombie," Baldwin said. "If it does, the only word it knows is *brains*."

"It's a draugr," Matt said. "A dead Viking warrior who guards treasure. It's sentient. Like a ghost. It can talk."

The draugr had deflated to human size now, which was still plenty big. But it stayed on the ground, watching Matt's hand. Matt could see an amulet around its neck. A Thor's Hammer.

"You're a Thorsen?" Matt said.

"I am," it said, its voice garbled, remaining teeth clacking. "Olaf Thorsen." Or that's what it seemed to say. It was hard to tell. Not all the consonants worked right when you didn't have half your teeth. Or most of your lips. Or a tongue. At least he seemed to be speaking English, which meant he must have been one of the early settlers.

"I'm a Thorsen, too," Matt said. "Matthew Thorsen. Of Blackwell. I need what you're guarding in that mausoleum. I need Mjölnir."

The draugr laughed. It was a horrible dry, raspy, chortling sound. "You think because you are a son of Thor you can wield his great hammer?"

"No, I think because I am the Champion of Thor, I can wield it. And I must. Ragnarök comes. The serpent stirs. The battle begins. I have been chosen to fight it."

As Matt said the words, he felt his heart stir. Noble words. Proud words. A champion's words. And, for perhaps the first time, he believed them. It would have been a truly perfect moment…if the draugr hadn't nearly burst itself laughing.

"You?" The thing cackled. "You are a child, not a Champion of Thor."

Baldwin leaped forward, saying, "Yes, he—!" but Matt cut him short.

The draugr continued, "You say you are the champion? We can settle this easily. Inside that crypt lies Mjölnir. Bring it to me."

"It's a trick," Baldwin hissed.

"Yes, it is a trick," the draugr said. "If the boy is truly a Thorsen, he already knows that. Do you think no one has found that hammer before now? They have. But they cannot lift it. It lies in its bed of stone, and only Thor's true champion can raise it out. Only the living embodiment of the great god himself."

"Uh, isn't that Excalibur?" Baldwin said.

Matt tried to shush him, but Baldwin said, "It *is* Excalibur. With the stone. I saw the musical." He lowered his voice. "I think his brains are rotting, too. He seems confused."

"The son of Balder, I see," the draugr said. "I *would* believe you are the living embodiment of Frigg's doomed son. As pleasant as a sun-warmed stone. And just as intelligent."

"Hey!" Baldwin said.

"He's being a jerk," Matt said. "He wants to test me. I accept."

Matt handed Baldwin his shield for protection and then marched toward the mausoleum. The sun streamed through the open doorway, and he could see inside easily now that whatever magic the draugr worked was gone. The crypt was empty, except for a single casket with a stone top. Getting that top off took some serious work, but eventually it slid back enough for Matt to see inside, and there lay—

A hammer. Which was what he expected. Except... well, he'd hoped for a little more. Maybe a flash of light. A bright jeweled handle. A gleaming bronze head. It was just a metal mallet. Not even a *big* metal mallet—maybe the size of one of the rubber ones in his dad's workshop. It was dull and tarnished, and the handle was too short. And it was that, the short handle, that made his breath catch, that made Matt stare at the hammer as if it truly were brilliant with jewels and fire.

The story went that Loki bet two dwarves they couldn't

beat their brethren's gifts for the gods. To be sure of that, he turned into a fly and bit them as they worked. He succeeded in distracting one dwarf, and when he pulled out Mjölnir, the handle was short.

That's how Matt knew this truly was the hammer of Thor.

Matt reached in and grasped the handle. It was just cold metal, not even wrapped with leather or cloth. He took a deep breath. The stories said that only Thor was strong enough to wield the hammer. Clearly, Matt wasn't stronger than other Thorsens. Which probably meant that they could wield it, too—once they got it out of here. That was the problem. The head was half-buried in the stone bottom of the casket. Matt could see scratches and nicks where others must have tried to cut it free. To no avail. This wasn't simple concrete. It was magic. Ancient magic.

Matt gripped the hammer and closed his eyes.

*I am Thor's champion. I know I am.*

He braced himself and, eyes still closed, he pulled—

His hands started to slide up the handle. Slipping off. His heart pounded.

*This is Thor's hammer. My hammer. All I need to do is pull—*

He staggered back, and as he did he opened his eyes and saw...

He was holding Mjölnir.

Matt let out a deep, shuddering sigh, and his whole body shook with it.

Holding the hammer in one hand, Matt walked out of the mausoleum. Baldwin stood about ten feet away from the draugr, watching it. The thing hadn't moved.

*No, not "the thing." I shouldn't call him that. He's my ancestor. Olaf Thorsen.*

As Matt stepped through the doorway, Baldwin glanced up. His gaze went to Matt's hand.

"Is that...it?" he said.

"It is."

"Are you sure? It seems kinda...small."

Matt could say that his glowing amulet proved it was the real hammer. Or he could point out the short handle and explain how it got that way. Instead, he stood on the stone slab outside the mausoleum doors and gripped the hammer, testing the weight of it. Then he swung back his arm and whipped it as hard as he could.

"No!" Baldwin said as the hammer flew through the air. "I didn't mean to throw it away! What if it *is* the right...?"

He trailed off as the hammer suddenly changed direction. Like a boomerang, it started coming back. Baldwin hit the ground facedown. Matt stood there, hand out. The hammer struck it, the handle smacking against his palm. He gripped it.

"Yep," he said. "This is Mjölnir."

"That. Is. Awesome." Baldwin hurried over and stared at the hammer. "Can I hold it? Oh, wait, no. You need to be worthy, right?" He gave a short laugh. "I probably don't want to know if I qualify."

"That's the comic book Thor," Matt said. "In the myths, only Thor is *strong* enough to wield it." Matt hefted it. "I don't think that can be true, either. I'm strong, but not superhero strong." He held it out. "You want to try? Keep your toes out of the drop zone, just in case."

Baldwin reached out. Matt handed him the hammer, then very carefully released his grip. It started to fall. Matt dodged to grab it, but Baldwin managed to grab it with both hands and stop it from dropping. He stood there, hammer a foot from the ground, his neck muscles bulging as he struggled to hold it up.

"That's what it means," Baldwin said, grunting with the effort. "I can hold it. I just can't wield it. Not unless I plan to drop it on someone."

Matt took the hammer back. It was heavy, but no more than he'd expect from a bronze mallet. That must be the magic, then. It didn't require actual strength to wield—just a magical kind. The strength of Thor.

"*Vingthor*," the draugr whispered.

Matt looked down at the hammer, his fingers wrapped around it, and in that moment, he almost believed Hildar.

He wielded Mjölnir. He could be *Vingthor*. He really could. He gripped the short handle tighter and it was as if he could feel that strength filling him.

Matt looked over. The draugr—Olaf—had dropped to one knee, head bent.

"You are Thor," Olaf said. "I doubted you. I mocked you. I offer my blessed Valhalla afterlife in penance. Wield the hammer. Send me to Hel."

"Your task was to guard Mjölnir," Matt said. "Which you did, and I am grateful for that. Now that I have the hammer, your services are no longer needed, and you may begin your true afterlife. Go to Valhalla. Take your place there, where you belong."

Olaf bowed his head again. "Thank you, *Vingthor*. I will be cheering you to victory from the great halls." He rose and started for the mausoleum. As he passed, he paused and looked at the hammer in Matt's hands. "May I hold it? For nearly a millennium, I have guarded it, but I have never been permitted to touch it."

Baldwin glanced over quickly, as if wondering what Matt would do. For Matt, there was no question. This man was his ancestor. A warrior who'd done his duty for almost a thousand years.

Matt held out Mjölnir. The draugr took it in both hands. It still dropped, as it had with Baldwin, but Olaf managed to lift it partway, bones rattling with the effort.

Matt chuckled. "I guess Thorsen blood helps."

"It would, if I had Thorsen blood. But I do not, *Vingthor*. I am Glaemir, king of the draugrs. I knew you would come for this, little Matthew Thorsen, and I did not have to wait long. While others may not be able to wield this hammer, I know many who'd pay dearly to keep it from your hands."

The draugr smiled, a horrible, grinning skull smile. Matt lunged to grab the hammer, but the earth under Glaemir's feet opened and he dropped. Matt jumped to go after him. The earth closed as fast as it had opened, and Matt hit the ground. Solid ground now. He lay there, staring at the upturned dirt that marked the spot where Glaemir had stood. Where he'd last seen Mjölnir. Swallowed by the earth.

# NINETEEN

## FEN

### "NOT A HERO"

The foul mood Fen had been trying to shake off wasn't getting any better. He decided that for right now silence was his best plan. He sighed and dropped to the rear of the group as his cousin tried to cheer everyone up.

"We'll get it back," she repeated as they left Saint Agnes. "We got Baldwin back, and we've accomplished so many other things! We'll figure this out, too."

He muffled a snort of disbelief. At the rate they were going, they'd be lucky to be *awake* when Ragnarök came. They had no idea how much time they had until the big doomsday event, but they weren't ready. They weren't even a little bit near ready. So far, they'd found the shield, lost the shield, and retrieved the shield; they'd found the location of the hammer, been taken captive, escaped, actually had the hammer in their possession, and lost it. They'd found and lost several of the descendants. They'd spotted more monsters than he even knew existed. The truth of it was that they were fumbling around in confusion, barely one step ahead of disaster most of the time. It was *nothing* like in the movies, where the heroes always seemed to have a plan. Maybe it was because they were kids, or maybe the movies didn't show how confused and beaten down the heroes were sometimes.

Fen didn't want to lose. He didn't want the world to end and everyone he liked to die. *He* didn't want to die. Things didn't look good for them, though. Even Matt was quiet as they went back to the camp to regroup and catch a few hours' sleep. Privately, Fen suspected that Matt was about as optimistic as Fen felt. The guy's own grandfather was the leader of the enemy, and a rotting monster had just duped him. Admittedly, Fen didn't think that having the Berserkers along would've changed that, but it would have been nice if they'd had some backup for that fight—and for whatever monster came at them next.

Once they returned to the campground where Owen had left them before he went off to deal with whatever his secret mission was, they all opened their bags from Helen to get out food and clean clothes, as well as the sleeping bags and camping lanterns that clearly should not fit in such small bags. This time, though, both Matt and Laurie also had first aid kits.

"You're hurt?" Fen flopped down beside her, his irritation gone at the thought of her being injured. "Where? Why didn't you tell me?"

"I'm not." She looked confused. "Are any of *you* hurt? Maybe it was supposed to be in your bag instead."

Baldwin poked himself in the chest with his thumb and said, "Invulnerable."

Matt held up his own supplies. "Got one."

They walked over to the bathrooms to wash off the stink of the draugr and change into clean clothes.

As soon as they left, Laurie turned her gaze on Fen. "That leaves you. Where are you hurt?"

She started fussing over him, trying to grab his shirt to lift it and then when that didn't work, she caught his arm and started inspecting it. "Maybe it's a bite." She reached for his ankle. "There are rattlesnakes."

"Did you check *your* ankles?" Fen's heart sped at the thought of his cousin being bitten by something venomous.

They both inspected their ankles. Nothing. They checked each other's shoulders, necks, and backs just to be sure. Nothing. They looked at their own stomachs. No bites, scrapes, cuts, or other injuries were visible on either Brekke.

"Maybe your bag's broken." Fen pointed at the first aid kit, feeling a little stupid but not having any other ideas, and really, the rules for magic things were new to him. "Put it back and try again."

Mutely, Laurie opened it and put the first aid kit into the bag. Then she reached inside. This time, there were a toothbrush and toothpaste, but the kit was still there. She pulled all three items out of the bag. "It *seems* to work."

Matt and Baldwin returned and sat down. Baldwin was eating some sort of sandwich that had sprouts and lettuce sticking out the sides. Matt was cleaning a cut with a disinfectant cloth that he'd pulled from his bag.

"I'm going to go over to the restroom." Laurie stood.

Fen stood, too. "Okay. Let's go."

"I can go by myself."

"But—"

"There's no one else here, Fen," she said very patiently. "You can see me the whole time I walk over, and the doors open to this side." She smiled at him before adding, "The worst thing I'll find is cold water or spiders."

"Fine." He folded his arms and stared at her until she reached the bathrooms. *What kind of a champion doesn't worry about his family?* After all the things that had happened, he couldn't forget that she was his first priority. Keeping Laurie safe had been his job before this whole hero business. He wasn't going to let that change.

Once she was settled in, they went to sleep.

A few hours later, Fen woke to the whoop of joyous

Berserkers. It didn't take a genius to suspect that those sounds could only mean one of two things: they and their freaky leader had been victorious or they were in the middle of a fun battle. Fen sat up and watched the Berserkers flipping and yelling as they entered the camp—waking everyone else up.

Within moments, Owen was perched on the picnic table like a king holding court, and Laurie was awake—and scrambling over to Owen like they were old friends. Baldwin was up and asking about one of the tricks the acrobatic fighters used, and Matt was heading toward two black-clad people who walked in the center of the crowd of Berserkers. The twins had returned.

"Goth Barbie and Ken, are you stopping in for a visit?" Fen asked as he came to his feet. "Just passing by?"

"Fen," Laurie cautioned him.

"No, it's fine. Wolf-boy felt abandoned," Reyna said. "We had a puppy once that misbehaved when we left it alone, and the trainer suggested a crate. Do we need a crate?"

"Funny." Fen bared his teeth at her.

Ray stepped up beside his twin.

Baldwin snorted in laughter, earning a dirty look from Fen and a smile from Reyna. "What?" he said. "It was funny." When Fen didn't crack a smile, Baldwin shrugged. "*I* thought it was funny."

"We're here to stay this time," Ray said quietly. "We can't run from this. We get it now."

"The monsters come after us whether we're with you or not, and we'd rather *you* fight them than have to do it ourselves," Reyna added in what might have been a joking tone.

Fen just stared at them with his arms folded over his chest. They had abandoned the team when Baldwin died; they hadn't been willing to go to Hel and rescue their dead friend. "You bailed on us when the team needed you," he said.

"Because things got...complicated," Reyna said. "Baldwin died. We freaked. Now we're back."

"You shouldn't have left in the first place," Fen said, glaring at her.

She shook her head and turned to Matt and Baldwin.

"What all did we miss?" Ray asked.

"The biggest thing is that I'm not, you know, *dead* anymore," Baldwin replied. "Oh, and they almost arrested Fen for it. Not cool."

"That's ridiculous! They should arrest Astrid for killing you," Ray grumbled.

At that, Fen offered him a small smile. Maybe Ray wasn't all bad. Reyna, on the other hand, was about as welcome as Astrid had been. *Except not evil.* Fen sighed. He might not actually like Goth Barbie, but he could admit that she wasn't evil. He tried to think like a hero should—looking at the most important things first. The twins could help in the big battle, and hopefully the other ones before it. They were supposed to be part of the team.

*Maybe their return is a good thing.*

Then again, his worry was that they would bail again when things got hard, and they *would* get hard again. He knew that as surely as he knew that they needed all the help they could get—and that they would probably still lose. He stayed quiet as he listened to them talk. Sometimes listening was the best plan. If you talked all the time, you missed all the hints and clues people gave out without meaning to.

Owen sat watching them silently.

Almost immediately, Laurie walked toward him with the first aid kit from Hel's magic bag.

"I think this is for you," she said.

Owen nodded and unwrapped a bandage from his leg. It was more a piece of torn cloth than a bandage, but as he uncoiled it, it was obvious that he'd been bleeding pretty seriously. He rolled up his bloodstained jeans.

"What happened?"

The blue-haired boy shrugged, but Reyna had overheard the question. She and Ray came over and started talking about a nykur attack. Alternating turns, they explained that some sort of water-monster-horse thing had tried to kill them, and Owen had been there to help save everyone. Reyna finished her story with, "If he hadn't arrived when he did with the Berserkers, at least one girl would've died, and...probably us, too."

"You made the right decision," Laurie said.

Owen shrugged, but he was smiling at her. Something in their exchange made Fen uncomfortable. He thought back to their private conversation.

"Did you know where he went when he said he had to go?" Fen asked, drawing all four gazes to him. "When he left us, did you *know*?"

She opened her mouth like she was going to say something and then closed it again. She looked at Owen and then just nodded.

"I can talk to Laurie," Owen said. "It's like in the myths. Our ancestors were close, and like Odin and Loki, we will be, too."

"Yeah, well, I'm his descendant, too, but don't go expecting us to be 'close,'" Fen said.

"I wouldn't expect that, Fenr—*Fen*." Owen smiled at him. "But I trust Laurie. I already promised that I would answer her questions when I returned."

Fen couldn't unravel the number of jabs that were in the things Owen said. He didn't care much, either. "Whatever, dude." He glanced at Laurie. "You, though? I expect more from you. You get angry if I keep secrets, but it's okay for you? How could you—No, you know what? I don't even want to hear it right now." Fen forced himself to stop there. It was either that or say something ugly to her. He tucked his hands into his pockets and kept walking past them without another word. He wasn't stupid, though: he paused beside

Matt and said, "I'm going to circle the campground...unless we're heading out soon?"

Matt shot a sympathetic look at Fen. "Not yet. Sorry. I'm still working on a plan."

Fen nodded and walked farther from the rest of the group. The Berserkers parted as he walked among them, not quite acknowledging him but not stopping him, either.

As he walked, Fen thought about the situation. He could admit that it was good that Owen was able to rescue the twins, but he couldn't see any reason that Owen couldn't have just *said* that to him and Matt. They could've had a plan—maybe sent the Berserkers to rescue the twins or kept some with the rest of the descendants.

*He knew the future. He* knew *that the twins were in danger.*

Fen stopped midstep. If Owen really knew the future, he also knew where the draugr would be, where Astrid was; so many things could be easier if Owen just told them what he knew up front. *That* was the plan right there. He also said he'd answer Laurie's questions, so they'd have her ask him some questions.

Quickly, Fen turned to go back to tell Matt, but he'd only gone a few steps when he heard Laurie's and Owen's voices.

"Where are your ravens?" Laurie asked.

"Learning things I'll need to know."

Fen ducked to the side of the bathroom, staying out of sight. He wasn't sure what to do. His first instinct was to walk up to them. If it had been Thorsen or Baldwin with her, he would've walked away, but Owen was a stranger—one who traveled with his own guard and kept secrets. It occurred to Fen suddenly: if Loki's representative could fight for the good guys, why couldn't Odin's be on the bad side?

"It's weird, the whole ravens thing and the knowing-the-future bit. If you see the future, why do you need ravens?" Laurie had the tone in her voice that said she was trying to be patient, but it wasn't going to last much longer. Fen was very used to that tone.

Owen was quiet so long that Fen thought he might have left. Then he said, "I don't understand all the details."

"About?"

"Fenrir," Owen said, just as Fen was about to step out and interrupt their conversation. Owen continued, "Where is Fenrir?"

Fen felt guilty for eavesdropping, but at the same time, it might be useful to hear what other nonsense Owen said. Something felt off. Either Owen was not really on their side or he had a thing for Laurie or something. Whatever it was, Fen wasn't leaving her alone with the guy.

"He'll be back," Laurie said. "He might be mad, but he wouldn't leave me."

Fen smiled to himself. *That* was the truth. His job—even before this whole Ragnarök thing started—was to protect his cousin.

"You don't need someone guarding you," Owen said. "You're not weak."

Fen almost growled. *Of course* she needed guarding! She was his family, his almost-sister, and he was Loki's champion. If he couldn't keep her safe, why would he want to try to save the world? His cousin was the only person in it that he'd thought worth saving when he'd left Blackwell. Admittedly, he'd changed a little since then. He thought Baldwin and Matt were worth saving, too. He'd gone to Hel for Baldwin once already.

"You have the bow, Laurie."

"Uh-huh. I know that."

At the well-duh tone in her voice, Fen smiled again. She might be sneaking off to talk to Owen, but at least, she still sounded like herself.

"The bow that you will use at the final battle...the one where I'll fight at your side." Owen spoke very calmly. "You are Loki's descendant, too. Think about it. Why do you all think *Fenrir* will fight next to Thor's champion?"

For a moment, Fen felt like all the air had left his lungs. It came to him in a flash; the day that the Norn pointed Matt to Loki's descendant, Fen had been with Laurie most of the afternoon. Matt had just assumed that she'd been pointing at Fen. They'd all believed it; they'd believed he was special. He wasn't. He should've known that by now.

He didn't stand around to hear Laurie's reply. In a daze,

he walked back to the campground, over to his sleeping bag, and sat down on it. Then, he stared at the sky, thinking about how colossally wrong he'd been to think that *he* could be special and good. He wasn't the hero here. He was the hero's *cousin*.

Fen stayed like that until Laurie came over to pack up her sleeping bag. Once she was done, she hugged him quickly. "Can we not fight anymore?"

"Good plan." He squeezed her tightly. "Come on. Let's go see where Thorsen is. See what the new plan is."

When she let go, Fen glanced at the picnic table, where Owen now sat alone.

The older boy saw him and gave him a sad smile. After glancing at Laurie to be sure she wouldn't see, Fen gave him a rude hand gesture in reply. He didn't need anyone's sympathy. Laurie might be the real hero here, but Fen was still her cousin, her family, and he wasn't going to stop protecting her.

# TWENTY

## MATT

### "UNEXPECTED ALLY"

Matt wandered off into the woods as the others milled about, adjusting to having the twins back and trying to make them feel welcome. Well, *Baldwin* was trying to make them feel welcome. Laurie was talking to Owen, and Fen was off on his own. Matt had wanted to talk to him, but he'd taken off before he could try. So Matt went for a walk. He wasn't feeling particularly sociable, either.

He'd had Mjölnir. He'd lifted it from its stone bed, proving he was indeed Thor's champion. He'd held Mjölnir. *The* Mjölnir. Had anyone ever told him he would one day wield it, he'd have...He didn't know what he'd have done. It was too far beyond anything imaginable. But he had. He'd held it, and he'd thrown it, and it had come back, just like in the myths.

Now he'd lost it. Had it. Held it. Lost it.

Matt stopped walking. He was far enough from the temporary campsite that no one should be able to see him. He put out his hand, closed his eyes, and concentrated on calling Mjölnir back to him. That was supposed to be how it worked. He threw the hammer, and it returned to him, no matter what.

*Except I didn't throw it.*

That shouldn't matter.

*It does. You know it does.*

Matt silenced the doubting voice. He imagined seeing the hammer. Imagined it flying toward him. Hitting his hand. He imagined what he'd felt before, the sting, the smart of it.

*Mjölnir. Come back. Come to me.*

Nothing happened.

*Mjölnir. Thor's hammer. My hammer. Return to—*

"What are you doing?"

Matt's eyes snapped open to see Reyna walking toward him.

"I was ... thinking," he said.

"That's a weird pose for thinking." She imitated him, closing her eyes and holding out her hand. Then she screwed up her face, like she needed to go to the bathroom.

"I was just—" He shook his head. "Go on back to the campsite. I'm fine."

"Oh, I wasn't checking to see if you were fine. What are you doing out here? Hoping the hammer will pop from one of these rabbit holes?"

Matt struggled against a retort.

"I'm glad you and Ray came back," he said evenly. "We all appreciate it. But I'd like a few minutes to myself. I don't mean to be rude—"

"Why not? I was rude to you." Reyna walked closer. "Why did you give that zombie guy the hammer?"

"I already admitted it was a stupid thing—"

"Just tell me. Why did you do it?" Reyna asked again.

Matt sighed. He'd explained this already. Obviously she hadn't been listening. Big surprise there. "I thought he was a Thorsen. He was in a Thorsen mausoleum. He was guarding Thor's treasure. He looked right and he had the amulet...I messed up, okay?"

"But why did you give it to him?"

"Because it seemed like the right thing to do. I thought he'd been guarding it all these years, and now he was off to Valhalla, and it was a nice gesture."

"Exactly. You wanted to be nice. And that's what you get for it."

Matt shook his head and started to walk away. Reyna jogged up beside him as he walked.

"You're too nice, Matt. That's your problem. You needed Ray and me, and you let us walk away."

He glared over at her. "What was I supposed to do? Force you to fight alongside us?"

"You could have argued more."

"I *did*. I argued; I explained; I even begged."

"You're Thor's champion. You're not supposed to beg."

Matt shook his head again. He didn't need this. Not now.

"And what about Astrid?" Reyna said.

Matt tensed. "Yes, I screwed up there, too. All my fault. Stupid mistakes? I have them."

"Hey, you're not the one who kept insisting the trolls were guys in costumes."

She smiled when he looked over, and it was an easy smile, like she was fine with mocking herself as much as she mocked others. Then, just as he started to relax, she said, "About Astrid," and he stiffened again.

"She played you," she said. "I know you're just a kid—"

"Excuse me? How old are *you*?"

"Thirteen, like you. But there's thirteen, and then there's *thirteen*. You're small-town. It's a whole different thing. Plus, you're a guy."

"What difference—?"

"Astrid was not small-town thirteen. She's probably not even thirteen. She totally played you, like a city girl would."

Reyna looked up at him and batted her lashes, her eyes round. "Oh, Matt. You're so big and strong and—"

"It wasn't like that," he said with a scowl, even as his face heated.

"Sure it was. I heard her."

"Okay, sure, she did that, but it just made me..." He shrugged as if trying to throw off the feeling. "I just...I felt bad for her. She seemed like she was trying to help, and Fen kept giving her a hard time, and no one really seemed to want her there. So I felt like I should do better."

"Exactly. You were being nice. I rest my case."

She was needling him, and no matter what he said, she was going to take it as proof of her point. Whatever that point might be. It seemed to change with every passing second.

"You need your hammer back."

"Really?" Matt said. "Huh. Thanks. I had a feeling I was missing something, but I couldn't figure out what it was."

"See? There. Doesn't that feel better?"

"Reyna, I appreciate whatever you're trying to do—"

"No, you don't. You want me to get lost. Go on. Tell me."

"Why? So you can leave again and then tell me it's my fault?"

She grinned. "Touché. You're getting better at this."

"Better at what?" He shook his head. "Never mind. You

want me to be mean? Go back to camp, Reyna. I'm trying to figure out a plan, and you aren't helping."

"Much better. For the record, that's not mean. It's honest. But either way, I'm not leaving. You need a plan, and I'm here to help you find it so you can stop moping and get us moving."

"I'm not mop—"

"How about brooding? Do you like that better? It has a more heroic air, don't you think?"

"Reyna..."

"You need to call the Valkyries."

He stopped walking and turned to her.

"What?" she said. "Do you have any idea how to find the hammer on your own? Besides digging for a very, very long time."

"It's not still down there. He took it. Somewhere."

"Exactly. *Somewhere.* You don't know where, and you *can't* know where, which is why you need the folks who tipped you off in the first place. Call the Valkyries."

He shook his head. "I've bothered them enough."

"When's the last time you called them?"

"I haven't. But they needed to rescue us just the other day. From the bison."

"They rescued you from—?" Reyna shook her head. "I don't want to know. So when else have they rescued you?"

"Well, never, but I'm supposed to do this on my own.

They told me where to find Mjölnir, right after they gave me my goats."

"Goats? No, again, I don't want to know." She paused. "Wait, actually, I do. You get goats?"

"Magical battle goats."

"Of course. So you get magic goats, a magic necklace, a magic hammer, a magic shield. You're like the favorite child who gets all the best Christmas gifts. What does Freya have?"

"Um, a magic cloak."

She waved that off. "Got it already. What else?"

"There's the boar, Hildisvini."

"Who? What?"

"Hildisvini. He's a boar. It's a wild pig—"

"I know what a boar is. That's almost as bad as goats. What else?"

"Um...swans, I think?"

"Swans? Great. You get killer goats, and I get pretty birds."

"Have you ever met a swan? They're vicious. I think I'd rather take my chances with a goat."

Her eyes lit up. "Really? Now that would be cool. Everyone would think they were just pretty birds and then they attack. Stealth swans."

Matt laughed. "I guess so. Well, we can always see if we can find your—"

285

"Uh-uh. You're not distracting me. Back to the Valkyries. The point is that they've only rescued you once, and you've never actually tried to summon them. Now you need to." Reyna lifted her hand as he started to protest. "You feel stupid, falling for that zombie's trick, so you want to fix this on your own. But it was an understandable mistake. The guy's a thousand years old. Of course he's going to be smarter than you. More cunning, anyway. You're a kid. You're going to mess up. The Valkyries know that."

"But—"

"But nothing. If you don't call them, then we're all stuck in a carnival fun house, banging around in the darkness, looking for the exit. I don't like fun houses. You can get us out of here, Matt, so do it. Before Ray and I decide to take another vacation and wait for your call."

"Um, pretty sure your last vacation didn't go so well."

"Yeah, yeah. Just call the warrior women. The sooner this is over, the sooner we can all go home."

Is that what she thought? That Ragnarök was a mere obstacle to overcome, like a final exam or a prize bout? Get it done and go home? No. When he looked at her, he saw the traces of worry in her eyes and heard a tremor in her voice. She was afraid it wasn't nearly that simple, but she'd pretend it was. It was easier that way.

"I don't know how to call them," he said, then hurried

on, in case it sounded like an excuse. "I'll try. I just don't know if—"

"I don't need the disclaimer, Matt. If you fail, there's no one here to make fun of you. It's just me."

"And that's supposed to make me feel better?"

"I won't say a word if you can't do it, okay? You get a free pass this time. Now go."

Matt closed his eyes and focused all his power on calling Hildar, and when he did . . .

Nothing happened. He didn't really expect it would, not that easily, so he kept working on it, kept calling her, in his mind at first, and finally, when he did start to get frustrated, saying the words aloud.

"I know I made a mistake," he said. "I lost Mjölnir—"

"Stop," Reyna said.

Matt opened his eyes. She was sitting on the ground, hands on her knees, palms up, as if she'd been using some kind of magic, trying to help.

"Stop apologizing," she said. "They're warriors. They don't want to hear you grovel. Not unless you're an enemy fighter, almost dead on the battlefield, and then they'll only run you through with a spear to put you out of your misery."

"How do you know they'd do that?"

She shrugged. "That's what I'd do."

Matt resisted the urge to step back and remembered that

Freya was said to be the true leader of the Valkyries. That might explain a few things....

"Okay, let me try again."

It took a while. He started asking nicely, and Reyna made him do it more forcefully and they kept going like that—back and forth—until he was practically ordering the Valkyries to appear.

And they did.

Matt heard them first, roaring through the forest. Before he could even see where the noise came from, the riders were upon them, galloping into the clearing and stopping short, with Hildar at the lead.

"You called, son of Thor?" she said.

"Um, yeah. I...well, I kinda lost—"

Reyna elbowed him and he cleared his throat.

"Mjölnir was taken from me. I was tricked by Glaemir, king of the draugrs. I feel foolish for that, but I need to get it back."

"You do."

"Which means I need to know where to find Glaemir."

"You do."

Matt took a deep breath. "Could you please help me find Glaemir?"

"We will take you to him when you are ready."

"Oh, I'm ready right—"

"You are not. Who is this Glaemir?"

"King of the draugrs."

"Which means you will not find him alone with his prize, will you? He has a legion of draugrs at his disposal."

"A leg—legion?" Matt's heart sank.

"Yes. However, most are not in his court. He will summon them, of course, to protect his great treasure, but they cannot travel as he does, flying through the earth. It will take time. Until then, he has only two score warriors."

"Two—two score? *Forty?*"

"Which is why you need to prepare. Summon your goats. Have Odin summon the rest of his Berserkers. Ready yourself for a difficult battle. Even we will fight alongside you."

"Can I get my swans?" Reyna asked.

Hildar turned to her. "Freya does not have swans."

"Right," Matt said. "I got that wrong. Sorry. Freya is said to be the leader of the Valkyries, who are swan maidens."

"We are not swan maidens," Hildar said, straightening and lifting her sword.

"But you can turn into swans."

"No, we are not swans."

"Not even vicious killer swans?" Reyna asked.

"No."

"Okay, but I'm still your leader, right? Like Matt said. Freya—"

"No." Hildar hesitated. "You are not battle proven. You may lead us one day. But we are still not swans."

"So what *do* I get?" Reyna asked.

"You already have the cloak."

"How about this boar Matt mentioned?"

"Not yet, daughter of Freya." Hildar paused, as if thinking. "There is the chariot drawn by cats."

"Cats? Like leopards? Tigers?"

"Just cats. House cats, I believe you call them."

"Are they vicious?"

Hildar eyed her. "The daughter of Freya seems bloodthirsty."

"I'm supposed to be your leader, aren't I?"

"It was not a complaint," Hildar said. "Merely an observation. No, for now, I believe the cloak is enough."

"And what about us?" said a voice behind them. It was Baldwin, coming through with Fen, Laurie, and Ray, who must have heard the horses. "Not to be greedy, but what do we get?"

"You can't be killed," Reyna said. "I'll trade my falcon cloak for that."

"But you also have magic," Baldwin said to her.

"What about me?" Ray said. "What does Frey get?"

"His sister," Hildar said.

"What?" Ray said, his face screwing up.

"You have your sister's protection and, if she deems fit, the use of her items."

"Oh."

"There's also a ship," Matt said. "Frey's ship. Skíðblaðnir."

"Try saying that five times fast," Baldwin whispered.

"Enough," Hildar said. "We are not celebrating Jarlstag early this year. You will receive the gifts that you require *as* you require them, *if* you require them. If you are questioning why the children of Thor and Loki receive more, their battles are the pivotal ones, and I do not believe any of you would wish to take their places."

"That's fine," Reyna said. "We weren't complaining. Just asking."

"Nothing wrong with asking," Baldwin said.

Everyone nodded, seeming satisfied with the answer. Or almost everyone. Fen hadn't said a word, but he didn't seem pleased.

"Are you sure I can't have the boar?" Reyna said.

"I am sure. Ask again, and you will get the cats, whether you wish them or not. Now let us prepare for battle."

# TWENTY-ONE

# LAURIE

## "TRUTHS, GOATS, AND BERSERKERS"

I need to talk to you," Laurie whispered to Fen, pulling him away from the others. "In private."

She took his arm and started tugging him back toward the camp. It wasn't really like they needed to be there, and Fen wasn't even speaking. She led him back to the camp, away from the others. She wished they had even more space—and more time—to have this conversation, but what she had was the woods where there were Valkyries and the rest of the descendants *or* the campsite where Owen and the Berserkers were. Neither Owen nor his people would interrupt her, so she walked toward the camp.

Fen followed silently.

Laurie knew he was already angry, as well as torn up over the almost arrest, but she couldn't keep this to herself. After Owen had told her that she was Loki's champion, she hadn't known what to say or do. She knew that it made sense—as much as it didn't. She didn't want to be left out of the final fight, didn't want her friends to fight without her, but she wasn't sure she liked the idea of being a champion. The myths said that Loki led the monsters, and although Laurie hadn't believed that Fen would, there was even less chance that *she* would.

She thought about everything that had happened since they'd left Blackwell. She'd been the one who had a new power, and she'd been the one who was able to use the ghost arrows. Helen had given her the map. Things that she'd thought were proof that she was a part of the team now seemed to mean more.

"Fen?" She spoke quietly. "I think I need to tell you something."

He walked over to his sleeping bag, glaring at Owen, who watched the two of them with a strange, sad look. He was a good guy; she saw that, but she understood why Fen acted like this. For years, his life had been about protecting her. He'd been even worse now that they were facing a pending apocalypse. He was fine with Matt and Baldwin and maybe even with Ray and Reyna being around her.

Owen bothered him, though, partly because he thought Owen *liked* her. She'd thought that, too, but now she realized that Owen had been so nice because he knew she was a champion.

She was terrified, more so than before. She'd gotten so used to arguing for the right to fight at Fen's side that now that she *had* to fight, she was unsure of what to feel. She could do it. She *would*. It was scary, though, especially if Fen wasn't with her.

When she didn't speak, Fen grabbed his sleeping bag and said, "Sounds like we missed at least one of the monster battles." He shook his sleeping bag before beginning to roll it up. "I think I'd rather fight horses than zombies. Too many dead things and gross things and—"

"Fen," she interrupted.

He stared at her, sleeping bag rolled and in his arms.

"What if another one of our great-great-whatever's descendants was the champion?" Laurie tried to keep looking at him, hoping that she wasn't going to lose her best friend and almost-brother. "I mean, when the Norn pointed at the fair, what if Matt thought she meant you, but..."

"What if she meant you?" Fen finished when her words faded.

Laurie nodded.

"Then I'd have to stop trying to send you home, where you're safer," he said with a shrug.

For a moment, she stared at him and frowned. "That's it?"

"You weren't going to go home anyhow," Fen added. "You have the bow now, too. That helps keep you farther from the worst of the fights."

"*Fen!* Be serious for a minute."

Silently, Fen opened his bag and pushed the edge of the sleeping bag into it. The bag worked almost like a vacuum, pulling the whole thing inside without any pushing or shoving on his part. Once that was done, Fen swung the bag onto his back. "I'm not exactly the obvious pick for a hero anyhow. I don't know why anyone thought it could've been me. Seems pretty stupid if you think about it."

"*I* don't think so," she objected. She wrapped her arms around him in a hug. When he didn't say anything else, Laurie did as she always had: she said the thing that would make Fen feel better. "He might be wrong about me, you know."

Fen snorted and pulled back from her. "Don't be ridiculous."

"Hey!" She head-bumped his shoulder.

He bumped her back. "I'm staying for the fight, though. I might not be all god-representing now, but Uncle Stig would thrash me if you got hurt, even if it is because you were stopping the end of the world."

She swallowed, trying not to think about the battle and being in the middle of it and the risk of failing. She felt braver when he was at her side, and she'd been afraid that he'd leave. All she could say was, "Thank you. I don't think I can do it without you."

"Of course you could. You won't need to, but you *could*."

They both looked up then as Matt and Reyna came toward them. Matt was smiling in that we-can-totally-do-this way again, and Laurie felt relief wash over her. Having both boys acting so glum had been hard. Fen seemed fine with her news, and he wasn't leaving her side. Now that they'd talked, it was almost as if his lingering upset over the arrest fiasco and Owen's attitude had vanished. Similarly, now that there was a plan, Matt was himself again.

"Come over here," Matt called as he went toward the table, where Owen was still sitting like one of the silent statues in Hel.

As they started over, Fen said quietly to her, "I still don't like Owen, and you don't need to be walking off alone with him. Uncle Stig wouldn't be pleased about *that*, either."

Laurie felt her cheeks burn. "Fen!"

"Seriously, that's three times now you've talked to him alone. Please don't do it again."

Mutely, she nodded. Now that she finally knew the secret Owen had been trying to get her to figure out on her own, there wasn't any reason for him to want to be alone with her.

"Okay, so Hildar said that Glaemir only has some of his people with him, forty or so, and I already told the . . . goats to meet us there." Matt paused sort of awkwardly. "Hildar gave me directions that the goats could follow, so they're on the move."

"The goats are on the move," Baldwin said in a low voice before cracking up.

The twins smiled at him. Fen rolled his eyes, but like everything Baldwin did, Fen thought it was fine. Even Owen's lips curled in a small grin.

"Owen, do you have more Berserkers or just these?" Matt asked.

For a moment Owen looked tense, but then he merely said, "I already had Vance summon the rest of the Berserkers on the way back from Evan's Plunge. They will meet us there. This was the next step."

"So do we win?" Fen asked.

The expression on Owen's face made more sense then as the frown that went with that tension appeared. "I am part of the planning now, Fen. Once I am involved, I can't see the possible futures. That's why I stayed away: so I could help more."

No one replied to that little tidbit for several seconds, and then Laurie clarified, "So you wanted to be with us, but you could help more by being away?"

Owen nodded. "And I had to wait because I was afraid I couldn't keep a secret from you."

The rest of the group looked from Laurie to Owen, and

she felt her face burn in awkward embarrassment: she didn't want to tell them about Fen, not now, not after he'd only just heard it himself. It seemed unfair somehow for him to have his change of role revealed already.

"What Owen is trying to get at and Laurie isn't saying is that *she's* the Champion of Loki, not me." Fen met her gaze as he said the words, and she hated that he must be feeling so horrible—and was grateful that he cared enough about her and about stopping Ragnarök that he was telling the others.

Laurie waited to see if anyone would say anything cruel, realizing that her hand was balled into a fist in anticipation. Matt met her gaze, and then she saw his eyes drop to her fist. He gave her and Fen a sympathetic smile.

"Huh," Reyna said. "Didn't see that coming."

"You're staying, right, Fen? I mean, you're not going to skip the big fight now, are you?" Baldwin asked.

Fen gave Baldwin a well-duh look. "All the more reason to protect my cousin. She's the champion, so she's in even more danger, *and* it's even more important nothing happens to her. I'll still be her bodyguard." He glanced at Owen and smiled. Then he looked at Matt and redirected the conversation to the current battle. "So we have goats, Berserkers, and...then what, Thorsen?"

"The Valkyries will take us there—and stay." Matt looked around at the assembled crowd of descendants and said, "Then we fight, and we win."

Baldwin nodded. "Straightforward planning. I like that about you, Matt."

The twins exchanged a nervous look, and Laurie told them, "We can do this. We've been to Hel and back. River of zombies. Giants. This is just a few draugrs, right?"

"Forty," Baldwin interjected. "That's what Matt said."

Before Laurie could try to comfort the twins, Reyna smiled. "Unfair odds for them, but that's what they get for stealing from Thor's champion."

Laurie looked around at the assembled group. They were finally all together, all of the descendants, and they were about to ride into battle with Valkyries, Berserkers, and... goats. It was pretty epic.

In a few short moments, the kids all joined various Valkyries and set off to the lair of Glaemir. Those with bags from Helen stowed their things in saddlebags. Matt had his shield in hand, and Laurie had her bow. Reyna had a cloak of feathers, which she fastened around her shoulders just before Hildar pulled her up onto her steed. The sight of the Goth girl with her feathered cloak sitting astride the massive horse made Laurie think of superheroes in the comics she used to read. *We* are *heroes!* She smiled as she looked over the rest of their fighting force. They might be kids, but they looked a lot like warriors right now.

That confidence stayed with her as the Valkyries carried them toward the draugrs. The ride was still exhilarating, but this time it also seemed less unusual. Laurie's confidence remained steady as they descended into a dark, damp tunnel that seemed to echo loudly. Every strike of hoof on stone seemed to pound like a drumbeat, and her heart wanted to beat in time with it.

It wasn't until the tunnel began to glow with a green light that her confidence faded some. The green glow emanated from slick swaths of some sort of fungus that clung to the damp walls. It was as if some oversized creature had sneezed repeatedly on the stone and dirt, and the snot still shivered there. The air grew thicker as the tunnel started to level out again, and Laurie didn't want to inhale deeply for fear of sucking in the rot.

As the stench grew more and more stomach-turning, she knew that they were almost there. Somewhere nearby, at least forty-one walking, decaying corpses waited. No one spoke. The only sounds were the steady inhalation and exhalation of the others and the hoofbeats on the ground.

Finally, they turned a corner and found themselves in a wide-open space. It looked like an underground arena. Stalactites and stalagmites speared down from the ceiling far overhead and up from the floor. Amidst these were what looked like the ruins of an ancient city. Walls and roofs, doorways and windows, they stretched out around the center space. From within those windows, draugrs looked out at them, and from beyond those doorways, still more draugrs walked.

"You're earlier than I expected," Glaemir said.

They all turned toward his voice. The draugr king had a throne built out of sarcophagi, and to either side, he had a guard that looked as rotten as he did. Their smiles showed missing teeth, and Laurie wondered briefly if those teeth had vanished before or after death. Vikings hadn't had the best dental care.

"Return Mjölnir to me," Matt said. He had to be as unsettled as Laurie was, but his voice sounded steady.

"No." Glaemir shook his head slowly. He had the hammer next to him on his throne, and his hand fell onto it as if it were an animal he'd pet. "You gave it away, boy, and coming here with a few children and girls on their ponies won't convince me to give it to you."

All around her, Laurie heard the Valkyries' responses to the draugr's jab. Most of them weren't in English, but they were harsh enough in tone that she suspected they were words she probably shouldn't repeat.

"Thorsen, where are the goats and Owen's clowns?" Fen asked in a low voice.

"The *Berserkers* will be here in a few minutes. The ravens went to retrieve them." Owen finally sounded exasperated, and Laurie felt bad for him. Now that Fen knew he could upset Owen, he'd be even worse.

"Son of Thor? Out of courtesy, we await your word," Hildar said.

"Are you certain you won't give it back?" Matt asked Glaemir.

The draugr's hand tightened around Mjölnir's handle.

"Then we'll take it," Matt said.

Immediately, the Valkyries surged toward the draugrs that seemed to pour from the ruins around them. Some stayed on their steeds; others leaped from the animals and charged. The kids dropped from the horses while the Valkyries spread out and attacked. Laurie lifted her bow and began firing. The twins had linked hands and were intoning. Baldwin let out a whoop, and Fen shifted into a wolf. As the fight started in earnest, Glaemir himself stayed on his throne, holding on to the hammer.

It wasn't the same as defending themselves against the monsters, which was the way most fights had gone. This was the first time they were going into a full assault on the enemy, and Laurie was energized by it.

The difficulty, of course, was that Matt had to reach the king, and with the way the battlefield was looking, by the time he did, he'd be exhausted from fighting. Glaemir, however, would be just fine. He sat on his throne and watched them with a smile.

Fen, in wolf shape, was by her side. He looked up at her and flashed teeth. Then he looked back at the king. She wasn't sure what *words* he was thinking, but she knew him well enough to expect that he had the same general thought she'd just had: get Glaemir.

She didn't have a clear shot at him, so they needed to get closer. Together, Fen and Laurie started toward Matt.

The fight had only just begun when Owen's two ravens swooped into the cavern, and in a blink the rest of the Berserkers came tumbling and leaping into the fray. Behind them was a veritable sea of fur and horns. Some of the draugrs seemed to hesitate when goats charged them, but their pause was brief. In a strange way, the goats seemed to be the perfect weapon against the draugrs: both were essentially deathless. The herd of goats all had the same power of Tanngrisnir and Tanngnjóstr to revive after death, and the draugrs could reattach their body parts when injured. It was a pretty even match.

The Berserkers swarmed into the middle of the fur and decaying flesh. They leaped and launched themselves, using even the bodies of the fighters on both sides as springboards. Stalactites were as good as horizontal bars to such gymnasts. It was utter chaos, even more so than the battle between the Berserkers and the Raiders. The Raiders, for all their temper and attitude, simply weren't as overwhelming as towering, rotting draugrs.

"Matt! Can you use your Hammer on Glaemir from back here?" Laurie called across the fight as she and Fen worked to get to his side.

His answer was lost under a roar as a draugr leaped toward them, and then they were separated from him in a growing tide of fighters. Fen stayed by her side, and every so often she saw Baldwin or the twins, but the chaos had divided them into small groups.

*Loki's champion*, she reminded herself. *I am Loki's champion*. She wouldn't fail her ancestor or the other descendants. She couldn't even consider it. She tried to ignore the growls, yells, bleats, and grunts. She had to do her part.

*One arrow at a time.*

# TWENTY-TWO

## MATT

### "VINGTHOR"

Battle. It's what Vikings were best known for, as if they spent their lives trolling the coastlines, shaking their swords, waiting for the chance to fight something. Steal something. Kill something.

Not exactly true. They were also farmers and explorers, and they spent more time in the villages than off raiding, but yes, Matt would admit that Vikings liked to fight. Not just one-on-one battles, either. They liked *this*.

He looked out over the battlefield. It was a seething mass of Berserkers and Valkyries and draugrs and battle-goats and the descendants of the North. A grand spectacle to stir the blood of any Viking. If he'd seen it in a movie, he'd have been glued to the screen, heart pounding, adrenaline racing. For a Blackwell kid, this was his version of a battle with pirates, ninjas, and zombies. It shouldn't get any better than that.

Except...well, this wasn't a scene in a movie. A week ago, he'd have admitted that a real fight would be terrifying. Now it wasn't so much the terror that made him wish it *was* a movie—it was the chaos.

It didn't matter if it was Berserkers and Valkyries and goats versus draugrs. It might have been redheads versus blondes for all it mattered from where he stood. It was chaos, utter chaos, with hooves flying and draugr body parts flying and Berserkers flipping overhead and dirt—lots of dirt, whirling up everywhere, from the horses and the fighters, dirt in his eyes and his mouth. He couldn't see much of anything after a while, just shapes whizzing past, sometimes overhead, sometimes underfoot, as he stumbled over the fallen. They smacked into him, too, jostling and grunting and knocking him off-balance, and he spun, shield up, Hammer at the ready, but they hadn't noticed him, just bumped into him and disappeared back into the fray.

Then there was the smell. Draugr, mostly. The stink of rot was so bad, it was practically a weapon itself. Matt stumbled over one of the younger Berserkers, who was retching from it, and Matt told him to go get some air. The kid's eyes lowered with shame, but his skin was nearly green with nausea. Yet it was another smell that turned Matt's stomach. The lighter scent, one he only caught now and again as he moved through the battlefield. Blood. As faint as it was, it was the truest reminder that this wasn't a movie scene, wasn't a game. It was real, and he was in the middle of it.

Yet it wasn't just him in the middle of it, and that was even scarier. There were the others, too, the ones he was supposed to be protecting—Fen and Laurie, Baldwin and the twins. While he knew he should be heading for Glaemir, he kept looking for them, to make sure they were okay, to see if they needed help. Looking and listening. But listening was nearly as futile as looking. The cacophony was enough to make his ears ring. Now and then he'd catch a distinctive noise—the snort of a horse, the battle cry of a Valkyrie, the clash of swords, the bleat of a goat—but mostly, it was just noise. Deafening noise.

This was a battlefield. A true battlefield. A true battle. And, frankly, Matt wanted nothing to do with it.

He suspected other Thorsens wouldn't feel the same. They'd be right in the thick of it, howling with the other warriors, their spirits soaring with long-dormant battle fever. Battle rage. Battle hunger. To them, it would be like a championship football game, just as chaotic and just as loud, just as smelly, and maybe just as bloody. They thrived on this. His brothers lived for it.

And Matt? No. He looked around and he remembered

why he never wanted to play football. That chaos didn't energize him like it did his brothers. Yet nor did he want to curl up in a ball, head down, hands over his ears. He was still a Viking.

He saw the battlefield, and he felt the stirring of his ancestors, but that stirring didn't make him want to leap into the fray. He wanted his own battle. Like in the boxing ring. One-on-one. Which was perfect, because that was exactly what he had to do. Fight one guy...who just happened to be king of the draugrs and, currently, lost in the middle of this seething battlefield.

When this all started, he'd known exactly where Glaemir was. He still did, hypothetically. In the middle. But he'd long since lost sight of him and was forced to rely on his necklace to lead him to Mjölnir. Just follow the vibrating amulet. Which would be awesome...if the entire earth weren't vibrating under his feet. So he had to walk with one hand holding his shield, the other clutching the amulet, gauging its vibrations and following them like a bat using echolocation.

No one left a path open for him. No one tried to stop him, either. They seemed too caught up in their own fights to notice—or care about—this red-haired kid who they'd smacked into.

Matt was so intent on his goal that he barely registered a draugr in his path. Just another zombie thrown out from the

fray. Except it didn't leap back in. It just stood there. Blocking his route.

Matt looked up. He had to. The guy was six feet tall—huge for a Viking. From the nose down, he was little more than a skeleton draped in ragged leather, which made the top half of his head seem like a weird skin-and-flesh cap rather than part of his head, the illusion even stronger because he wasn't wearing a helmet. Tangled dark hair fell from that "skull cap" to his shoulders. Dark eyes peered at Matt, one filmed over, as if blind. Under his nose, his head was a grinning skull with a surprising number of teeth intact. Those teeth clacked as he opened his mouth, and Matt was sure that clacking was all he'd hear—how could you talk without a tongue...or a throat?

But somehow, this draugr could, though the words were guttural and hoarse, even harder to understand than Glaemir's speech.

"So you are the one who thinks he is the great god Thor?" the draugr said.

"Not exactly," Matt said, keeping his voice calm as he surveyed the situation, trying to see an easy way out. He needed to save his energy for Glaemir. "'Living embodiment' is the phrase, which means I'm kinda Thor and I'm kinda not. It's confusing."

"Do you mock me, boy?"

"No, I'm just correcting you. But if you're asking if I *am* the living embodiment, the answer is yes. Now, if you'll excuse me, I need to get my hammer."

"*Your* hammer?" The draugr seemed to spit, which was really hard to pull off without saliva. Or lips. "You are not this Champion of Thor."

"Yes, I am. I can prove it, too."

The draugr snorted in derision.

"I can. Just help me clear a path to Glaemir and take Mjölnir. I'll show you that I can wield it. That should settle the matter."

The draugr let out a grating laugh. Then he charged.

Trolls were so much easier to trick.

Matt slammed his shield up into the draugr's face, which made him stagger back, one eye bulging like it might have lost its moorings. It also might have ticked him off. The draugr roared and inflated to double his size. He charged again. Matt tried to throw his Hammer, but it fizzled. He did manage to get the shield up in time, but that had worked better when the draugr wasn't twelve feet tall. The shield only hit the zombie's thigh. The draugr swung one massive arm. It connected with Matt's shoulder and knocked him onto his butt, making him skid backward across the ground.

As Matt scrambled up, he could see the draugr bearing down, his hand reaching out to grab Matt, and he knew he wouldn't make it onto his feet in time. Then an arrow hit the draugr's leather chest-plate. It didn't do any damage, of course, but the zombie stopped and looked down at it. That's when a wolf lunged from the crowded battlefield and clamped down on the draugr's leg. As Matt sprang up, Laurie stepped from the fray. Still biting the draugr's leg, Fen gave her a look, as if to say *About time.*

"Hey, my arrow beat you," she said. "Technically, I was here first."

The draugr turned on her and roared and when it did, it seemed to get even bigger. Then it charged. Matt saw this thing—a fifteen-foot-tall zombie warrior, not even caring that a wolf was still gnawing its femur, barreling after Laurie, who was armed only with a bow—and he found the rage he needed to launch the Hammer. Launch it with a *crash* and a *bang* and an explosion of force clear into the battlefield. It also knocked down Laurie and sent wolf-Fen flying. They were ready for it, though, and bounced back while the draugr was still lying there, shaking its head as if to say *What just happened?*

"You still doubt I'm Thor's champion?" Matt said, advancing on the draugr, which had deflated when it hit the ground. "I—"

The draugr leaped up, surprisingly agile for a leather-bound skeleton. "The true champion would never have let Mjölnir slip from his grasp. You are an impostor, and I will put you in the earth, where you belong."

It was a great speech. The draugr even followed it up with

a roar, ready to reinflate. Except...well, the problem with battlefield speeches? If you're talking, you aren't fighting.

So when the draugr began to roar, he got it from all sides. An arrow in the back of the head. A wolf clamping down on his arm bone. And Matt running full speed and slamming him in the face with the shield. This time, it was like hitting him with a shield made of solid brick. There was a horrible cracking noise. Then a *rip* and a *snap* as the draugr fell backward, and Fen ended up with a detached zombie arm in his mouth.

The draugr hit the ground flat on his back. His face *looked* like it had been hit with a brick shield—the bone cracked, nose lying flat, a couple of teeth dangling loose. Still, he struggled up and ran at Fen, snatching his arm back and magically reattaching it. Then he went after Matt.

The fight continued. Laurie pelted the draugr with arrows. Fen chomped down on whatever bone he could reach. Matt slammed the draugr with both shield and Hammer. He called on Tanngrisnir and Tanngnjóstr, and they joined in, butting the draugr mercilessly. Yet, like a horror-movie zombie, the draugr just kept coming. That's when Matt realized he was in trouble. He was wasting his strength and his powers on one insignificant draugr while the real battle waited.

Angry and frustrated, Matt felt the rage build inside of him, amulet burning hot.

"Get out of my way!" he shouted finally, as he faced off

with the draugr, arrows sticking from its armor like porcupine quills, Fen hanging off its arm.

The draugr laughed. "The little boy grows tired? I am a warrior, fool; I will not step aside for—"

"Thor!" Matt roared. "You will step aside for Thor."

He didn't even need to launch the Hammer. Like in the cabin, it launched itself, a massive ball of blue light hurtling from his body. Fen saw it coming and let go, twisting out of the way. The draugr stood there, jawbone hanging. The ball hit him in the breastplate and—

And shattered him like a baseball hitting a vase. He broke into a hundred bones, flying like shrapnel, everyone ducking to avoid the pieces. Then...

Quiet. All around them, the battle stopped. Berserkers, Valkyries, and draugrs alike turned and stared at the arrow-ridden armor lying on the battlefield.

Matt strode forward, bellowing, "I am the Champion of Thor. I come for Mjölnir. Stop hiding behind your army, Glaemir. Face me!"

The silence rippled outward, the fighting stopping even beyond those who could see what had happened, even beyond those who could hear Matt's words. A hush fell and the crowd parted, and at the end of it, he could see Glaemir, rising from his throne, Mjölnir now at his feet.

"You want Mjölnir?" the draugr king said. "Come and take her."

Matt continued walking, aware of the crowd on either side of the path, in case someone jumped him, all the while not taking his gaze from the king. Fen and Laurie helped, walking on either side of him, as did Tanngrisnir and Tanngnjóstr.

"Your friends and your pets stay there," Glaemir said as Matt approached the throne.

"And your guards?" Matt said.

Glaemir waved the two back. "You will give me your word that your side will not interfere, and I will vouch for my warriors. This will be between us. A fight for Mjölnir."

"You have my word."

Matt caught Fen's eye. Fen tilted his head discreetly, asking if he should jump in when he could, but Matt shook his head. If he broke his word, the draugrs would break theirs. This was the way it should be. The way he understood. Warrior versus warrior.

He climbed the steps onto the massive raised stone slab that held the king and his throne. He didn't need to defeat Glaemir. Just get to Mjölnir, less than ten feet away, the handle sticking up, as if waiting for him. Then keep the draugr king at bay long enough for the Valkyries to snatch him up. Easy.

Glaemir reached down and, for a heart-stopping second, Matt thought he was reaching for Mjölnir, that he'd somehow learned to wield it. But no, his hand went past the hammer and under his throne to pull out—

A sword. It was four feet long and nearly four inches

wide. The hilt looked a thousand years old, dull and tarnished, the carvings nearly worn smooth from use. Yet the blade? The blade was clean and polished and sharp.

Matt's heart thudded. Until now, the draugrs had fought mostly unarmed, a few wielding clubs and cudgels, but nothing with a blade. A blade...

He swallowed.

A blade made this a very different kind of fight.

"I don't have a weapon," Matt said.

"Yes, you do," Glaemir's half face contorted in a terrible smile. "It's right here. Come and get it."

He brandished his sword, smile growing to a skull-head grin.

"Unless you lie," Glaemir said. "Unless you truly are an impostor."

"You know I'm not. I—"

"Come and get it, then, Atli Thor." *Thor the Terrible*, said with a contemptuous twist of what remained of his lips.

"I have no weapon," Matt said again.

"You have a shield."

"And you are invulnerable. You don't need a shield."

"You have your amulet. Are you going to continue whining like a child? Or do you intend to fight me?"

Matt charged. Glaemir smiled and swung back his blade, and Matt heard Laurie shout, "No!" but at the last second, he flung up his shield and the sword clanged off it, as if it had turned to metal. The plan had been to block the blow and grab the hammer. Except the hammer wasn't there. When he grabbed for it, the stone slab beneath it shattered, as if hit from below, and Mjölnir dropped out of reach.

Matt heard Laurie shout again and twisted just as Glaemir swung the sword for another blow. He barely blocked it this time, the impact slamming through his arm with a jolt of pain. He could hear Laurie shouting suggestions, which would be great if Fen's helpful growls weren't drowning her out.

Matt scrambled to the side before Glaemir swung again. He leaped up and blocked the next blow, then raced out of Glaemir's reach and hit him with a Hammer strike. It was decent enough. A week ago, he'd have considered it a success. But he was spoiled now, after the megablows in the cabin and here on the battlefield, and it seemed like lobbing a basketball when he expected a cannonball.

The Hammer strike hit Glaemir. The draugr king stumbled back. It was no more than a stumble, though, not even enough time for Matt to get two steps closer to Mjölnir, now on the edge of the broken stone slab under their feet.

The fight continued. Slash. Dodge. Hammer blow. Recover. Hack. Block. Repeat. The whole time Matt's focus stayed fixed on Mjölnir, even when he pretended otherwise.

Glaemir wasn't stupid, though. He knew that's where Matt was heading and kept cutting him off and driving him back.

Finally, Matt realized he had to change tactics. He wasn't getting that hammer without inflicting some serious damage on the zombie king. So he concentrated on the Hammer that he *did* have—his amulet. He managed to get in some serious blows, too. Blasts that nearly knocked Mjölnir off the slab with their force. The same blows would have exploded a lesser draugr. Or one with less flesh on his bones. The most Matt managed was to knock small, nonessential parts off Glaemir. An ear. A tooth. A few bony fingers. It wasn't enough.

The trick, as Matt realized midway through a slash-dodge sequence, was to aim the Hammer blasts somewhere other than Glaemir's chest. He blocked a sword thrust and danced backward, nearly to the other side of the slab, purposefully balancing on the edge. Glaemir grinned as if Matt didn't know where he stood. The draugr barreled toward him, sword out, pointed straight at the shield, his only goal to knock Matt back a step and onto the stone below.

But Matt was ready. He fired a Hammer blast straight at Glaemir's left knee—bare bone under his ragged trousers. It was a good blast, too, complete with a crash and flash that sent the nearest bystanders reeling. The hurtling ball of light hit its target dead-on...and half of Glaemir's left leg shot across the slab, leaving the rest of him standing there. For a split second, he didn't seem to realize what had happened. Then he fell.

Matt raced across the slab, skirting the draugr king as Glaemir bellowed for his guards to find the rest of his leg. Matt was five feet from Mjölnir. Four. Three. He heard Glaemir roar and dropped into a slide, stomach hitting the stone slab, skidding over it as it sliced through his shirt, into his skin, the sudden pain excruciating, but he didn't care. Mjölnir was there, right there—

The slab edge crumbled, and the hammer dropped. Matt could see it, just a few feet below, the handle still up. He could push off the edge and—

"Matt!"

He didn't need Laurie's warning. He sensed Glaemir and flipped to see the draugr king's sword coming straight at him while Matt's shield twisted awkwardly beneath him, useless.

He fired a Hammer blast instead. It knocked Glaemir back, just enough for the sword to sing over Matt's head. Matt leaped to his feet, ready to scramble down off the slab, but Glaemir slashed again, this time cutting through Matt's shirt, just missing his skin. Matt yanked his shield up. Below, he could see Mjölnir, lying there on the ground. . . .

No, wait! It *wasn't* just lying there. It was moving. Rocking. Vibrating. Matt reached out his hand, trying not to be obvious. Mjölnir rocked harder.

He focused on calling the hammer to him. Which would

be a whole lot easier if he wasn't also focused on not getting skewered, stabbed, or sliced. He dodged a sword thrust and blocked another. The whole time, Mjölnir rocked but never so much as lifted an inch from the ground.

"You will not get Mjölnir, boy," Glaemir said. "It is not yours."

*Yes, it is. I pulled it from the rock. I threw it and it returned to my hand. It's mine.*

*Now return to me, Mjölnir!*

It rocked once. Only once. Glaemir noticed and laughed.

"As I said, it is not yours, impostor."

"You know I'm not—"

Glaemir swung, cutting him short. Nearly cutting his hair short, too. Matt dodged, then blocked, then sidestepped.

*He knows I'm Thor's champion. He knows I freed Mjölnir. He's lying. For some reason, he's lying.*

Matt realized that, and fresh rage shot through him. He'd proven himself. He had. He absolutely had, and if there was any doubt—

No, there was no doubt.

"I am Thor!" he roared as he continued blocking Glaemir. "*Asa-Thor. Atli Thor. Oku-Thor.* I am all of those. I am *Vingthor.* Battle Thor. Mjölnir! Return to me!"

The hammer shot up. It hit his hand so hard his arm whipped back with the force. But his fingers instinctively wrapped around the handle. He gripped it, and he heaved it, swinging it straight at Glaemir. It hit the draugr in the shoulder, his arm bones exploding. Matt didn't wait to see if that was enough. He hit him again, the hammer like a stone mallet, splintering bone under dried flesh. The second blow knocked Glaemir onto his back. Matt hit him again, in the other hand, sending Glaemir's sword whipping through the air. Then he stood over the draugr king, Mjölnir raised over Glaemir's head.

"I am Thor!" Matt shouted, and he lifted his head, looking out at the crowd, braced for the first sign of attack from the draugr's warriors.

But they weren't attacking. They were bending, down on one knee, heads lowered.

"*Vingthor!*" one shouted.

Another took up the cry, and it echoed across the ruins and through the field of dead warriors.

*Vingthor.*

Battle Thor.

# TWENTY-THREE

# FEN

## "DEATH STEPS IN"

Fen shed his *wulfenkind* form and stood next to his cousin as the draugrs all bowed to Matt and cheered. He wasn't going to get all touchy-feely and say anything aloud, but it was pretty amazing. The fighting had all stopped, like a wave of stillness swept over the crowd, and Thorsen stood poised over the fallen leader of the draugrs.

"We won," Laurie said. "He has Mjölnir."

Even as the room had come to an almost reverent stillness, Baldwin was still irrepressibly bouncy. He came over to stand beside Fen. "This god-representative thing is the most epic thing ever. We've battled dead guys and nasty wolves."

Fen raised his brows as he looked at Baldwin. "Wolf here."

Baldwin made a dismissive gesture with his hand. "Not the nasty sort, though. Doesn't count."

Fen had to smile. He was really glad Baldwin was alive again.

Matt turned and looked pointedly at them and then at the twins. He tilted his head in a beckoning gesture.

"Thorsen wants us." Fen lifted his arm in a sweeping arc, gesturing the others forward, and then shot a guilty glance at Laurie. "Sorry. Used to being the second-in-command, but I guess that's you now."

Laurie rolled her eyes. "Don't be stupid. We're a *team*."

As the others joined them, they all made their way up to where Matt had overcome Glaemir. Once the descendants were at his side, Matt looked at the silent dead, who were bowing to him. "I am not an impostor; neither are they. These are Loki's descendants." He looked at Fen and Laurie.

The cousins exchanged a confused look but then lifted their heads and stared out at the draugrs, who now watched them. Matt obviously had a reason for what he was doing. They trusted him enough to go along with it.

"And Frey and Freya's."

The twins stood with linked hands, ready to use their magic if things got violent again.

"And Balder's."

Baldwin gave a cheery wave. "Hi! It was great fighting you."

"And Odin's. He has the god's Berserkers."

Owen, who was already surrounded by several of the Berserkers and once more had the two ravens perched on his shoulders, lifted his head and looked out at the subdued draugrs with his one good eye.

"The impostor here is Glaemir." Matt glared down at the draugr. "He's misled you, made you fight *against* the truth. He convinced you that I wasn't really the rightful descendant of Thor, even though he knew I was."

The draugrs started grumbling, words of anger mingled with shock.

Glaemir said nothing.

"You've stayed here, defending a power-hungry king instead of going to the next world." Matt held Mjölnir steady in his hand, but Fen saw his hand tighten like he wanted to lift it. He was a good guy, not likely to beat even an enemy in anger, but he was also all about justice, and as he talked, Fen understood that what Glaemir had done was even worse than trying to steal Mjölnir.

"He's lucky Aunt Helen isn't here," Fen muttered. "Messing with the dead that should be hers. He'd get what for."

"I wish she *were* here, then," Laurie said just as quietly.

"Me, too." Fen felt sad for the decaying fighters. Only a few moments ago they'd been the enemy, but now that he knew the truth, he realized that they were victims. If *he* had a weapon like Matt's, he might not be so good about resisting the urge to lower it on Glaemir's head.

"If I had been invited by my dear family sooner, I would've dealt with Glaemir by now," said a voice behind them.

"Aunt Helen!" Laurie exclaimed.

"Niece." The ruler of Hel wore another living dress, this one covered by death's-head moths. Aside from the tiny little skull shape on the backs of the moths, they weren't particularly odd. Helen's habit of dressing in living things, however, was a bit creepy.

"Speak of the devil," Fen murmured.

Helen laughed and shook her finger at him. "Now, now, Nephew. I'm standing here with the godlings. Would I do that if I were a devil?"

"Hey, Helen," Baldwin said.

She turned her smile on him. "Are you adjusted to living again?"

"Oh, yeah. Epic battles. Camping." Baldwin grinned and nodded. "It's all good."

The twins and Owen remained silent, but when Helen's gaze fell on Reyna and lingered there, Reyna took a small step back. Several of the Valkyries strode through the room to stand near the girl protectively.

Helen laughed. "I was merely examining her."

"She will ride with us," Hildar said. "She will never be yours."

Fen, like a lot of boys in Blackwell, thought warrior girls were cool, so he knew that Freya rode with the Valkyries. Between them, they took the battle-dead. Helen took the rest. What he hadn't realized was that it meant that Helen and the Valkyries weren't very fond of each other. He wondered briefly if some of his instinctive dislike for Reyna was because he was related to Helen. It didn't really matter. Reyna was a disappointment in terms of the warrior girls he'd imagined, and the Valkyries were a bit *intense*.

"I have no need of her sort," Helen said regally. "Or yours."

Then the ruler of Hel waved a hand dismissively at the Valkyries and stepped forward, positioning herself in front of the kids but still with them. Even here among the dead, the goats, and the gods' descendants, she stood out as something remarkable. Her plastic-like skin looked even less real here in the odd greenish light of the cavern, and her beetle-colored eyes shimmered as the light emphasized their iridescence. She was the actual daughter of a god, a ruler in her own dimension, and as both of those, she was someone to fear—and she was about to let them know it.

"This world is not your place. The dead do not belong in Midgard," Helen told the draugrs in a voice that was not unkind. "You will be sorted. Those of you meant for Valhalla can go with *them*." She gestured toward Hildar. "The rest will come with me to Hel."

The Valkyries appeared to be in agreement with Helen, although they still watched her warily.

"What if we don't want to leave Midgard?" one of the draugrs asked.

"You'd rather stay here rotting?"

There was a grumbling among them at Helen's words. Finally, the same draugr said, "What if the gods need us?"

"We're not gods," Matt interjected.

Helen sent him an amused look. "*If* the godlings need you, they can summon you from Hel . . . at least those of you who opt to come with me. My niece and nephew can call out to me—as you've just seen." She held out her hands as if they were children to be summoned to her side. "I pay attention to my family. It is what my father would want. These two are my family."

Laurie glanced at Fen, her expression clearly asking for his opinion on approaching Helen. He shrugged. He was pretty sure there was something more going on here, that Helen had an angle he couldn't quite see. She was, of course, one of Loki's children. That meant she probably had an angle on *most* things. Fen understood that; he usually had an angle, too.

After a deep breath, Laurie took one step forward and slid her hand into Helen's. Fen muttered a word that elicited a scowl from his cousin and a quirk of a grin from Baldwin, but then he stepped forward and stood on the other side of Helen. He didn't take her hand. That was just strange and girly, but he stood at her side. "We, uhhh, can reach her like she said," he told the draugrs. "If we need help, we could call her."

"But you have earned your rest," Laurie added.

Matt, Reyna, and Ray had moved closer to the Valkyries when Fen and Laurie stepped up beside Helen. Baldwin bounced in place between the two small groups, lost in whatever it was that he thought about in his quiet moments. None of them could make the choices for the draugrs. They merely waited.

After a moment of silent contemplation, a few of the decaying warriors moved over to stand with the Valkyries or in front of Helen. Once they'd done so, the rest followed. It was odd how they knew which woman to approach. A couple tried to go to the Valkyries, but it took only a quelling look from Helen or Hildar before they turned and went to their rightful groups.

"You've earned some rest, too," Helen told Laurie and Fen. "Go on, then."

"Thanks for helping or whatever," Fen said, feeling more awkward with her now than when they were in the land of the dead. In Hel, she was an obstacle, someone who stood in the way. Now she was a relative who was being nice. Plus, she was a god of a sort. It was intimidating.

"Father Loki would like you, Fenrir." Helen patted his head, and then turned away.

Laurie shivered at that pronouncement, and Fen shot her a look of agreement. He wasn't so sure that being liked by Loki was a *good* thing. Laurie obviously agreed.

Once everyone returned to camp, it felt like a party of sorts—one that Fen didn't want to attend. He was happy for everyone. They were one step closer to being ready for the big fight, possibly *several* steps closer. The group was all at the camp together; they had the shield, the hammer, and even Reyna's cloak. He knew he should be happy.

He also knew he couldn't stay around them just now. He took off into the woods. Fen wasn't sulking or hiding. He just had an itch under his skin, and sitting around with the others wasn't working for him. He felt good, proud of Laurie and of Matt, and yeah, he felt a little bummed that *he* wasn't the one to stand in for Loki. It really wasn't a huge surprise, though: he was a bit of a screwup, and if the Norns were going to pick one of Loki's descendants to be a hero, Laurie was the very best choice.

*It still stings.*

He walked a few more minutes in silence and was just debating shifting so he could go for a good run when he heard a growl. *Seriously?* Fen was starting to think that there would never be time to just rest again until they survived Ragnarök—assuming they *did* survive.

When Fen turned, he saw an unpleasantly familiar wolf watching him. The big gray wolf parted his teeth in a menacing smile of sorts. Fen sighed. This wasn't what he needed... oh, *ever*.

"Skull."

The wolf padded closer. Seeing this cousin in *either* form was never a good thing. They hadn't ever been friends, and that had only gotten worse when Skull started trying to force Fen to do things to help him in his lame mission to end the world.

"I expected to see your ugly face when the Raiders attacked us, since you've been up in the thick of their craziness," Fen said.

Skull shook off his fur and stood on two feet. "I had other things to do."

His scarred arms had a few fresh bruises. One particularly ugly yellowed bruise vanished partly under his torn shirt, but that was standard for any leader of a Raider pack.

Fen glared at him. "And you're working for Mayor Thorsen? How does that even make sense? I thought you hated them."

"You seem to be working for a Thorsen, too. At least I'm working for the *right* one." Skull took a step toward Fen, as if he could intimidate him with his size. "I told you, Fenrir: the final battle is coming. We can take this world for ourselves."

"Would everyone *stop* calling me that! My name is *Fen*. Three simple letters." Fen ground his teeth.

"Fenrir is who you *are*," Skull objected. "You've been confused. You have to see by now, though. You should be with the *wulfenkind*, not them." Skull gestured vaguely to the woods behind Fen as if the other descendants were there.

"Whatever, meathead," Fen scoffed. "I *like* the world, and I'm not going to help you try to destroy it."

Provoking Skull probably wasn't the brightest idea, but over the last few days, Fen had faced a cave bear, dead warriors, the police, and buffalo. Skull didn't seem as frightening anymore. Fen might not be the one who would fight in Loki's place, but he had faced monsters straight from myth and had an aunt who ruled Hel, and Skull was just a bully.

"You don't understand." Skull kept advancing. "The survivors of Ragnarök will rule the world. We'll get the respect we deserve. Any humans left will obey us, and the monsters will be freed from their shackles. Our family, the children of the great Loki, will have our own kingdoms. The strong will prosper, and the weak will serve."

"So the big plan is to do what? Trust Mayor Thorsen to treat you fairly after he sacrifices his *grandson* to a big snake and lets the world fall apart?" Fen stared at Skull. He'd expected something more elaborate than *let the world end* as a plan. What kind of person actually believed that the end of civilization was a *good* idea? "People will die. Millions, *billions* of people will die if we don't stop Ragnarök."

Skull shrugged. "Humans."

"I'm human. You are, too." Fen folded his arms over his chest. "Our families, friends, everyone we know."

"No. We are *wulfenkind*, but we exist on their scraps. We're the children of a *god*, Fenrir." Skull had a wide-eyed look that made his words sound even crazier. "And you're ready to lead us now. I had to wait, but now that you know that you're not a hero, you can take your place at the front of our forces."

"Say what?" Fen took several steps backward. "Have you been drinking something? Alcohol isn't a good idea. I mean, aside from you being a kid, it's just bad for your brain. Or maybe you ate some bad meat? Or—"

"I wanted it to be me, Fenrir," Skull interrupted.

"*Stop* calling me that," Fen snapped.

Skull laughed. "You're not a hero. You're the one destined to lead the monsters, Fenrir. Owen knew it, too. Soon they all will, and we'll trample them under our paws."

"Thanks, but I'll pass," Fen drawled, trying to sound calm, hoping that his rising panic wouldn't show. Maybe Skull was as scary as the monsters after all. He was crazy *and* a bully.

"The mayor explained it to me, and I understand now. It's

obvious that it's you." Skull rolled his shoulders. "You saw Helen herself. Went to see the queen of the dead, and you came back. She will lend her dead to you, and we will—"

"Seriously, stop." Fen looked around for the best escape route as Skull advanced. He thought he saw one of Owen's ravens watching, but being sure he was seeing a black bird in the shadows of the trees wasn't easy.

Skull sighed. "I'll be your top lieutenant. Hattie will be at our side, too."

"I'm. Not. Joining. Your. Pack." Fen snarled at Skull. If the older boy was anything other than a Raider, Fen would call for help, but there were rules among *wulfenkind*, and whether or not Fen liked them, he was bound by them. You don't call on outsiders to settle a dispute.

"You are. In fact, you're going to *lead* it," Skull said, and then he punched Fen square in the face. "It's your destined role."

"Dude, stop!" Fen scurried backward. He hoped that he *had* seen one of the ravens, and that it would get help, because if he did this one-on-one, there was no victory possible. If he defeated Skull in a one-to-one fight, the rules dictated that he'd be in charge of a pack of Raiders—which meant doing what was best for them. He'd be exactly where Skull wanted him: separated from the descendants of the North and bound to do what was in the best interests of the pack. If Fen *didn't* defeat Skull, he'd be beaten until he was too weak to even flee and be held as a captive.

"I don't want to fight you *or* take the destined monster-leader role!" Fen yelled.

"It's not a choice." Skull swung at him again, this time hitting him in the stomach. "I'm going to get a few good hits at you, but then you'll win. It *has* to happen like this. You can fight now or later," Skull said as he punched Fen in the face again. "Hit me back, Fenrir. You're *wulfenkind*."

Fen dodged the next swing, but he still refused to lift his fists. Skull lashed out with another hit; that one made contact. The feel of it knocked Fen backward.

"I can make you fight," Skull snarled.

As Fen tried to dart to the side, Skull kicked. His leg arced out, and the connecting blow made tears come to Fen's eyes. The older boy's strikes were meant to be painful, to anger Fen until he reacted.

"No." Fen hated the idea of taking a beating, but he could handle it. Decision made, he met Skull's eyes and said, "I won't fight you."

Skull stood perfectly still for a moment, staring at Fen, and then he asked, "Do you really think you can keep Laurie out of our reach?"

"She has nothing to do with this." Fen growled. His hands fisted almost of their own accord. "My cousin is—"

"She stands with our enemy. The Raiders will take her if you don't fight back, and they'll beat her for every punch you should've thrown. You have a role to play in the battle,

337

Fenrir. You either accept your fate, or we do what we have to in order to help you find acceptance."

Fen had to warn Laurie. He started to turn around, to try to get back to the others, and Skull threw himself at Fen, tackling him and beating him until Fen wondered if he was going to die.

*If he kills me, they can't use Laurie to make me do anything evil. They have no reason to hurt her.*

"Fight back," Skull said between punches. "I'll stop once you're unconscious. Then we'll talk again. While you're out, I'll get the others, and we'll take Laurie. She met Helen, too. She could lead us, too, you know."

Fen growled. "Stay away from my cousin."

"Make me."

Fen shifted into a wolf and squirmed out from under Skull. He could run, reach her, *warn* her, but when Fen turned to flee, Skull kicked him hard in the side.

"In a fight for control of a pack, no one walks away," Skull reminded Fen. "You are *wulfenkind*, Fenrir. There are rules. You can't run from a fight for dominance."

Fen growled again, and then he attacked.

Although Skull stayed on two legs, he was still an able opponent. He was, however, not as agile as a wolf. Fen's shape—and his teeth—gave him an advantage. It wasn't an easy fight, but Fen felt like he was stronger than usual, like reserves of power were his. The others had gained gifts from their god ancestors. Was Fen finally gaining something because he was doing what he was destined to do, even if it meant potentially joining the side of the villains? Was that the way it worked? Gifts came when they accepted their fate? Even as the thought occurred to him, Fen rejected it. If he had to be on the wrong side to be stronger, he didn't want it.

At the realization that by winning this fight he was losing everything, Fen stopped. He just stopped. He shed his wolf form and told Skull, "No. You're not defeated, but I'm not staying here. I'll break that rule. You can declare me a rogue or whatever it is. The pack can hunt me if they have to, but I won't do this."

Skull shook his head. "You can fight me, or I will beat you until you can't move. Then I'll go after your sweet cousin."

Fighting hadn't worked, and accepting the beating hadn't worked. Fen needed help. He opened his mouth and let out a howl. It wasn't entirely wolflike, as he was in human form, but he hoped that one of the others would hear and come to investigate. It was against every *wulfenkind* rule to do as he just had, but somehow, following pack rules wasn't quite as important when the battle for the end of the world was coming.

He saw the raven then. It swooped down low enough that Fen could almost touch it. "Get the others," he called, feeling a little ridiculous talking to a bird, even though it was probably Owen's bird, but he was desperate enough to try.

The raven made no sign that it was even the *right* raven, but Fen clung to the hope that help was coming. Hope wasn't enough, though, so he resumed hitting Skull back. It was an odd sort of fight in which neither one of them was trying to truly win. Fen was trying to buy time, and Skull was trying to only put up enough resistance to make it a valid challenge for domination.

The others didn't come, and Fen was growing tired. They'd already had a full-out battle that day. He'd *started* the fight tired. He howled again, hoping that Thorsen or Baldwin or even Owen would come. He even said, "Aunt Helen? I wish you were here." No one came.

He kept trying to not win the fight but not get too injured, either.

Still, no one came. If the raven understood, it hadn't brought help. Helen hadn't appeared. None of the others came to see where he was. He was alone and tired, and Skull wasn't going to stop until Fen beat him or was too beaten to keep fighting. Then they'd do it all over again when he healed. There was no rescue for him. Fen finally accepted that he had no other choice: he had to beat Skull. He had to win this fight to keep Laurie safe.

Soon, Skull was on the ground in front of Fen. He stretched his neck out, baring his throat to Fen, and said, "My pack is yours. I am yours."

At that, Fen felt a series of connections to people set-

tle onto him. He felt his pack, his new *wulfenkind* family, lift their heads and muzzles as they felt him, too, and he heard their howls as they gave voice to the desperation that Fen felt.

He was well and truly trapped, bound to the enemy, compelled to look out for their needs and their well-being... which was the exact opposite of what he wanted to do. Now he'd have to put the good of the pack first, and they wanted to bring about the end of the world.

"I can lead you home," Skull said in a weirdly meek voice.

*Now what do I do?* Fen thought he'd been trapped by being Loki's representative in the final battle, was almost embarrassed when he found out he wasn't, and now was terrified that he again seemed to be the god's stand-in—but this time, for the wrong team. By winning the fight, he'd lost so much more: now Fen would have to lead the monsters against his friends.

## ACKNOWLEDGMENTS

We want to thank:

- Meghan Lewis, Breanna Lewis, and Dylan Marr, for coming up with titles for the books;

- our agents, Sarah Heller and Merrilee Heifetz, for believing in the project (and us);

- and our kids (Marcus, Alex, Julia, Dylan, and Asia) and our assistants (Laura Kalnajs and Alison Armstrong), for feedback.